I0674279

AUTUMN
FALLS

A.R. KINGSTON

Keen Quill Press

Denver, CO

Copyright © 2021 by A.R. Kingston

All rights reserved. No part of this publication may be reproduced, distributed or transmitted in any form or by any means, including photocopying, recording, or other electronic or mechanical methods, without the prior written permission of the publisher, except in the case of brief quotations embodied in critical reviews and certain other noncommercial uses permitted by copyright law. For permission requests, write to the publisher, addressed "Attention: Permissions Coordinator," at the address below.

A.R. Kingston/Keen Quill Press
8547 E Arapahoe Rd
Ste J-397
Greenwood Village, CO 80112
www.arkingston.com

Publisher's Note: This is a work of fiction. Names, characters, places, and incidents are a product of the author's imagination. Locales and public names are sometimes used for atmospheric purposes. Any resemblance to actual people, living or dead, or to businesses, companies, events, institutions, or locales is completely coincidental.

Book Layout by Creative Indie
Book Cover by Disgruntled Unicorn Designs

Ordering Information:
Quantity sales. Special discounts are available on quantity purchases by corporations, associations, and others. For details, contact the "Special Sales Department" at the address above.

Autumn Falls/ AR Kingston -- 1st ed.
ISBN 978-1-7342400-0-9

CHAPTER ONE

"The sinister, the terrible never deceive: the state in which they leave us is always one of enlightenment. And only this condition of vicious insight allows us a full grasp of the world, all things considered, just as a frigid melancholy grants us full possession of ourselves. We may hide from horror only in the heart of horror. –**Thomas Ligotti, The Medusa**

Tendrils of fog snaked across the small island, choking out the visibility in its slowly congealing mist. Stopping at the edge of a small field, a man glanced up to observe the halos of streetlamps distorting in the milky vapor. Shrugging, he stepped into the street glistening with the droplets of the evening rain. He did not need to see where he was going; he knew this island by heart, it had been his home for over thirty years. Surrounding shadows and the cackling of crows coming from the nearby woods swallowed up his thundering footsteps as he approached the spires of the wrought-iron gate separating him from his destination.

Pushing on the rusted gate, it let out a groan and nudged open just enough for him to slip his way in through the crack. Stealing a glance at the time-worn burgundy bricks of the old hospital, he stuffed his hands in the pockets of his gray wool pea coat and continued his stroll down the eroded dirt path. The sand and stone crunched beneath his boots while the cawing of crows—which sounded like laughter—echoed through the desolate space and rolled back to him like thunder.

Stepping over the split curb onto the grass, he drifted to the vine-covered walls and crouched in the shadows. Continuing to creep along the outer edge of the building, he paused beside a dust-hazed window with thin veins of cracked glass and peeked inside. Flickering light from the white candles pooling onto the floor splashed across the glazed cream tiles, and the shadows of flames danced on the lustrous walls. There, at the far corner of the room, a woman sat in a steel basin filled to the brim with crimson blood.

The curves of her body skated across the deep maroon surface and distort in the ripples as she scooped up the precious liquid. She brushed it across her porcelain skin, and he watched in awe as her wrinkles faded and the whites of her hair turned jet black, transforming her into the woman he had always known. He had observed this ritual for years, trying to figure out how he had never noticed her decay, but he was still no closer to finding the answer. Had he known what she was, what this island had become, he would have escaped before things turned sour, and perhaps he could have watched his child grow up instead of leaving her without a father. But, in the end, his soul was a small price to pay to ensure his family's safety.

Turning away from the window, he backtracked to the opposite end of the building and into the old burial ground adjacent to the building. Crossing the lawn speckled with limestone bricks, he briefly glanced about at the numbers etched into their weather-sculpted surface. This was a remnant of a time when the islanders still buried the people whose lives the witch had stolen, but that was way before his time, and it was not what he came there to see. Having crossed the field of graves, he paused and inhaled the rotten egg smell of sulfur, filling his lungs with the caustic substance. Smiling to himself, he faced east and headed towards the back of the hospital to check out his handy work.

In the ominous, heavy silence, he glances across the soggy, sun-bleached lawn to a crack splitting the ground a few steps ahead of him. Observing the black smoke seeping from the fissure to meet the bright orange moon veiled by fog, he let out a sigh. He pondered how long it would be for the entity contained inside to be set free to wreak havoc on the inhabitants of the land. Too long had the witch imprisoned the creature inside—forcing it into her service—but soon enough it would take its revenge. These were the events he set in motion twenty-five years ago when he gave it his soul freely, a soul which the woman inside the hospital planned to sacrifice all along to keep the demon bound for another quarter of a century.

With his hands in his pockets, he continued to gaze up at the night sky with the striated clouds hiding the stars until he heard a branch snapping behind him. Letting out a snort, he shifted his attention to a small ship bobbing on the horizon, and the figure behind him let out a melancholy groan. He did not need to turn to see who was behind him, he could hear the voice resonating in his head. It was the same creature who offered him the deal years ago, sparing him from a fate far worse than death, but in the process tying him to the island permanently. Smirking, he continued to glance at the navy horizon until the robed figure came to stand beside him, probing his brain with questions.

"So," he finally let out a sigh and peered at the man covered in a black hood beside him, "you've come to check on the crack yourself, have you?"

The creature did not speak—it couldn't speak since it lacked a human tongue—but it let out a groan and nodded its head to let him know he was correct in his assumption. Then, it asked him a question by telepathically projecting its thoughts into his head, and the man nodded while scrunching up his lips.

"Don't you worry, my cursed friend; I'll keep up my end of the deal. But remember, you have to promise me that nothing will happen to her, that was our agreement. And don't you go telling me I have nothing to worry about. I know the witch is plotting to lure her here like she did me all those years ago. She needs her blood to complete the ritual, or the monster breaks free and her time here is up. Not to mention, I don't want you taking her soul either, since our deal was for her to stay safe and live a long, happy life."

The thing beside him moaned and assured him he would keep up his end of the bargain before it retreated into the shadows and vanishing from sight. The man nodded and recalled how he exchanged his soul for the assurance that his wife and daughter would be safe, and that the witch would never lay claim to his girl's blood. Back then, he believed he was doing the right thing, but now the twenty-five-year mark for the Feast of Shadows was fast approaching, and she'd need that blood to complete her ritual or risk being dragged off to hell where she belonged. In a few more months, he would finally be free from his obligation, he just hoped his sacrifice would not have been in vain as he could sense his daughter getting closer. Shaking his head at the work ahead of him, he turned on his heels, and walked towards the tree line, vanishing into the mist.

CHAPTER TWO

"Nothing ever begins. There is no first moment; no single word or place from which this or any story springs." –Clive Barker, Weaveworld

A crisp, salty breeze hit her face, tousling her auburn hair as the fog enveloped the ferry on all sides. Closing her hazel eyes, Charlotte Briggs clutched a hand around the turtleneck of her cream cable-knit sweater. Inhaling the stale, sulfur aroma, she felt oddly calm despite the circumstances of her move. It seemed as if eons passed since she'd been to New England, and this isolated, fog-locked island in Maine was far removed from the hustle and bustle of Seattle that she had become accustomed to. But the change of scenery was just what the doctor ordered, and it got her as far away from the past she was so desperate to escape.

She thought of giving her mother in Boston a call before moving back to the East Coast, but she did not want to worry her. Eleanor Briggs had always been adamant about Charlotte staying out of Maine, claiming it was the land of the devil. She figured it would upset her mother if she knew about her making a home there, but she did plan on having a talk with her eventually. She just needed a bit more time to gather her nerves to call her. Exhaling the ocean from her lungs, she felt a small hand insert itself into the nook of her arm, and she glanced down at her son staring up at her. With his short black hair and steel-gray eyes, Kevin was looking more and more like his father each day. Seeing so much of *him* in their son made her heart ache. And yet, Charlotte cherished the boy, and the memories all the same.

"What is it, baby?"

"Are we almost there?" Kevin looked out at the congealing mist and frowned. "We've been on this thing for what feels like forever."

"I... I think so." Charlotte strained her eyes as the veil of fog lifted a bit to reveal the worn, ivory brick lighthouse of Autumn Falls sitting eerily still on the horizon and sweeping the ocean with a pale beam of golden light. "Probably another ten minutes or so if I was to take a guess."

"Still think this will be a good move for us?"

"I hope so. At least I will be able to make enough money to get our own place."

"I guess that's a plus." The boy sighed and stared at the island coming into view. "Is it always so cold here?" He shivered and tightened his navy windbreaker around himself. "It's still late August, but it already feels like mid-winter."

"It will always be a bit colder than what you are used to, but I promise it will be warmer once we get off the ferry. It's always a lot colder on the ocean."

"I sure hope you're right. I hate the cold." Kevin pouted and snuggled closer to her for warmth. "And I *really* hope Bret doesn't follow us here or try to get you back... again."

"Me too, baby, me too."

Cringing from the thought of her ex following her, Charlotte turned to glance back to the horizon and suppressed a shudder trying to break its way down her spine. She met Bret back in Boston seven years ago when she was just starting EMT school. Back then, she was an eighteen-year-old kid with an almost two-year-old child of her own. Having faced so many obstacles as a teenage mother, she was convinced no one would ever want her, until Bret Miller came along. He was four years older than her, more mature than anyone she encountered beforehand, and she fell for him hard. At first, he seemed like the perfect gentleman, always doting on Kevin, and bringing her flowers. Even her mother was convinced he was the one, and she encouraged Charlotte to take the plunge. Blinded by the notion of having a family, she accepted his proposal to move to the West Coast after three years of dating.

That was when the trouble started, she reckoned, the moment they moved to Seattle. After another year of bliss together, she finally realized what a monster he was. Isolated from her friends and family, Charlotte saw a hidden side to Bret, a dark side like she'd never seen before. At first, it was the small things; keeping tabs on her at all times, not allowing her to spend time with co-workers, cutting off her contact with her lifeline in Boston, telling her what to wear, and controlling what she could spend their money on. She put up with it, tried to rationalize the change in him, but then, the abuse got worse. It started out with snide insults about her being a teenage mother, or her looks, but it quickly escalated into physical altercations. For years Charlotte covered up the bruises and pretended everything was fine until Bret did the one thing she could never forgive him for. He slapped Kevin over spilling some milk on their new counters.

After years of tolerating the abuse, Charlotte had had enough when the well-being of her child was on the line. She had Bret arrested the same day, then she quietly packed her bags and left before he got out of jail and tried to keep her with him. Unfortunately for her, being a single mother on a paramedic salary in Seattle was near impossible, and the two of them lived out of small hotel rooms for almost a year. And, to make matters worse, Bret began stalking her. He would show up at her job, at the coffee shop she frequented, and in the hotel lobbies. Even the restraining order she got against him was doing little to keep her safe, and he focused on harassing Kevin at school by showing up unannounced and trying to take the boy with him. She thought of moving back to Boston, live with her mother for a bit and figure things out when the strange call came in.

The woman on the phone claimed the small island town of Autumn Falls was looking for a daytime paramedic to take over an open position, and according to her LinkedIn profile, she fit the bill. It was all well and good, and Charlotte was happy to take the job, except for one slight problem—she didn't have a LinkedIn profile—at least, she didn't think she did. Still, the lady on the other end was very insistent, going so far as to tell her about the job, and the town she would be living in.

Autumn Falls was a small island between the coast of Maine and Nova Scotia, and the only way to get to it was to grab a two-hour ferry ride from Cutler. It was an old, historic town, full of intrigue, not to mention it was extremely safe and had great schools. The woman on the phone told Charlotte that she would be paid her normal Seattle salary, plus moving expenses, and be provided with a hotel room until she found a place of her own. To sweeten the deal, she also informed her that she'd only deal with an occasional emergency here and there as the island was one of the safest places in the United States. The offer sounded almost too good to be true, but it was exactly what she needed to return closer to home and get away from the man making her life miserable. Accepting the job on the spot, Charlotte and Kevin packed up and were on the next flight out to Bangor, where a bus took them to the ferry terminal.

Now, well on their way to the secluded island encased in mist, Charlotte grasped her hands around the slick rail of the ferry and leaned over to look at the dark blue, foam-crested waters below. She was watching her crooked reflection bob in the waves when the sudden, low moan of the foghorn signaled they were getting close to shore. Looking up, she watched the clouds part to reveal a lush island blanketed with trees which were turning gold, orange, and maroon. Boats and small private docks covered the pristine harbor while on the island itself, through the foliage, specks of Victorian and Colonial homes came into view, greeting their new visitors. Unable to figure out why, Charlotte's skin got covered in gooseflesh, and she wanted to turn around and run.

With no escape possible, she watched as the boat pulled up to a red weather-beaten shack decorated in frayed fishing nets and colorful buoys. White picnic tables sitting beneath wind-torn umbrellas lined the pallid dock. On a dusty, plate-glass window cracked gold letters declared the building to be a general store and boat rental. Slinging her black trauma bag over her left shoulder, Charlotte grabbed hold of her roller suitcase and nudged her son, who snatched his faded black duffel bag off the metal bench just as the ferry jolted to a stop. The rest of the passengers shuffled off the boat in unison, with Charlotte and Kevin trailing behind them.

Standing on the pier as people floated around them, Charlotte glanced about and noticed six crows sitting motionless on the piling, staring at her with their black glass eyes. A feeling of dread crept up inside her as the dark statues turned their heads to study her. Her head was screaming at her to run, but she held tight and continued to look for the person who was supposed to be picking her up. Spotting a man with graying hair standing at the end of the dock holding a sign, Charlotte stepped forward causing the birds to take off in a sea of iridescent blue and green feathers melting into the sky. Jumping back with a yelp, she pressed a hand on her chest to steal her beating heart and turned to study the man who had gotten closer. He squinted his brown eyes, chiseling canyons into his spotted face as he pressed a hand against his forehead and lifted the white cardboard with her name written neatly in bold, black letters.

"Hello." Charlotte waved and approached the stranger with Kevin in tow. "I'm Charlotte Briggs."

"Pleasure to meet you, miss. I'm Cyrus. And..." he glanced down at the boy while furrowing his brow, "who might this young man be?"

"I'm Kevin, her son."

"A bit young to have a child this old, aren't you?"

"I..." Charlotte paused and rubbed her free shoulder while glancing down at her feet, "I had him when I was sixteen."

"I see." Cyrus shook his head with a soured expression. "Well, no matter, Autumn Falls is a great place for kids to grow up, with it being so safe and all. I'll be shuttling you, and your fellow co-workers around until you are all settled, and you can ask me anything you want about the island. The other two arrived earlier today and are already settled at the hotel. You will meet them tomorrow." Glancing at the bags by their feet, he lifted his eyebrow and leaned to glance behind Charlotte. "Is this all the luggage you have?"

"Yes." She chuckled. "I'm afraid we don't own much. It made the move easier."

"Very well then," Cyrus grabbed hold of the roller suitcase and waved his arm, "follow me."

Taking hold of Kevin's hand, Charlotte followed her guide to a green, roofless Jeep Wrangler waiting nearby. Leaning over the large spare tire in the back, Cyrus wedged their bags behind the rear seat. Lifting the boy up to sit in the back, he motioned to Charlotte with his head, and she got up front to sit beside him. Smiling at her, he revved the engine to life and started off down the paved road, which was smooth as glass. At first, Charlotte said nothing, but as a brick building on a hill came into view, her curiosity took over, and she turned to stare at her driver.

"Say Cyrus..." she stole a second glance at the three-story building sitting behind black iron gates, "what's that ivy-covered building there. The one with the white columns forming five arches?"

"Oh, that be the old Mercy Hospital. It was built back in eighteen sixty-three and shut down sometime in the seventies in favor of the newer model we have on the island today. But I still say it was something else that brought the old place down."

"Like what?"

"Oh, well, there be rumors and all, stories of an old doctor who worked at Mercy and liked to experiment on her patients. A great many people died behind them walls and are now buried on the same grounds. Rumors say that at night you can still hear the pleas from the dead and see apparitions. Then, there are stories of all the accidents that happen on hospital grounds. The locals claim the land to be cursed, and no one dares step foot in that place. But you know, they are just stories, so probably no need to worry or nothing."

"Right," Charlotte laughed nervously and swallowed the rock forming in her throat, "stories."

"No need to worry, Miss. Briggs. It's an old island, full of stories, just like any other town in America. It keeps things interesting."

"Guess you're right, but..."

"You don't like ghost stories?"

"Oh, no, I love them. It's just..." Charlotte peered at her wistful reflection and swallowed the pain coming over her in waves, "well, I guess it's just personal."

"I understand. You can talk about it any time you feel ready, if you want. Plus," Cyrus stopped the Jeep and put it in park, "we have arrived at our destination."

Stepping out of the car to grab Kevin and their bags, Cyrus left Charlotte to stumble out her door and through the porte-cochere as her eyes rose to take in the place she'd be calling home for a while. The five floors of the grand hotel climbed to meet the pastel blue sky with its sangria-colored roof. Two towers flanked the sides and a small one rose from the center of the roof, tickling the wispy cloud floating by. It reminded her of the hotel she stayed in Disney World on a trip with her mother, and she felt the air catch in her lungs at the thought of not living in some shady motel again until they got settled.

"All right, miss." Cyrus put a firm, gentle hand on her shoulder and handed her the roller suitcase he had wrestled out from the back. "If you go on inside the woman at the front desk will give you the keys to your room, which has already been paid for the month. Inside you will find an envelope with a card that is your daily food allowance. I think the town gives you a hundred per day. Feel free to check out the restaurants at your leisure, and if you need anything, you can give me a call, I left my number in the pocket of your suitcase. I'll be by tomorrow at seven-thirty to pick you up and drive you, and your colleagues to orientation."

"Thank you, Cyrus."

"Of course. It's my pleasure. Now off you go. Go on, get settled, and relax. You have a full day ahead of you tomorrow."

Giving Charlotte a wink and a wave, the man hopped into the Jeep and drove off, leaving her standing in a cloud of dust. Coughing, she turned and stared at the two massive French doors before her and wondered if that was the entrance she was supposed to use. But as Kevin took hold of her hand and dragged her along, a young man in a red uniform swung a door open for her, inviting her to go inside.

CHAPTER THREE

"Celebrate endings—for they precede new beginnings." –
Jonathan Lockwood Huie

Stepping into the open interior of the hotel, Charlotte felt the blood drain from her head at how opulent the place was. A green paisley rug covered the sprawling snow-white marble floor, with an enormous crystal chandelier hanging at the center, above a lacquered grand piano. The whole entryway was flanked in white, from the pillars and railings, to the dividers and small coffee tables breaking up the winged velvet sofas. Sucking in a lung-full of air, Charlotte grabbed hold of Kevin's hand and headed for the reception desk where a hook-nosed woman in a gray suit was waiting for her.

"Miss. Briggs, I presume?" The white-haired woman curled her paper-thin lips into a grin and adjusted her thick cat-eye spectacles.

"That's right."

"Very good. We have been waiting for you." She reached into a cubby and slid two keys with a brass medallion on them over to

Charlotte. "You will be in room one o three. It is down the first hallway on your left, all the way towards the end. I hope you find your stay enjoyable."

"Thank you very much."

"Oh, and Miss. Briggs," Charlotte turned back to look at the woman, "I was told to inform you that your son has been successfully enrolled in Horizons Academy. He can start tomorrow morning. It is a short walk from here, so you will have absolutely nothing to worry about. Someone will wait at the school to greet him."

"Oh, uh, great. Thank you again."

Charlotte turned back and walked towards the first hallway while pondering the odd exchange. She thought it rather strange that her son was being enrolled in school so suddenly, or that she did not need to be there with him, but as she rounded the corner, her worries faded away. A paisley runner like the rug in the entrance stretched down the glowing tunnel of white doors. It was a tad dated, but a pleasant change from the puke green and neon orange abominations she had grown used to over the past year. There was no buzzing of a dying ice machine, nor a flicker of lights in a dimly lit hall. All there was to greet them was serene silence. Walking down toward the end, she found the door with their number on it and stepped inside their temporary home.

The interior was as nice as the outside with its clean mocha walls and soft maroon carpeting. The two queen-sized beds were neatly done with cream comforters that were free of cigarette scars and semen stains. A plush ruby sofa sat facing a flat screen TV and to the side, in front of the sliding glass door leading to a patio, was a round oak table with three Oxford chairs tucked into its nook. They were the same color as the sofa, and free of any spots— which, unlike their last place— might be misconstrued as bloodstains. Turning to her right, Charlotte flicked a switch on for the bathroom and leaned her head in to peek inside.

At first glance, the bathroom appeared even better than the room. White brick lined the bottom of the wall with pale sea-foam paint on top. A double vanity with a marble top waited for her below a large gold framed mirror. Straight ahead, a small door led to a room housing the toilet, and to her right was an antique claw foot tub. This clearly had not been updated recently, but it still smelled clean and had no broken hardware, or signs of mold. Shutting the lights off, she went to put her stuff away and spotted Kevin laying on the bed closest to the patio, looking at her with his face propped on his hand.

"All right. I know that look, young man. What is it?"

"Don't get me wrong." He sat up and wrinkled his nose. "I think this place is great and all, but... do we have to live in another hotel?"

"Not for long," Charlotte smirked and opened her suitcase. "I'll start looking for a house or an apartment as soon as I get paid, and we replenish our bank account." She went over to the dresser with an armful of garments and began putting them away. "And you know, my offer of having you stay with your grandmother in Boston still stands, at least until I get settled."

"No way, I'd rather be with you. Together till the end, right?"

"Till the end." She turned and smiled at her son. "Now, want to grab some room service and settle down for the night?"

"Sure." Kevin opened a navy-blue leather booklet and peeked inside. "I'll have the baked macaroni and cheese. And... as soon as we get a place to live, I want a dog."

"All right, a big old golden retriever, I promise. Now let me order the food, I'm starving."

Picking up the phone on the nightstand, Charlotte dialed the number for room service and waited. It had been a long time since she had something other than fast food or some questionable concoction she picked up at a gas station, and she was sure looking forward to having a fresh Caesar salad. On the bed beside her, Kevin flipped through a small booklet he found about the hotel history while he waited for her to get done. Having finished her order, she placed the receiver back in the cradle and sat down on her bed to observe the boy who was frowning at his pamphlet.

"Read something interesting?"

"Did you know they constructed this hotel in nineteen o nine?"

"No. But I'm not surprised given its splendor."

"Well, I bet you also didn't know that it was built on the ruins of the original Eldawood Hotel, which burned down in the great fire of nineteen o three."

"There was a fire in nineteen o three?"

"Yes. According to this, it took out the hotel and half a city block. A total of three-hundred people were killed."

"Oh my. And they build this place on top of it?"

"Yup. Right on the ashes." Kevin paused and heaved out a sigh. "Seems like this whole island is shrouded in tragedy."

"Well, yes, but it's as Cyrus said, every old place has its history."

Smiling, Kevin nodded his head in agreement just as a knock came on their door with someone on the other side announcing it was their dinner. Grabbing the silver tray from the man in a red uniform, Charlotte gave him a tip and sat down to enjoy her salad. Once they had finished their food, she set the tray to the side and drew closed the burgundy curtains overhanging the glass door. Settling down for the night in preparation for the long day ahead she lay her head on the memory foam pillow and went to sleep.

CHAPTER FOUR

"Nothing else wounds so deeply and irreparably. Nothing else robs us of hope so much as being unloved by one we love." – **Clive Barker**

C*harlotte* woke up with sweat beading on her brow and her red shirt clinging to the moisture of her skin. The room felt like she had stepped into a sauna. Tossing off the tangled, sweat-soaked bed covers, she rolled out of bed, muttering at how Kevin must have turned up the heat again. Pressing her feet to the soft fibers of the rug, she rubbed her eyes as they adjusted to the darkness. Standing up, she shuffled over to the thermostat, which was one of the new digital ones, and tapped on the down button. A soft green light glowed on the display, and she frowned at what she read. According to the indicator screen, the temperature was left at sixty-eight degrees she had set it to, but the room itself was a sweltering one-hundred and ten, and climbing.

"Impossible." She muttered to herself.

Shaking her head, she walked over to the sliding glass door, hoping to nudge it open a crack and let the crisp night air into the room. Pushing one of the red and gold curtains to the side, she froze, and the air caught in her lungs. She wanted to turn and run, but she couldn't move. Something held her in place as her lungs continued to sting without fresh breath. Outside—despite it being a moonless night—the courtyard overlooking the ocean appeared to be surreally bright. Squinting, Charlotte rubbed her eyes and stared out at the swirling clouds of fog beyond the glass. She tried to come up with a reasonable explanation for what she saw, but no matter how much she tried to rationalize it, the area outside was not as she remembered.

Releasing the stale air from her lungs, she took in a deep breath and continued to observe the spectacle on the other side. The world beyond had lost its luster, appearing to be almost as gray as an old-time movie. A dusty cobblestone street flanked by iron lanterns replaced the garden path of intricately placed slabs of concrete and lush green lawns she remembered. Inside their houses, behind crazed glass, flames of candles flickered and danced about the walkway. Stone houses puffing clouds of smoke upwards to the blackened sky had replaced the maze of shrubbery and rhododendrons from earlier in the day. Watching a horse-drawn carriage roll by a short distance away, Charlotte thought she spotted movement out of the corner of her eye, lingering on her porch. Leaning forward, she attempted to steal a glance at the figure beyond the door when an all too familiar voice called her name from the hallway, causing her blood to run cold in her veins.

"No..." she whispered, "it can't be."

Frowning, Charlotte grabbed her pink robe off the nearby chair and slipped it on. Inching closer to the door, she pressed her ear to the polished wood, and listened closely while holding her breath. Once again, she heard the voice from her past calling her name, and she swallowed the rock forming in her throat. It was impossible. There was no way he'd be there, she knew that, but she could not help it. Before she knew it, she was removing the chain from the door and pulling it open a crack. A blast of hot air singed her cheeks, and she strained her eyes to see past a plume of smoke filtering into the room. The hall on the other side was almost a perfect back—the seashell scones on the wall appeared to have vanished—the only source of light was a faint carmine glow coming from the end of the tunnel to her left.

Fearing there might be a fire, she grabbed a key from the pocket in the door and slipped it into her robe. Stepping through the crack, she coughed as smoke enveloped her on all sides, and she shut the door tightly behind her to keep it out of the room. Turning towards the direction of the glow, she got paralyzed in her spot by the man standing before her. Flooded by long-forgotten memories, she felt the tears pricking the corners of her eyes as he took a step closer to her. He was older now, but still as handsome as he was back then with his messy black hair and only a small bit of stubble on his square jaw. She would have recognized him anywhere, even if she hadn't seen his picture on the back of one of his books. It was Zack, her Zack, and the sight of him made her knees wobble.

Zack Campbell was her high school sweetheart, and in her mind, the one that got away. She could recall every detail of their first meeting as if it happened yesterday. It was her Freshmen year at the Silver Oak High School. She was a shy, awkward nerd with glasses who preferred the company of books over people. Zack was a Junior and the captain of their school's football team. She first laid eyes on him one crisp October morning during study hall at the library. He came in wearing his red and white varsity jacket, tossing his ball in the air. Charlotte was the only one there, and he approached her, asking if she would help him find a book which she gladly did. As he thanked her and left, she thought that would be the end of their encounter, but he came in the next day asking her for help with his homework.

That was how all of this started, with a few tutoring sessions which quickly blossomed into romance over the course of a few weeks. By Halloween, the two of them had officially become a couple, and Charlotte became the envy of the entire school. Not that she blamed everyone for being jealous, even she did not understand what he saw in her over a peppy cheerleader with the perfect legs. But Zack, who was her first boyfriend, had quickly become her everything. For him, she took down her walls, let him into her private world, and gave herself to him in ways she could never imagine. Looking at him now, every cell of her body suddenly recalled the memory of their first time together. Her skin crawled with the sensation of his touch, and her lips remembered his fiery breath as they consummated their feeling for one another.

Back then, she thought there was a future for the two of them, planned out a life they would have together. Little did she know her world would come crashing down around her when he dumped her a week after his graduation. He was going off to UCLA in the fall on a football scholarship, and he didn't think it was fair to have her in a long-distance relationship, especially since she had always talked about becoming a surgeon. With an aching heart, Charlotte recalled how he told her they were on a different path now, but if it was meant to be, the road would bring them back together. That was the end of it, at least for him—but for her it was only the beginning—she learned she was pregnant with Kevin a few days later.

Glancing up at his steel-gray eyes, Charlotte recalled the stew of emotions that flooded her as the two red lines appeared on that darn stick. She remembered bawling her eyes out as she told her mother—a single parent herself since her father died while she was still a baby—and how her mother was willing to support her no matter what she decided to do. At first, she considered putting the baby up for adoption. After all, everyone around her had convinced her that Zack should not know he was a father. But as she held her son at the hospital and stole a glance at his face, she knew she could never be apart from him. He looked too much like his dad.

For years, she thought the only memory left of Zack was the one found in their son. She let him go that day, convincing herself their path would never cross. And yet, here he was, standing before her with pleading eyes, or at least some version of him, one which was not entirely human. The Zack before her, while retaining the image of the man she once loved, was nothing like him. Her knees buckled beneath her, and she fell against the wall, clutching her chest as his once gray eyes turned to a glowing shade of deep ruby red. Clouds of shadowy smoke poured out from his body and he reached out a hand to her, tilting his head.

"Cherry, is that you?"

"Yes..." Charlotte chocked down her sadness as the hot tears streamed down her face, "it's me."

"Please," Zack's voice was distorted and distant, "help me?"

"What's wrong, Zack? What do you want me to do?"

"Save me... please...."

"How?" Charlotte pushed herself off the wall to get closer to him. "Tell me what you want me to do."

"Save me, Cherry. Please, help me. You are the only one who can."

He said nothing more, he just continued to stand with his hand stretched out towards her, and she felt herself getting pulled closer to him until she was melting into his body. She missed him so much, she wanted to hold him again and comfort him in his hour of need. Embracing him in her arms, his body stiffen at her touch and the muscles ripple beneath his cotton shirt. She buried her face in his chest sobbing and noticed he had a strange smell of sulfur to him. He reached around to hold her, but as he wrapped his arms around her back, a blood-curdling squeal rang through the hallway.

Charlotte felt the temperature suddenly drop and glanced up to Zack, evaporating in her arms until there was nothing left. She was left standing, holding on to the smoke seeping through her fingers, and for the first time, she noticed that she could see her breath in front of her. The scones which had reappeared on the cream damask walls flickered faintly around her, and the room slowly spun and whirled like something in a fun house mirror. Feeling queasy as her head floated with the room, she leaned a hand on the wall and swallowed down the sour taste of bile lingering in her throat. At the end of the hall, she could hear shallow grunts and groans, and she squinted to try to see in that direction, not expecting to be greeted by a grisly sight.

On the far end, a black cloth-clad torso wiggled towards her at an alarming rate. Its legs did not seem to work, as it walked—if you could call it that—with one arm in front of the other as it pulled itself along the paisley rug. The thing was slowly closing the distance between them as its human arms picked up pace with every stroke. A human torso, that was not entirely human, carried on its shoulder the scar-painted face of a white pig. Its snout twisted as it let out groans, and Charlotte could see that its eyes were vacant socket; dark and lifeless, still oozing blood across the pink skin.

Clutching her chest, her heart raced faster as the air slowly drain out from her lungs and caused her head to spin even more. She wanted to scream, but nothing came out except the sound of the wind escaping her throat. The horrible creature was almost upon her as it ran on its arms to eat away the space that separated her from it. Turning around, Charlotte urged her legs to move as she attempted to run for the door of her room, but every step she took felt like she was walking in Jell-O. She aimlessly jabbed the key into its slot, jiggling the lock and praying it would open. The smell of carrion crept into her nostrils, and she could feel the creature's hot breath as she pleaded with the lock, and with God to be spared from what it had in store for her.

Finally, as if by the grace of God upon hearing her prayer, the door handle turned, and Charlotte flung herself into the safety of the room. Slamming the door behind her, she wheezed and pressed her back to the wood. Closing her eyes, she took a few deep breaths and thanked God for letting her live. With trembling hands, she turned to slide the door chain into position with the grunts resonating continuously from the other side. She attempted to tell herself she was going crazy, and convinced herself to peek through the peephole to prove it. Pressing her eye against the small hole, she could see nothing but a dimly lit hall, until a bloody eye socket popped up from the ground to meet her gaze. Letting out a yelp, Charlotte fell to the floor and scrambled back towards her bed.

Pulling herself up to the soft mattress, she sat with the covers pressed up against her and continued to pant. Hours seemed to pass by with the creature sniffing at the bottom of her door until it let out a shriek and moved away. She could hear it dragging itself along the floor as the sound of its grunts slowly grew distant and muffled. Charlotte waited until she heard nothing but the hum of the radiator and laid her head down on the pillow with the comforter still pressed to her face. Telling herself it was only a dream, she closed her eyes and urged herself to return to sleep, so she could wake back up in her world and forget about the horrible nightmare which just transpired.

CHAPTER FIVE

"What looked like morning was the beginning of endless night"—William Peter Blatty, The Exorcist

L ost in an uneasy sleep, Charlotte felt herself being nudged awake. She recalled the strange nightmare she had, glad for it to be over, but as she attempted to move, she realized she was still wearing her robe. Straining open her eyes, still heavy with sleep, she saw her son shaking her awake. Strange thoughts flooded her mind, and she tried to recall exactly what happened last night, or what she thought happened, but no rational explanation came to mind. Sitting up in bed, she yawned, stretched her arms, and allowed her feet to hit the floor before turning her head to stare at Kevin.

"What time is it?"

"It's already seven, mom, you slept in. If you don't hurry, you'll be late for your first day of work."

"Oh, damn." Charlotte shot up and ran to the bathroom. "Did you have breakfast yet?"

"No. I was going to grab something from the hotel café on the way to school."

"All right," Charlotte poked her head out as she threw on her shirt, "Just be sure to grab your key and return right back to the room after school. I don't want you running all over this island just yet."

"I know, mom." Kevin rolled his eyes. "That has been our routine for the last year, or did you forget?"

"No, I did not." Charlotte fumbled out of the bathroom while attempting to put on a sock. "But I'm your mother and it's my job to worry about you."

"I know, I know. But it's not like Bret is going to follow us here. He doesn't even know we left Seattle."

"I realize that, but..." she paused and wondered why she was so apprehensive. "I guess I just want to make sure he is gone for good before I feel safe about letting you be out on your own, or at least until you have friends with parents who I can trust."

"Yeah, yeah, I get it. Can't have big, bad Bret coming to kidnap me or anything. I promise to come right home and lock the door until your shift is done. Now hurry before your ride leaves and you have to walk to the station. Something tells me that Uber isn't a thing around here."

"Okay, fine, I'm out." Charlotte went to leave but paused in the doorway to steal a backward glance at her son. "Are you sure you'll be all right here by yourself until I get back?"

"Yes, mom. We got four restaurants here at the hotel, plus

cable, and I have my iPad and Nintendo Switch. Not to mention I will probably have like ten hours of homework to keep me occupied until bedtime."

"You know, my previous offer still stands. You can go live with grandma in Boston until I get settled and know for sure that Bret won't come after us again."

"No way! I already told you, I want to stay with you. Plus, I doubt he'd go unnoticed if he came looking for us. The population here is all of like five-hundred people, and they all know each other."

"Well... I guess you're right. Okay, be good, stay out of trouble, I'll call you as soon as I can. Love you, Kev."

"Love you too, mom. Stay safe."

Shutting the door behind her, Charlotte glanced towards the end of the hall and shuddered. She gawked at the exact spot where the pigman stood, but in the daylight the only thing that was there was the dappled light coming in from the side door and dancing on the wall. Stilling her racing heart, she tiptoed down the hall until she pushed through the glass door to the welcoming freedom of the outdoors. Autumn's breath tickled her neck as she turned to spot the familiar green Jeep waiting for her in the parking lot. It was filled with fresh faces. A burly young man around her age with short brown hair and dark brown eyes sat chatting up a petite redhead beside him who was substantially younger, perhaps only nineteen, a kid starting out in the world. She was far too young to be her new partner, thought Charlotte, and she was curious to find out why the girl was with them.

Cyrus was waiting by the passenger door, kicking at the murder of seven crows which had gathered by his feet. At first, the birds refused to move, but as Charlotte approached, one of the black fiends turned to regard her with its beady, unblinking eyes. It stared at her all of but a heartbeat until it let out a caw, ruffled its shimmering onyx feathers, and flew off, taking all of its companions with it. She stopped and watched the dark flock clog up the sky in murky darkness as they vanished from sight, and she thought how particularly strange it was. But as much as she wished to ponder the meaning of the birds, she remembered she had to get to work and sprinted the short distance between her and her ride.

"Well, good morning, Miss. Briggs." Cyrus waved at her with a smile that crinkled his face. "Glad you're able to join us."

"Sorry. I guess I slept in. I promise it won't happen again."

"No need to apologize, it happens to the best of us. Now, allow me to introduce you to your co-workers. This young lady here is Iris Chapman, the new dispatcher for your shift. And the young man sitting beside her is one Charles McCrae, your new partner."

"Hello." Charlotte mumbled as she averted their gaze. "Nice to meet you all."

"Hey there." Iris leaned past Charles and waved. "I can't wait to get to know you better. I didn't get to meet many lady paramedics back where I lived, now I get to be friends with one."

"Howdy partner." Charles looked up at her and frowned. "Where is your trauma bag? I was told we needed to bring our own."

"Back in my room." Charlotte peeked over her shoulder in the direction she came from. "I thought today was only orientation."

"You are correct, Miss. Briggs, today is only a meet and greet. You are not required to have your bag."

"Still, you may want to grab it anyway, you know how these places are. The last orientation I went to turned out to be a full-on shift. Plus, no use in dragging it in tomorrow when you can drop it off at your locker today."

"Oh, right. I guess you have a good point. I can always go back and get it. If that's okay with you, Cyrus?"

"Yes ma'am, but hurry, we don't want to be too late."

"Sure, not a problem. I'll be back in a jiffy."

Charlotte turned to head back to the door. She could have easily gone in through her patio door, but in her paranoia over Bret, she kept it latched and even used the safety bar that was provided. The thought of going back through the hall caused her insides to churn and prick, but she had no other alternative. It was daytime after all. Everyone knew nothing scary ever happened during the day. Such things were reserved for the midnight hour when the visibility was low, and your eyes played tricks on you.

Tricks, that was all last night was, an elaborate illusion created by her panic-stricken brain. Convincing herself of her own delusions, she reached for the door when a cackle of crows came from above her head, rooting her to her spot.

CHAPTER SIX

"Darkness always had its part to play. Without it, how would we know when we walked in the light?"— **Clive Barker, Abarat**

harlotte's trembling hand hovered over the door rail as the crows continued to caw above her. Their spooky, high-pitched cries blended into the laugh of a mad man. She wanted to tilt her head up and observe them, count how many there were, but her muscles refused to move despite her best efforts. Shutting out the melancholy cries of the birds, she depressed the metal bar and pushed her way back inside the hotel. Standing in the hall, she looked toward her door and her heart dropped into her ankles as the space seemed to elongate into an unfathomable eternity.

Lights flickered around her as the hallway stretched further and further away from her, and somewhere in the distance, she heard the tolling of a bell. Listening to its mournful clang, a splitting headache assaulted her out of the blue. Her brain throbbed as if someone were digging a knife into it, and all she could do was clench her teeth to stop the bile that was burning a hole in her esophagus from making its way to the floor. The room rocked and swayed like some ship caught in a raging storm, and black smoke filtered in around her. Overcome with nausea, she leaned against the wall, which quickly gave way beneath her, sending her toppling to the cold ground below.

She pushed herself up and realized that the paisley carpet beneath her had transformed into a cobblestone street. The world appeared to be drenched in a shade of sepia and streams of people flowed by her, none of which stopped to help. Passersby continued to float around her, and some through her, and that was when Charlotte realized that she was not actually there. She was transported to a world outside her time, merely a spectator to the ghosts of the events which had long since passed. Alone in a world she did not belong to, and with no way to return back to her time, a pang of pain radiate through her heart.

"Get up, Lottie." A distant male voice called to her. "You have to get up."

Lottie, her heart missed a beat. Only her mother had called her that, and that was not her. Straining to stand up, an invisible force weighed her down. It was as if someone was sitting on top of her, keeping her there. No, she thought, I won't let this end here. Clenching her jaw, she struggled to stagger on to her feet until she could glance in the voice's direction. A strange man with curly black hair in a dark blue paramedic's uniform stood by one of the stone houses, pointing to its door. He seemed so familiar, a specter from some long-forgotten memory which no longer existed, and Charlotte wanted to run into his arms.

"Come on, Lottie." The man continued to point to the door. "You don't belong here. You must get out. Focus on what keeps you living. Focus and you will find your way back."

With wobbling knees, Charlotte stumbled forward, pushing her way through figments of people who had long left her world. The stale, greasy air made it difficult to breathe, let alone think, and her muscles screamed in agony with her every step. She felt like she was dying, and perhaps she was. But she urged her legs to move forward, down the street to where the man stood, and she focused on Kevin, who would be lost without her. Her vision was growing dark from the pain when she reached the house the man had been standing at. The stranger had long evaporated, but as she focused on the door, she let go a cry of relief. There, on chipped and faded lacquer, was the number one-hunderd and three.

Grabbing hold of the ornate doorknob, she twisted it in her hand and fell inside just as she lost her grip on reality. Laying on the floor, she opened her eyes and saw that she was back in her room, her bag sat right beside her. Releasing the tears building in her eyes, she looked about the room. It was empty, Kevin must have left for school already. Walking to the glass door, she peeked outside and saw Cyrus standing by his Jeep. A sigh of relief escaped her lungs, and she wiped away her tears. Grabbing the bag off the floor, she slung it around her shoulders and went to open the door when she suddenly stopped. She needed to get back outside, but the thought of going back in the hallway terrified her. Still, there was no other way out, and she held her breath as she went to pull open the door.

CHAPTER SEVEN

"Because God is never cruel, there is a reason for all things. We must know the pain of loss; because if we never knew it, we would have no compassion for others, and we would become monsters of self-regard, creatures of unalloyed self-interest. The terrible pain of loss teaches humility to our prideful kind, has the power to soften uncaring hearts, to make a better person of a good one." — Dean Koontz, The Darkest Evening of the Year

Gawking into the hallway beyond the door, Charlotte wondered when it was going to change and send her back into the hellish world she came from. But aside from her pounding heart, all she heard was a muffled hum of a vacuum cleaner to her right. Peering around the corner of the door frame, she spotted the maid in a black and white dress, vacuuming the floor a few doors away from her. Rationalizing that nothing would happen with another person there with her, she stepped out and shut the door behind her.

Glancing down to the end where specks of light from the door were on the wall, she found the panic welling up inside her. Not daring to be in the hall any longer than she had to be, she clutched her bag to her chest and sprinted for the other end. Bursting through the door she sent a black mass of crows soaring into the air as they croaked in protest at her haste. Paying no attention to the flock leaving glimmering green and purple feathers in their wake, she continued to run for the Jeep. Having crossed the lawn, she spotted her salvation in sight and nearly fell on her face as she tripped over the curb in a rush to escape from the hotel.

"Well, dang." Charles glanced up at her frazzled face and scratched his head. "That was quick."

"Yeah." Charlotte heaved and wheezed. She hadn't run that fast since she was a kid. "Told you I'd be quick. Now let's go, we wouldn't want to be late."

Hopping in the front seat next to Cyrus, Charlotte put her bag between her legs and stilled her shaking hands before pulling her seat belt around her. The others continued to stare at her, and she hoped they wouldn't catch on to her fear, or her general unease of being on the island. She didn't understand what was going on with her, nor could she explain the ominous feeling she got from being in Autumn Falls, and she did not want these strangers to think she was crazy. She needed this job more than anything and did not need to be dismissed on the account of being clinically insane. That's all she was, insane, a loon who needed to be locked up and medicated, but with her being Kevin's only parent, she couldn't afford to be hauled away to a cushy state hospital for treatment.

"What are we waiting for?" She turned to Cyrus and smiled. "Let's get moving."

Frowning at her, the old man started up the car and drove out of the hotel parking lot, heading west on Cottage Lane. Charles and Iris were hitting it off in the back, chatting and flirting while Charlotte stared out the windshield in silence, ignoring their playful banter. She never did much like people, and while she was always cordial with her co-workers, she never formed the close-knit relationship the others had, mostly because Bret wouldn't allow it. Resting her elbow on the side of the door, she leaned on her hand and heaved out a sigh. She was busy marveling at the colorful Victorian cottages lining the street when the distant wail of an ambulance getting closer drew her attention. Sitting up in her seat, she noted the Jeep had slowed down and watched as a boxy white ambulance streaked between two brick buildings in front of them, heading east up Emerald Beach Avenue.

"Cyrus..." Charlotte frowned as she continued to listen to the cry of the sirens grow distant and finally stop. "I thought they said there was only one ambulance crew per shift."

"Oh, there is. You on the first shit, one second shift, and one on the night shift." Cyrus said unfazed and turned left to go in the opposite direction of the ambulance. "That was sixty-five seventy -four that you saw just now. It crashed almost twenty-five years ago, killing everyone on board."

"Are you trying to say Char saw a ghost ambulance?" Charles leaned in between the seats and tapped Charlotte's shoulder. "You don't mind if I call you Char for short, right?"

"Sure. As long as you don't mind me calling you Chuck."

"Fine by me. I actually kind of like that nickname. Now," he turned to face Cyrus, "about that ghost ambulance. Was that thing for real?"

"It was as real as you or me, but it was no ghost..." Cyrus glanced in his rearview mirror with a soft scowl, "no, that was more of an echo."

"An echo?" Iris mumbled from the back seat and stole a glance over her shoulder. "What's the difference, if you don't mind me asking?"

"A ghost is the spirit of a deceased person; one you can interact with. They are sentient beings who understand they are dead and are sticking around because they have unfinished business to attend to. An echo on the other hand is an imprint on the environment, like a photograph or a film reel. It happens when an event is so traumatic it burns itself into the fabric of reality and keeps playing itself repeatedly, on a loop. You can't interact with it, and you can't change it, just watch it run its course."

"So..." Charlotte paused. "We just keep seeing a glimpse of it making its last run, is that right?"

"Correct, Miss. Briggs. It got t-boned by a truck and went off a cliff less than a mile up the road. By the time the auxiliary crew got to the scene, both of the medics and the patient they were transporting perished."

"That's so sad." Charlotte glanced down at the hands on her lap. "Did any of them have children?"

"Just Sinclair. His partner was a single guy at the time. Yup," Cyrus nodded and stared out beyond the glass of his windshield, "it was a dark day for the first responders of Autumn Falls. We lost our two medics in the morning. Then ten firefighters died that afternoon in an explosion over at the fish processing plant. And that night, one of our officers died in a hit-and-run up on Ocean Avenue."

"How horrible... for everyone involved. I can only imagine what it was like for their children having to deal with losing their parents like that. Not that I would know, since I lost my father when I was still a baby, far too young to even remember what he looked like. Still..." Charlotte glanced out her window and held back a tear, "I constantly worry about what would happen to Kevin if he lost me. I'm all he has."

"What happened to his dad?" Iris said in a half whisper while avoiding Charlotte's gaze. "If you don't mind me asking, that is."

"Oh, well..." Charlotte studied the leaves fluttering in the trees and pondered how she should phrase the next part of her sentence. "You see, his dad doesn't exactly *know* about him."

"What?" Chuck yelled, leaning in closer to her as if he was suddenly interested in their conversation. "You mean to say that never told the guy he was a father?"

"Not a word."

"Damn girl," he shook his head, "that's just cold."

"Enough, Charles!" Iris glared at him and whacked his shoulder with the back of her hand. "I'm sure Charlotte had a good reason for not telling him. We shouldn't pry into her life like that. I'm sorry I even asked, this is my fault really."

"No, it's no big deal. Don't feel bad. It's truly a non-issue, I promise."

Iris did not reply, she turned her head away with downcast eyes, and Charles sat looking out his window, still rubbing the spot on his shoulder where she hit. An awkward silence befell the Jeep as no one dared speak more on the subject of Kevin, or his father. Even Cyrus kept his mouth shut the rest of the way to the station house. It wasn't until they reached the small brick building with Mullioned windows that he broke the silence as he parked in the small parking area at the back.

"Well, here we are. The station contains all the emergency services for the island. Let's go meet Miss. Owens. I saw her waiting for us upfront."

Grabbing her bag, Charlotte trailed behind the others as they rounded the corner of the building and walked past the two large garage bay doors where six crows had gathered to watch. Pacing by the glass entryway was a tall woman wearing a fine, navy-blue Italian suit. Her raven hair was wound tightly in a neat bun, and she stopped to push the sleeve of her jacket and steal a glance at the watch on her slender wrist. Turning on the stiletto heels of her black leather boots, she spotted them approach. Pursing her thin cranberry lips, she narrowed her blue eyes and stormed towards them, her heels clicking rhythmically on the stone.

"You're late." She hissed.

"Sorry ma'am," Cyrus tipped his hat to her, "but Miss. Briggs wished to grab her bag, and then we got stuck at some lights."

"Fine. I shall accept that excuse, but only for today. Just see to it that it won't happen again."

"Yes ma'am, of course. I'll deliver them to you on time from now on." Turning to leave, Cyrus waved at Charlotte and her companions. "Off you go kids, follow your new supervisor, Victoria Owens. I'll be back to pick you up at four. You have fun now."

Watching him leave, a sickening sense of dread filled Charlotte and as she turned to shake the woman's cold, lifeless hand she felt a chill rake through her spine. There was something about her new boss she simply did not like. Perhaps it was her haughty, upper-class attitude, or the ice in her voice and the dark glint in her eyes, but she was on edge while she was around her. The others seemed to not notice something off about the woman, or the station house while they gleefully introduced themselves to their supervisor, and Charlotte was left clutching her bag while all her instincts were screaming at her to get away.

CHAPTER EIGHT

"The oldest and strongest emotion of mankind is fear, and the oldest and strongest kind of fear is fear of the unknown." — **H.P. Lovecraft, Supernatural Horror in Literature**

Six crows had gathered on the eve above the door to the station and twisted their heads down to peer at Charlotte. One of the black birds ruffled its feathers, blinked, and let out a cry which reverberated through the street. The luster in the bird's eyes appeared cold and ominous, causing a shiver to creep down her spine and a rock-hard lump to form in her stomach. Turning her gaze to Victoria, she noted the woman's face crinkle as she glanced up at the birds and hissed for them to scram. Seemingly listening to the command, the birds flapped their feathers and took off, settling back down on a striped awning of a candy shop across the street. There was something not right about the whole thing, a primitive fear she could not explain crept up inside her.

"All right you three, enough lollygagging." Victoria ignored the birds, and Charlotte's tension as she turned and waved her hand. "Come now, follow me. Let me give you a brief tour. Then, since you two have your bags, you can go out on your first run and get to know each other as partners while I give Miss. Chapman a break down on how we do things around here."

Flinging the glass doors open, Victoria led the trio inside the three-story building's warm reception room. The polished herringbone oak floor led the eyes to an antique reception desk crafted of cherry, and speckled with the morning sun. A young blonde in a cream blouse with a tight French twist looked up past the thick black rims of her glasses. Twisting her lip into a partial smile, she adjusted the neatly done bow on her neck and went back to typing on her keyboard without saying a word.

"As you can see," Victoria continued, "the bottom floor is our reception area. To the left, you have the stairwell and the vehicle bay. "We have a total of four fire trucks and three ambulances here. You two will drive number thirty-six fifty-five, which is parked upfront. I will let you load it up as soon as we get done here and you can go explore the town."

"What's on the right?" Charlotte stole a glanced towards a solid oak door at the other end.

"Oh, that is our police department and jail. You will probably have little dealings with them. We don't have the type of violence you have grown accustomed to in the city. Our boys in blue are just here to deal with obnoxious teenagers making our life a living hell. Now," Victoria nudged open another solid door and held it open for them, "how about we check out the rest of the building?"

Nodding silently, Charlotte shuffled in behind Chuck and Iris into a narrow concrete stairwell where a fluorescent bulb flickered and hummed above their heads. The bulb did little to illuminate the dim space, and if it wasn't for the metal door with a small window leading to the parking lot out back, the area would feel suffocating. Walking around past the door, Victoria ushered them to follow her up the stairs to the next floor. Charlotte waited for everyone else to go and hearing the echo of heels clicking in the hall, she trailed up behind them. After two flights of stairs, Victoria opened another door, and they stepped into an open area with two more doors in front of them and a line of vending machines to their left.

"We reserved this floor for emergency medical services. The fire department is on the same floor behind us, but they have access through the garage bay, so you won't have to worry about them lingering here. The dispatcher's office is the door on the left. This is where Iris will handle most of the emergency calls for me. The door to the right is the locker room, bathroom, and showers. Your lockers have your name on them, so feel free to put anything you'd like in there, like a change of clothing if you wish to take your showers here. I have also put your uniforms in them, so do change before you go out on patrol." Victoria opened the door again and motioned her head into the stairwell. "Let's go check out the common break area before I let you loose."

Returning to the stairwell, they followed their boss up another two flights of stairs to the last floor of the station. On the other side of the lone oak door was a short hallway filled with pictures and newspaper clippings. Following the Arenberg parquet floor, Charlotte peered through the picture windows into the break room. The space reminded her of a fishbowl as she watched the two firemen playing at a Foosball table. Beside them, on the blue striped sofa, a man sat cross-legged in a blue officer's uniform with his face buried in the morning paper as he sipped coffee from his Styrofoam cup.

"This is the common break room." Victoria continued, not moving. "Inside we have a TV, a Foosball table, and a fully stocked kitchen. Use it on your off time, which I am sure you will have plenty of. Officer Johnson over there makes the best pot of coffee around, so I suggest grabbing some first thing in the morning, before it's all gone."

Half listening, Charlotte bobbed her head in acknowledgment as she ambled alongside the wall, studying the framed prints that hung on its burgundy walls. Stopping at one section, her eyes trailed up and lingered on a small pine frame with a photograph of four paramedics standing arm in arm behind the glass. The young man in the middle caught her attention, and she could not look away from him. He was oddly familiar with his dark curly hair and a bright smile on his face. Leaning closer, she squinted to make out the name tag on his jumper, *C. Sinclair*, she mumbled to herself. She knew him, despite never having seen him before, and she felt compelled to reach out and touch him, getting a shiver down her spine as if remembering something she had long forgotten.

"Who are the men in this photograph?"

"Oh, them." Victoria answered coldly. "That was the original crew from twenty-five years ago. They took this photo when they first started working here, six years before that horrible accident that took the lives of Sinclair and his partner, Neewer. The other two men still work the night shift, though they are getting ready to retire. But that is ancient history, one we don't much care to talk about it. Let us go to work now, Iris will come with me to learn the ropes, and you two go change and grab your ambulance to explore the town."

Not willing to press the issue of the lost medics further, Charlotte followed the rest of the group downstairs. Watching Victoria guide Iris into the dispatcher room, she shuffled into the locker room where Chuck was already half naked. Pocking his head from behind his metal door, he smiled at her, and she responded with an awkward wave as she opened the locker with her name on it. There was something unsettling about the metal box, and she ran her finger across the ancient tape marks on the door as her partner continues to strip down behind her.

"All right, Char, I'm going to go take a quick shower before we head out. That okay with you?"

"Yeah, sure." Charlotte broke away from the familiarity of the blue painted steel. "Take your time. I'll go stock the bus and meet you downstairs."

"Thanks, partner."

Waiting for Charles to head into the shower room, Charlotte donned on her blue uniform and shut the locker door. Heading through the door to head downstairs, she paused in the stairwell, consumed by fear. The bulb above her pulsated, and she thought she saw movement in the shadows coming from the top floor. She tried convincing herself she was being hysterical, but as a low moan floated from the top and reverberated around her; she let out a yelp and dashed down the stairs. With her heart galloping in her chest, she flew down three steps at a time and burst through the door into the garage bay without ever trying to glance behind her to see what could be following her.

CHAPTER NINE

"Just when you think you've hit rock bottom, you realize you're standing on another trapdoor."—**Marisha Pessl, Night Film**

L eaping through the jamb, Charlotte startled a fireman who was hanging up equipment on the rack opposite of her. The man with the salt and pepper hair turned around as the door slammed behind her with a frown, and she tried to downplay it by saying that the door got stuck. Nodding his head while she laughed nervously, the man simply said it happens and returned to work. Red hot from the embarrassment of letting her nerves get to her, she tracked down her ambulance—a shiny white bus with red and gold lettering that read 'Autumn Falls EMS'—and opened the back doors to step inside.

Just as the outside appeared brand new, the inside was a state-of-the-art model with all the bells and whistles that were not even on all city ambulances. This town, despite claiming to be a safe haven far removed from the life she had known, spared no expense when it came to its emergency services. Pulling open a clear navy-blue door of one of the cabinets, she noted it was fully stocked with everything a medic would need, including all the optional equipment. She was wondering what they could possibly ever need half of it for when a bang on the metal door caused her to jump and shriek in surprise as she whirled around and spotted Chuck standing behind her, leaning on one of the doors.

"Sorry, didn't mean to startle you. You all right?"

"Yes. I'm fine. It's just this place. It got me all freaked out for no good reason."

"I hear you there, partner." Chuck handed her his bag, stole a glance over his shoulder, and dropped his voice to a whisper. "That stairwell makes me feel uneasy, as if someone is watching me."

"I got the same notion in there just now, and our hotel isn't any better."

"You noticed that too, huh? Yeah, I hate that place, feels so oppressive despite how luxurious it is. But..." Charles cocked his head to peer at the group of firefighters gathered at the back, "perhaps we should talk more about this elsewhere. Ready to ride?"

"Yeah, let us get the hell out of here. I'll drive first and grab our first call if it comes in, since you know, seniority and all."

"Fine by me. Shall we go hunt down a cup of coffee?"

"Sure. I saw a cute little café not far from here. We can see what they offer."

Jumping out from the back of the ambulance, Charlotte shut the door behind her and got in the truck's cab. There was something unsettling about the firemen who stood cross-armed at the far wall, burning a hole in the back of her head with their glares. Ignoring the nagging feeling that something was wrong in this ideal town, she started the engine and drove out of the bay, heading for the Jumping Java Café that they passed before turning onto Ocean Avenue. In the passenger seat, Chuck fidgeted with his thumbs and stared out the window into the rear view mirror. Once away from the station, he turned and looked straight at her.

"Hey, I'm sorry about making that comment about your kid's father. It's just, I guess I'd want to know if I was him. I didn't mean to step on your toes or anything."

"I know. And I don't blame you for reacting the way you did. Truth is, I wanted to tell him, I really did."

"So, why didn't you?"

"We were so young back then, just kids ourselves. He was going off to college to live his dream on this big football scholarship. He was going to be a journalist, you see. Everyone around me was telling me how selfish I was being for wanting him to know. His sister told me it was my decision to have a baby, but I shouldn't drag him into it, and his mother told me to not ruin her son's life because I was a whore who couldn't keep her legs closed. After a few weeks of this, and some extensive bullying from his family and friends, I figured he didn't need to know, at least not while he was in school."

"Why didn't you tell him after he graduated?"

"I had moved on by then. I was living with a guy who I thought was a great man, and who at first treated Kevin as his own son. Little did I know that as soon as we moved to Seattle, things would change. Once he isolated me from my support system, he couldn't care less about Kevin, and he enjoyed controlling the hell out of me. By the time I escaped that nightmare, Kevin's father had become a famous guy with loads of money and probably the same amount of women begging to be by his side. And well..."

"You just didn't want him to think you were some gold-digger after his fortune."

"Precisely. Plus, I couldn't expect him to accept responsibility for a kid he was not aware of for nine years, right? I mean, what kind of guy would want that?"

"I guess you have a point. But as a guy, I'd like to think that I'd want to know. Still, what you do with your life if your choice, Char.

Smiling at her partner, Charlotte pulled over and went inside to grab their coffee. This was the first time she opened up to anyone, and it was great to unload the things eating away at her off her chest. She trusted Chuck more so than she trusted her previous partners, like there was an unspoken bond between them, and for the first time since setting foot on the island, she felt relieved. Bringing out their complimentary coffee and pastries back to the ambulance, she climbed in and asked him where he wished to go. He didn't have a clear destination in mind, and they drove down

Ocean Avenue, enjoying the sites until they pulled up to a red light.

Sitting idling at the intersection, Charlotte observed another murder of crows sitting lined up on the horizontal bar spanning the road above them. Their glass eyes glistened with the late morning sun as they twisted their heads, looking down on her. She counted them. Seven in all, ruffling their feather and continuing to study them with a stony gaze. Strange, she thought, they only come in groups of six or seven, but why? Were the birds trying to tell her something, or were their numbers just a coincidence? The light turned green, and she drove through the intersection and parked in a small lot overlooking the ocean.

"Hey, have you noticed," she looked over at Charles, "how the crows here seem to only come in groups of six or seven?"

"No..." he paused and glanced out to the seven who had followed them and were now sitting on the bench across from them. "You for real? Or are you just messing with me?"

"No, I mean it. I thought it was strange how they are always in large groups, so I have been counting them since we got on the island." She paused and took a sip of her coffee. "Six or seven, that's the only number they come in. Don't you think it's a tad, peculiar?"

"I guess." Chuck continued to stare out the windshield and recounted the birds on the bench. "Reminds me of a silly counting rhyme my mom taught me when I was a young boy. Let me see if I remember how it goes... oh yes... one for sorrow, two for joy, three for a girl, four for a boy."

"Yeah, that rhyme was originally used to count magpies over in England. My mom taught it to me too, but hers was a bit different from yours."

"How so?"

"Hers went like this: One for sorrow, two for mirth, three for a funeral, four for a birth, five for heaven, six for hell, seven for the devil, his own self."

"A bit dark for a kiddie rhyme, don't you think?"

"Perhaps." Charlotte glanced at him and smirked. "But my mom always claimed that it was far more accurate than the improved version you know."

"So, what are you saying? These birds are telling us we are in hell and that the devil is amongst us?"

"Who knows, maybe, or maybe they are just birds. I just find it strange how their flocks are only in those numbers, that's all."

"You know... now that you mention it, have you noticed something else strange about this place?"

"Like what?"

"Like how the *only* birds on this island *are* crows? There isn't even a single seagull here."

"You're right, that is strange." Charlotte flexed her hands on the steering wheel and continued to stare out the window. "Come to think of it, I watched the gulls turn and head away from the island when we were still three miles out, almost like they dared not venture here."

"Shit Char, now you're scaring the shit out of me. What if..."

"EMS thirty-six fifty-five," The radio crackled, making Charlotte and Chuck jump in their seats. "EMS thirty-six fifty-five, please respond to fourteen o eight Ocean Ave for a thirty-five-year-old male who injured his leg in his garage. This is a priority call."

"Dispatch," Charles picked up the receiver, looking over at Charlotte who was still panting, "this is EMS thirty-six fifty-five, we copy, responding to fourteen o eight Ocean Ave." Hanging the radio back up, he nudged Charlotte whose knuckles were turning white from gripping the wheel as she continued to shake. "Ready to go?"

"Yes. Sorry. It just startled me. Let's go."

Flicking on the lights and sirens, Charlotte backed out of her spot and headed up the road to the address. Onlookers stood on the sidewalk and watched as they flew by them with their lights spinning and their ambulance wailing. Slowing down for a sharp turn, she rounded the corner and pulled up into the driveway of a white Cape, which seemed oddly silent. There were no neighbors or family to welcome them and show them to the injured man, just the still calmness of a tomb, or a funeral parlor. It was almost as if someone made a prank call and was hiding out inside, and if they just made it up a few more feet, they would discover no injured man and absolutely nothing to worry about.

CHAPTER TEN

"There are black zones of shadow close to our daily paths, and now and then some evil soul breaks a passage through. When that happens, the man who knows must strike before reckoning the consequences." __ **H.P. Lovecraft, The Thing on the Doorstep**

The wind whistled eerily through the trees as Charlotte walked up the winding stone walkway to the white house with the forest-green shutters and a matching green door. Something about the space unnerved her, and in her gut, she sensed an ancient evil as she rang the bell and waited for someone to answer. Nothing. She waited a few minutes and rang the bell again. This time she heard shuffling on the other side and the door opened to reveal an elderly lady in a yellow, blood-spangled house dress. The woman looked over at the two medics with her bulging gray eyes and smiled.

"Yes. Can I help you?"

"Sorry to bother you ma'am," Charlotte stole a glance behind her at a tabby cat sitting on the sofa yowling in her direction, "but we received a call about a man injured at this address."

"Oh, yes," she bobbed her head and the curly wisps of white hair on her head bounced with every motion, "Mickey is in the garage, follow me."

The woman left the door open and went deeper into the house. Charlotte stole a glance back at Chuck, who shrugged his shoulders, and she stepped into the cozy cottage. Once inside, the scrawny, mangy looking cat hopped off the floral sofa it was sitting on and hissed at her before swiping at her leg with its sharp claws. Startled, she leaped back with a yelp and the feline ran off to hide under the skirt of the pastel pink recliner.

"Oh, don't mind Mr. Figgins, dear. He just doesn't like uniforms. Come now, Mickey is this way."

The calmness in the woman's voice was uncanny, and Charlotte was wondering if this was all an elaborate prank to hoodwink the rookies until she stepped through the door into the garage, and her heart sank into her stomach. The first thing she noticed was the blood-streaked wall, with the spray fanning up to the ceiling and running down the white paint in streams. Following the carnage, she spotted an ash-gray foot sitting beside a miter saw which was still spinning with a loud hum, blood congealing on its polished steel platform. Behind it, a man sat up against the wall, humming while the stump of his right leg continued to spurt blood which pooled on the concrete beneath him.

"Jesus..." Charles muttered.

"Jesus doesn't live here anymore."

Charlotte turned back to glance at the disheveled old woman who was grinning from ear to ear, pulling back her lips into a sneer. The white hair flying around her made her appear insane with her bulging eyes as she went back inside the house with a cackle, shutting the door behind her. Bewildered by the encounter, Charlotte wanted to bolt through the nearest door, but she knew she'd have to treat her patient despite the panic pooling up inside her stomach. Turning to the man in question, she swallowed her fear and rushed to his side. Throwing her bag down beside him, she kneeled to assess him while she put on her latex gloves.

At first glance, the man was sweating profusely, beads of perspiration glistened on his ashen brow, and his lips were turning blue. His breath was shallow and rapid as he turned to glance at her with his sunken brown eyes. Taking his clammy wrist into her hand, Charlotte could feel his pulse weakening, he was going into hypovolemic shock, she had little time to move.

Yelling for Chuck to preserve the foot, she reached in her bag and pulled out a tourniquet. Placing it just above the cut in his leg, she tightened it to stem the flow of blood and covered the man up with a thermal blanket to keep him warm. She was busy applying a pressure bandage to the bloody stump when her partner walked up to her with a foot held inside a bag filled with an ice saline solution. Instructing him to run an IV and provide the patient with some ketamine for the pain, she glanced back up at the man who seemed to be getting worse.

"Sir, can you tell us exactly how this accident happened?"

"Accident?" The man glanced up at her, grinning. "Who said anything about an accident?"

Tilting his head back, the man laughed almost hysterically, chilling Charlotte to the bone. Nodding her head at Chuck, they managed to get the man on a back board and secure him to the stretcher as he continued to howl with laughter, thrashing against the straps that held him down. Trembling, she shouted for her partner to open the garage door as their patient continued to act irrationally, telling her all about how his mother helped him cut off his foot. Her heart raced, even as the door clanked above her head. Running up to her, Charles threw the bagged limb on top of the patient and grabbed his bag.

"Ready to go?"

"Yes," Charlotte put her bag over her shoulder, "let's transport him while he's still somewhat stable."

"Should we tell the old woman that we are leaving?"

"No. I'm sure she will figure it out once she hears our siren. Plus, I don't want to stay here longer than we need to. Something about this whole thing just don't feel right."

"No, kidding." Charles peered at the foot on the stretcher. "All right, let's go."

Wheeling the patient to the back of the ambulance, Charlotte glanced up and spotted the old woman standing at the bay window, watching them through a pulled-back sheer panel. There was a huge grin on her face, and she slowly waved at them before turning back to head into the house. Swallowing the hard lump in her throat, she couldn't help but think how calm the lady was, almost as if they were taking her son on a fun ride and not like he had life-threatening injuries. Perhaps they both suffered from some form of mental illness, and she intended to have Iris instruct the officers to check it out as soon as they got going. Relaying her concerns to Chuck, he assured her he would take care of it as he shut the door behind her, leaving her in the back with the man who was still hooting and hollering.

CHAPTER ELEVEN

"The real world is where the monsters are." — **Rick Riordan**

*I*n the back of the ambulance, Charlotte continued to work on her patient as it sped down the winding island streets. The man had calmed himself, and she was able to turn away from him to a bag of fluids which she intended to administer to him intravenously. Turning back to the stretcher, her heart nearly leaped out of her chest. What was once a human man had transformed into a hellish creature straight out of a nightmare. Its gray skin clung loosely to its elongated bones and his once brown eyes were as dark and lifeless as black holes. Opening its mouth to reveal rows of needle-sharp fangs, the creature grabbed hold of her wrist with its bony, ape-like fingers and pulled her in closer.

"We're coming for you."

His voice was hauntingly melodic, as if he were trying to sing her to sleep with his very threat. The breath that caught in her lungs was burning and Charlotte's scream came out as nothing more than an inaudible whisper. Thrashing and twisting, she attempted to pull away from him, but he held tight. Then suddenly, he let go of her, sending her falling to the floor, hitting her elbow against the metal counter. Standing up, she rubbed her aching joint and studied the man passed out, breathing heavily just as the ambulance pulled up to a stop.

She waited for Charles to open the door to the sweet freedom beyond the cramped confines of the cabin and was getting ready to jump out past him before her professionalism took over. Wheeling the man out, a group of nurses who were ready to take possession of the patient greeted them. Following the ladies in pink scrubs through the bay doors, Charlotte relayed information to a stout woman with short gray hair and a friendly smile.

The nurse assured her the man was in expert care and put a hand on Charlotte's shoulder. She noted how cold and lifeless it felt, and for the first time she noticed how the smell of death seemed to cling to every person who worked at the hospital. Not a fresh scent you might expect at a trauma center, but an old one, akin to a rotting corpse or the stale earth of a burial ground.

Transferring the patient to the hospital bed, Charlotte left her paperwork with the nurse and wheeled the stretcher back to the ambulance. Having cleaned up the mess in the cabin, the two partners sat on the back bumper and stared up at the clear sky. She continued to shiver from her encounter, despite the afternoon sun warming her skin, and wondered what Charles would think of her if she told him.

"Hey, what's this?" He lifted her elbow, pointing to the bruise which started to blossom on the flesh. "You okay, partner?"

"Oh, that, yeah, I'm fine. The guy just attacked me while I was inside, I fell down trying to get away."

"What? How is that possible, we strapped him down before we left?"

"I know, but it was not him that attacked me..." she paused, wondering if she should continue, "he seemed possessed or something. I don't know how else to explain this, but he seemed different."

"How so?"

"I guess he was more like some alien creature, or a demon. But perhaps I'm just going crazy and imagining things."

"No, I don't think you are. Did you notice the smells in that place..." Chuck glanced over his shoulder at the red-brick building behind him, "they were not normal for a hospital?"

"You're right. Most hospitals smell like bleach and antiseptic, but this one smelled... damp and mildewy."

"Right... I also noted the sour, metallic scent of blood floating in the air. I suppose it's not all that uncommon, but I've never got a whiff so strong before. And it was as cold as the tundra in there, or a tomb."

Tomb, Charlotte nodded, deep in thought. She didn't make that connection before, but now that Chuck brought it up, she had to agree that the interior of the hospital appeared to be more like a mausoleum than a place of healing. There was an odd silence to the place, a somber one which reminded her of a cemetery or a morgue. Normally hospitals were a bustling place with chatter, phones ringing, and news anchors on TVs spouting the latest events as they happened. But Wilson Memorial had none of that. It was as hushed as the vacuum of space.

"EMS thirty-six fifty-five," the speakers on their collars crackled simultaneously, "please respond to thirty-six hundred Prospect Street for reports of a deceased female on premises."

Frowning, Charlotte picked up the radio and pressed down the button.

"Dispatch, this is EMS thirty-six fifty-five, please confirm you want us to respond to thirty-six hundred Prospect Street?"

"That's correct EMS thirty-six fifty-five."

"What's wrong, Char?"

"That's the site of the old hospital. Cyrus said the locals dare not step foot on those grounds. So why would there be a dead body on premises?"

"No clue, maybe someone dumped it, want to go check it out?"

"We have to. It's our job."

Getting up from the bumper, Charlotte and Chuck shut the cabin doors and headed for the front of the ambulance when another crack from the radio rooted them to their spots.

"EMS thirty-six fifty-five, this is dispatch," Victoria's icy voice hissed through the radio, "disregard that last call and return to the station house... immediately."

"Yes, ma'am." Charlotte spoke into her collar. "We'll be right over."

Next to her, Charles gave her a shrug of his shoulder and walked to the front of the cab.

"Guess the boss lady has spoken. Off to the station we go."

Not daring to say anything, Charlotte got in the passenger seat of the cab and stole a glance out the window. There, above the ambulance bay, were six crows perched neatly in a row, watching them leave. An ominous premonition filled her, a primitive dread or some ancestral memory which was telling her to leave the island or come face to face with death. She pondered what she should do on their short drive back to the station, but she was no closer to finding an answer. While the temptation was great to go back to Boston and start over on familiar ground, Charlotte was not ready to admit defeat just yet. That, and she wanted to get to the bottom of the mysteries enshrouding the island.

CHAPTER TWELVE

"What humans want most of all, is to be right. Even if we're being right about our own doom. If we believe there are monsters around the next corner ready to tear us apart, we would literally prefer to be right about the monsters, than to be shown to be wrong in the eyes of others and made to look foolish." — David Wong, This Book Is Full of Spiders

P ulling back into the garage bay of the station house, the first thing Charlotte saw was Victoria pacing back and forth by the wall. Upon hearing the ambulance pull in, she stopped, turned, narrowed her eyes at them with pursed lips, and tapped her foot on the floor. Charlotte felt uneasy around her and waited for Chuck to hop out first before she carefully opened her door and followed slightly behind him.

"What's up boss lady?"

"This is nothing against the two of you, personally." The chill in Victoria's voice matched the icy luster in her eyes as she spoke to the two of them. "But I will tell you exactly what I told Miss. Chapman when she was too hasty to give you that ludicrous call;

you are under *no* circumstances to go near that abandoned hospital. Is that understood?"

"But ma'am." Charlotte piped up, stepping forward from behind Chuck's back. "What if someone was seriously hurt there? Isn't it our job to respond to every call?"

"Your job, Miss. Briggs," Victoria spat out her words as her nostrils flared, "is to help the injured and the dying, and occasionally, transport the dead. I can with the utmost confidence assure you that there was no one hurt at that hospital. Furthermore, there will *never* be anyone who will get hurt there. The calls we get about that condemned structure are nothing more than prank calls by local hooligans who want to stir things up and scare the bejesus out of us given the building's colorful history. Rest assured, Miss. Briggs, the grounds of that place are entirely off limits, to anyone, and the area is locked down tighter than Fort Knox. You are to stay away from that old hospital if you know what's good for you. Are we clear on that?"

"Yes ma'am. Absolutely. You won't hear about it from us again."

"Good. See to it that I don't. Now off you go. Go finish your shift. I want you to drive around some more, meet the locals, and learn about the island while you have some downtime. I'm sure your one rouge call is probably all you will ever get in a given day."

"Yes. ma'am"

Charlotte watched Victoria turn on her spiky heels and storm through the door for the stair well. Once the echo of the clanking heels faded, she turned to Charles, who silently motioned for her to get back into the ambulance. They drove away from the station house to a nearby park they had passed on the way back from their call. Sitting on the park bench, soaking up the sunshine, they counted to groups of crows gathering around them and chatted about the unpleasant lecture until the clock before them struck three and it was time for them to return.

CHAPTER THIRTEEN

"There are no explanations for human evil. Only excuses." —
Dean Koontz, Intensity

C *leaning* off their ambulance to prepare for the next day, Charlotte grabbed her bag out from the cab and exited the station. Walking for the spot where the Jeep was waiting for her, she crossed the parking lot when something caught her eye and froze her in her tracks. Putting a hand to her racing heart, she continued to gawk at the black-clad figure standing next to a large oak tree across the street. She knew that creature too well by now; it was her mythical pigman, staring at her through its empty eye sockets. It did not move from where it stood, it simply tilted its head and raised a hand, pointing at something. She traced the lines of the bony finger and her eyes landed on the vine-covered brick building sitting atop the hill in the distance. Returning her gaze to the tree, she was hoping to get a better look at the figure, but it was gone as quickly as it appeared, and she could finally exhale the stale air trapped in her lungs. Stifling a scream, she turned and ran for the Jeep where Cyrus would be waiting for her.

Throwing her bag to the floor, she opened the door and hopped in panting. The old man turned to frown at her, and she just smiled at and claimed she couldn't wait to get home. With a snort, Cyrus turned away from her, and she leaned her head on her hand, counting the six crows which gathered on a ledge of the station house above them. It was not long before Charles and Iris strolled out together, chatting and laughing. Having climbed in the back of the car, Chuck leaned over the seat and patted her on the shoulder.

"Not going to leave your bag in your locker, partner?"

"No." Charlotte glanced over her shoulder with an awkward laugh. "I like having it on me in case I need it. A force of habit really since in Seattle they expected me to bring it home."

"Fair enough."

"Hey, so guys, are we going to talk about Victoria's blow out today?"

"You mean when boss lady flipped her lid over the call to that old hospital today?"

"Yeah, and she was being nice to the two of you, I know cause I listened in after how she went off on me. Why, I thought she was going to rip my head clean off when I told her I called it in to you." Iris glimpsed down in her lap with a pink tinge to her cheeks. "You should have seen how red her face got when she heard the location. She spent the next ten minutes lecturing me about how I should ignore all calls for the hospital and how I should forget the place even exists. At one point, she threatened to fire me if I ever take a call for that place again."

"Really?" Charlotte glance back at the building looking over the island beneath the lighthouse. "Chuck and I were actually talking about that place ourselves after our lecture. I mean, I know they condemned the place, but there is no way that no one dares to go in there. Even in large cities we have kids and urban explorers breaking into nuclear power plants and other dangerous areas. I have a hard time believing that such things don't happen here to a lousy old hospital."

"Oh, I'm sure they do, Miss. Briggs, but *if* they do, we probably won't get any calls about them getting hurt there."

"How come?"

"Because legend has it, that if you are to go into that place, you won't be getting out alive."

"Legend?" Chuck leaned in closer to Cyrus. "Now *that* I have to hear. Tell us, old man, what is this legend?"

"Well, the first thing you should know is that the Natives called this place the isle of the great devil. It was rumored that men who fished too close to this island often got lost in the fog, never to find their way back, and the natives believed that a great evil spirit dwelt here." Cyrus started up the Jeep and drove down the winding road. "Then, when the first settlers got here, stories began to circulate about how they banished a witch here, and how she made a deal with the devil to extend her life in exchange for human souls. After the hospital was built on that hill there, and that doctor started her experiments, it didn't take long for locals to claim that they built it on the site of the witch's cottage and how she now haunts the place, hunting for souls to give to her master. Today, aside from a few brave kids and some tourists, no one dares to go there, and those who do, don't stay long."

"Fascinating," Charlotte glanced at the old building growing closer as they drove, "so, everyone stays away from it out of superstitious fear?"

"Not fear my girl, more of a primitive instinct or a need for self-preservation. Don't believe me?" He glanced over at her with a smirk. "Well, you just get near the gates of that place and you will understand what I mean. The oppressive energy will grab hold of you and suck the air right out of your lungs the moment you're near and your skin will begin to tingle. For most people, that is enough proof that something evil dwells there, and they run away as fast as their feet will carry them. To this day, I don't think a single person has managed to get anywhere near the door to even stick their nose inside and poke around." Parking the Jeep by the side door of the hotel, Cyrus cut off the engine and gazed up to the sky, still smiling. "But enough of old ghost stories and urban legends. I'm sure you kids have better things to do with your evening. I'll see you guys tomorrow at seven-thirty sharp."

"Bye Cyrus, I'll see you tomorrow." Iris jumped out and waved. "You have a good night now."

"Night, Miss.Chapman."

"Night, man."

"Thank you, Cyrus, for the ride and the stories." Charlotte grabbed her bag. "Take care now."

"You too, Miss. Briggs. And keep an eye on that boy of yours, this island can be rough for newcomers."

Holding the straps of her bag, Charlotte watched Cyrus drive off into the distance, getting sad at not getting to hear more of his stories until the next day. She turned to walk inside and spotted a giggling Iris lean over and whisper something in Charles' ear before running off into the hotel. Lowering her gaze, she went to go through the side door when Chuck called out to her and made her stop halfway to her destination.

CHAPTER FOURTEEN

"Maybe all the schemes of the devil were nothing compared to what man could think up." —**Joe Hill**

Turning, she waited for her partner to walk over to her. She always hated this part, where people would try to befriend her. It's not that she didn't want friends, she craved them, but after living with a man who forbid such luxury, she was still nervous about forming deeper social connections. Evidently Bret still had a hold on her, and she was not entirely free from his brainwashing, but she waited for Charles to approach her, regardless.

"You got plans tonight, Char? Cause Iris and I were going to go out and check out the bar down the street, and we wanted to know if you want to join us."

"Thanks, Chuck, but I can't leave my kid behind. Plus, I think we are going to have pizza and watch *Night of the Living Dead* tonight."

"All right, suit yourself. Enjoy your night with your boy. Iris and I will see you tomorrow. But if you change your mind, you know where to find us."

"Thanks, man. I'll see you tomorrow. You guys have fun."

Waving at Chuck, Charlotte headed for the door but stopped when she remembered what happened to her in the hallway that morning. For a moment she entertained the idea of going to the patio and knocking on the glass door, but she didn't want to scare her son, or worse, give him the idea that his mother was crazy. She had no choice, and she pulled open the door and held her breath as she stepped into the peaceful hall. Darting her eyes around between the two walls, she noted that nothing strange was happening. The only sounds were the dings of the elevator and the muffled whispers of footfalls on the carpet from people going into their room. Feeling safe, she exhaled and hurried for her door.

Inside, she found Kevin sprawled on the bed with his Switch in hand, playing Mario Kart from the sounds of it. His book bag was parked on the stool by the door, as flat as it was the night before. Charlotte was puzzled. Normally his bag would be bulging from books, and he would be sitting at the desk feverishly scribbling amongst a mound of scattered worksheets. If Kevin was any other kid, she'd think he skipped school, but her kid was far too responsible for that. He had aspirations of becoming an engineer when he grew up, and he worked hard to keep his grades up. Parking her bag next to his, she took off her shoes and shut the hotel door behind her.

"Hey kiddo, how was school?"

"Freaky." Kevin finally looked up from his screen and sat up to greet her. "Do I really have to go back there?"

"Yes, you do, young man. Seriously, what has gotten into you? How bad can your school possibly be?"

"Horrible. There are all of like ten people in my class, and they are all weird."

"How so?"

"For one, they just sit, and do their work quietly. Then there is the teacher." Kevin sat up and whispered. "She doesn't teach anything, she just put's up our assignments on the blackboard, and we do them. And let me tell you, these kids, they don't talk, they don't look up, I'm pretty sure they don't even blink. They just sit and work like a bunch of mindless zombies, or some freaky living dolls."

"Huh, so your teacher doesn't give lectures?"

"No! She just sits at her desk, humming this creepy tune with a smile on her face and her head in a book. She doesn't even glance up to see if we are working. I think I could have left and come back before lunch without her taking notice."

"That is a bit strange."

"Oh, you haven't heard the rest of it yet. When they break for lunch, they all just reach under their seats, pull out the same lunch—plain bologna sandwich, celery sticks, an apple, and a carton of low-fat milk—and they just eat it in silence at their desk, in the same order. They don't talk to each other, and they don't go outside to play, they finish their food and return to work. It's like they aren't even kids. It reminds me of that movie you love about the robot wives."

"So, I take it you didn't make any friends then?"

"Nope, I don't befriend robots, or aliens."

"What about homework?"

"Don't got any. I asked the teacher if she was going to assign us some, but she just laughed and said homework is for inner-city kids. Said something about keeping them inside and off the streets and how that's not an issue in Autumn Falls. Then she told me we learn all we need to learn in class."

"I see." Charlotte plopped on the edge of her bed to consider the unsettling irregularities happening all over town. "Well, if it's any consolation, my day wasn't any better. I responded to a guy who cut off his own foot with the help of his mother."

"What? Like, on purpose?"

"That's what it seemed like. They were not even the least bit concerned about his injury. And then, in the ambulance on the way to the hospital, he grabbed hold of me and wouldn't let go. I think it was just the adrenaline talking, but it freaked me out nonetheless."

"What if it wasn't adrenaline? What if there is something wrong with this island?"

"Like what?"

"I don't know. Maybe everyone here has an alien parasite

embedded in their brain. Or maybe it's like in that book where there is an ancient bacterium that consumes people and creates phantoms from them so it can hunt more prey."

"Sounds like you have been watching far too many sci-fi movies and reading too many adult horror books."

"Yeah, maybe..." Kevin stared at her biting his bottom lip, "but you have to admit that this place is odd. I don't know what it is, but I feel on edge here, like someone is constantly watching me with hungry eyes, waiting for the right moment to strike."

"Yeah, my Spidey sense is tingling here too. But lets at least give this place a chance before we pack up and run. Maybe this is just the way island life is, and we'll get used to it."

"I don't want to get used to *this*. I want my brain intact, thank you."

"All right, all right." Charlotte got up from the bed laughing and ruffled her son's hair. "How about I order us some pizza, and we forget all about today over a movie?"

"Anchovies and extra cheese?"

"You got it. I'll go down to the corner store and grab the pizza. Why don't you go to the lobby and grab a movie from the red box that they got sitting next to the soda machine?"

"Deal. See you back here in a bit. Watch out for them zombies, or body snatchers, or whatever they are."

"Will do. You stay safe too, kid."

Watching Kevin leave, Charlotte went to order their pizza.

The rest of the evening was uneventful with nothing frightening or unusual happening to either of them. The two enjoyed their dinner while watching old horror movies and laughing. By the time bedtime rolled around, they had both forgot all about the events of their day and settled in for the night. Breathing a sigh of relief, Charlotte settled down on her pillow and drifted off to sleep, eager to put the day behind her.

CHAPTER FIFTEEN

"We're too much ourselves. Afraid of letting go of what we are, in case we are nothing, and holding on so tight, we lose everything else."—**Clive Barker, Imajica**

A loud ringing pierced through the silence, ushering Charlotte to abandon her pleasant dreams and wake up in her room. Shaking off sleep, she glanced at the red light blinking on the screaming phone, and then moved her heavy eyes to the digital clock beside it. Three in the morning, she thought to herself. Who would call this late at night? Still, the phone was unrelenting, and she picked up the receiver before it woke up Kevin as well.

"Hello?" She waited for someone to reply, but the only thing on the other end was heavy breathing and the hollow sound of rain in the distance. "Hello, who's there?" Still, no reply came, only static. "Bret, is that you?" More raspy breathing came as a reply. "Bret, if that's you then you better listen; I don't know how you tracked us here, but it's over between us. Forget I ever existed. And Bret... I swear, if you come after us, I will kill you myself with my bare hands. You stay the hell away from us, you hear?"

She expected him to reply, but no one did, only the sound of heavy panting and the rasp of raindrops in the distance came through from the other end. Frustrated, she slammed the receiver back on the phone and sat in bed gripping her sheets. Cold hard fear stirred inside her, she was terrified he was going to come after her again, try to steal Kevin like he did that one time. Thinking she was going to give her mother a call in the morning, she noticed something else for the first time, the hissing of static coming from the living space. Getting up from the bed, she stared at the snow flickering on the television. Thinking they forgot to shut the screen off before going to bed, she reached for the remote on the small coffee table.

"Cherry." Zack's voice called her, and she fumbled with the clicker, which slipped out of her hands. "Help me, Cherry."

Looking at where the voice came from, she spotted a face forming in the black and white lines of the screen, bulging, trying to escape. Slapping a hand over her mouth, she swallowed a scream and fell onto the couch. The face twisting and pulling at the glass, moaned, and a hand formed next to it, trying to escape. Quickly pressing the red button on the remote, she watched the screen go black and the form disappeared. Dropping her arms down, she stared at the blank screen, taking a deep breath as her heart slowed from a gallop to a light trot. Standing up on shaking legs, she was about to go crawl into bed when something outside caught her attention.

Tick. Tick. Tick.

Charlotte was chilled to the marrow and her heart skipped a rhythm as she realized that the sound was coming from outside. Someone, or something was tapping on the glass pane of her door. She waited, praying for them to go away, but then she heard it again.

Tick. Tick. Tick.

Her stomach cramped with fear, paralyzing her in place. Still, the ticking continued on the glass, and she turned to fling back the curtains. Greeting her from the silver moonlight hanging in the curdling mist was the pigman, tapping at the door with his long black fingernail. Upon seeing her, the creature let out a shrill yell and sent her stumbling back to the floor. It pressed its snout to the door, fogging up the glass and making it squeak as it moved around. Charlotte scrambled back up against Kevin's bed and watched at the thing pointed behind him, to where the old hospital sat. She half expected him to bust through the pane and take her, but to her surprise the creature turned and walked away, leaving her sitting breathlessly in the dark.

Not daring to get close to the door, she crawled up into bed next to her son, and draped her arm around him. She pressed herself closer to him and held him tight, fearing losing him to the demon outside if she was to relinquish her grip. The boy was everything she had, and her heart twisted in agony at the thought of something bad happening to him. So, Charlotte gripped him tighter, as silent tears ran down her face from the thoughts plaguing her mind, and she fell asleep with a heavy heart and a sickening feeling in the pit of her stomach that something horrible was going to happen to him.

CHAPTER SIXTEEN

"I don't know which is worse. The terror you feel the first time you witness such things, or the numbness that comes after it starts to become ordinary."—**Tasha Alexander, A Fatal Waltz**

Although they could have stayed at the station house and waited for a call to come in, Charlotte and Chuck agreed to go grab a coffee from the café instead of being anywhere near Victoria. Both had agreed that the woman made them uneasy, and that she had an ominous aura around her which made the blood run cold. Having grabbed their drinks, compliments of the nice elderly lady behind the counter, they sat on a nearby bench at the park across the street, glancing up at the lighthouse sweep its dim-washed light across the horizon. Taking a sip of her coffee, Charlotte nudged Charles with her elbow and motioned her head to the seven crows gathering in the grass beside them. Knitting his brow, he leaned over, picked up a small rock, and chucked it at the birds, making them scatter in a flood of angry cries.

"Damn, birds." He muttered and sipped at his coffee. "I'm *really* starting to hate them."

"You and me both."

"So," he glanced over at her, "what's up with you sporting those dark half-moons under your eyes?"

"Oh, so you've noticed." She tittered. "I thought I put on enough concealer to cover it up, but I guess not."

"You resemble a drunken raccoon. Did you not sleep well?"

"Nope, not at all."

"For real? I slept like a baby. Want to tell me what's keeping you up?"

"I got a phone call last night at three in the morning. I picked it up, but the person on the other end didn't answer. All I heard was heavy breathing."

"And you think it's your ex?"

"That's my fear." She glanced up at him. "What if he found me again? What if he comes after me?"

"Then you give old Chuck a call in room one fifty, and he will come running to punch that bastard in the face."

"Thanks." She glanced at her lap, giggling. "It sounds like we are becoming friends."

"Well, yeah. Aren't partners supposed to be friends?"

"I don't know. I wasn't allowed to have friends of any kind when I was with Bret, especially not the male variety. He always thought that every man out there was looking to fuck me. Hell, he freaked out when a cashier smiled at me and told me to have a good day. Claimed he was flirting with me, and that I was flirting back by smiling and saying thank you."

"He sounds like some unstable asshole with serious mental issues."

"No kidding. I still can't believe I put up with his shit for so long." Charlotte glanced down at her lap, playing with the paper cup. "But enough talking about me. I want to know your story."

"What do you mean?"

"Well, you know why I'm here, but how did you get on this island? Surely being a medic in Phoenix beats some Podunk New England town any day."

"I suppose if I was any regular medic, then city life is where it's at. But when the call came, I was already looking for a place a bit slower, with fewer trauma calls and more taxiing old ladies to the hospital kind. In Phoenix, I was beginning to think like I wasn't going to cut it. I was starting to regret ever going into emergency medicine."

"How come?"

"You sure you want to know?"

"I wouldn't have asked if I didn't."

"Promise not to laugh at me if I tell you?"

"Why would I?" Charlotte peered over at Charles, who was studying her carefully and fiddling with his thumbs. "All right, fine, if it makes you feel better, I promise not to laugh."

"Okay then." Charles took a deep breath. "Here it goes. As you know, I've been an EMT since I was nineteen, much like you. I loved this job back then, constantly feeling like a god when I was able to pull people back from the brink. But three years later I was given a harsh dose of reality on how little control I actually had.

"This happened a few months after I got my medic's license. Things were going great, and I loved the job, and the additional responsibility that came with it. Then, the call came in, one none of us want to hear. The radio chirped and the dispatcher in a grim voice told all units to respond to a mass casualty event. My partner and I didn't know what to expect, and nothing prepared me for what I saw when I got there. Come to find out an overturned eighteen-wheeler caused a sudden traffic back up near the train tracks. There were two cars on the tracks themselves, and due to some act of God, the lights on the crossing were not working that day. The train barreling down the tracks had no time to stop and hit the two cars almost full force, derailing, and taking out six more cars stuck in traffic.

"There was debris everywhere—tires, glass, clothing, twisted hunks of metal—I couldn't make heads or tails of things. I heard shouting and glanced over to see a fireman wave us over a few feet down the tracks where the worst of the carnage was. We passed by what remained of a blue corvette, sitting on the tracks. It was a heap of scrap at that point—its roof flattened, the tires bent, and the hood ripped clean off and flung into the woods—there was a white tarp over the windshield, and I knew they didn't even try to cut the bodies out.

"A few feet down the tracks, a green minivan lay on its crumpled side, cracked open like a tuna can by the jaws of life. I spotted an infant car seat in a ditch behind it and ran over to see if it was occupied. I lifted it up and my heart sank when I saw him, all broken and bruised, and only a few months old, but I came far too late to save him. Later, my partner told me the poor baby didn't stand a chance when the train hit, that he was dead on impact. But as I covered his little body, I couldn't help but blame myself for coming too late, and I felt sick to my stomach thinking of his last moments.

"The rest of his family didn't fare better—the father's head got cut off by a piece of metal and the mother suffocated while waiting for help—but as the firemen finished cutting the roof off, they yelled for us to hurry as they had a live one. A small five-year-old girl got pinned in her seat, probably from not wearing her seat belt when the train hit, and was thus spared from the brunt of the impact. She had a broken leg, and a fractured skull, but we stabilized her and got her to a hospital before returning to the scene. We worked that disaster for eight hours. Sixty people died that day, fifteen of them on scene and the rest at the hospitals.

"When I got home that night, all I wanted to do was forget, but the scene continued to haunt me. Every time I closed my eyes, all I could see was the twisted metal. I actually smelled the burning rubber intermixing with the metallic scent of blood and the pungent aroma of spilled fuel. When I tried to fall asleep, the screams and moans of the victims plagued me, and in my dream, that baby, with his cracked open skull, looked up at me and asked me why I couldn't save him. Night after night he continued to haunt my dreams, begging me to not let him go. After a week of sleepless nights, I could no longer handle it, I began to drink... a lot.

"I know it was wrong, but I needed something to take the edge off, anything to get away from the nightmare. I never drank during my shift, but as soon as I got home, I buried my head in a bottle until I passed out. After a few months, I thought of calling it quits or finding a better job elsewhere. That's when I got the call. A job offer here, in a quiet island town where almost nothing ever goes wrong, and the calls are few and far between. I saw it as my opportunity to continue doing what I loved and get a break from the horrors eating away at me. So, here we are, stuck on this little cursed island, still dealing with death, but at least it's on a smaller scale."

"I see, you had your burn out, I guess." Charlotte continued to gaze at the white and brown cup in her lap. "Do you still see that infant in your dreams?"

"Occasionally he still visits me. It has gotten far less since I got here though, and he no longer blames me for his death. I know this sounds nuts, but it's almost like something about this place is taking away the guilt from me."

"Maybe you are just coming to terms with what happened that day."

"Maybe you're right."

"You still drink?"

"Yes, but not to forget. I drink for fun now, and not to the point where I'm blackout drunk. I only have a drink or two and call it a night." Chuck stared across the lawn at the crows glaring at him from the shimmering black lump they formed on the sidewalk. "Does this change things between us? Or are you still fine with having a former drunkard as your partner?"

"I don't think I could have asked for a better partner and friend, Chuck. We all have calls that haunt us, it's part of the job. To this day I still flinch when I get OD calls after failing to revive a fifteen-year-old who took too much heroin. Deep down we know we can't save everyone, but it doesn't stop us from hurting when we fail, we're only human after all."

"That's true. And I bet as a mother calls concerning children are your worst nightmare."

"They sure are. My heart aches every time a child gets injured or dies. It reminds me I can't protect my baby all the time, and definitely not forever. And every time I go home, I hold him tighter because I don't know what the next day will bring."

Charlotte and Chuck continued to sit in silent reflection, watching the sun glisten on the window of the bakery. There was a quiet understanding amongst them, one which only comes from dealing with trauma on the scale on which they had. She still worried about being isolated on the island if Bret came looking for her, but Charlotte knew she found a reliable friend in Charles, and that he would not allow that monster to hurt her the way he previously had. Rising from the bench, she smiled and took his cup, walking over to the nearby trash bin to throw them out when the radio on her lapel chirped to life.

"EMS thirty-six fifty-five, please respond to fourteen twenty-eight Meridian Ave for a potential suicide."

"Dispatch, this is EMS thirty-six fifty-five," Charlotte exchanged glances with Chuck, "please confirm that you want us to respond to fourteen twenty-eight Meridian Ave for a suicide?"

"Correct. According to the caller, a man appears to have shot himself... with a spear gun."

"That is seriously messed up." She remarked to her partner before depressing the radio button again. "Ten-four, we are on our way."

Rushing for the ambulance parked across the street, Charlotte hopped into the passenger seat as it was Chuck's turn to drive and tend to the patient. Knowing the man's story, she turned and asked him if he was all right to take this, to which he assured her he was. He turned on the lights and the sirens and their vehicle flickered to life, signaling for the cars and pedestrians to move out of their way. Looking out her window as they pulled out of their spot, she noted a peculiar calmness to the people. Back in Seattle, when people heard the wailing of the sirens, they glanced up, turned their heads and tried to discern where the vehicle was going, or what emergency was taking place. But not here. Here the people continued to sit around unfazed, eating their muffins and chatting amongst one another with blank faces, looking up only to smile at them and nod their heads. Kevin was right. There was something unusual going on in Autumn Falls, something that was out of this world.

CHAPTER SEVENTEEN

"We'd stared into the face of Death, and Death blinked first. You'd think that would make us feel brave and invincible. It didn't."—**Rick Yancey, The 5th Wave**

C *harles* took a sharp corner onto Ocean Avenue heading for the fishing pier, and Charlotte noted something else that seemed unusual. The cars before them had parted like the red sea, which in itself wasn't strange, but the fact that they were all perfectly pulled over was. In the city it was not uncommon to see cars scattering in every direction as they approached, and some cars even disregarded that an ambulance was trying to make its way through. But not here, not in Autumn Falls. Here, the road cleared for them with precision, so they never had to slow down even once. Beside her, Chuck ignored the Utopian phenomenon outside and sat muttering as he took another sharp corner onto Meridian Avenue.

"Come to Autumn Falls, they said. There are fewer calls here, they said." Charles grumbled under his breath. "What they apparently neglected to mention, is that all my calls would deal with crazy people and their self-inflicted injuries." He pulled over to a spot close to the docks. "I mean, who the hell shoots themselves with a goddamn spear gun?"

Shrugging her shoulders, Charlotte grabbed her med bag and hopped out from the cab. Charles led the way to the docks, situated beside a red, weather-worn fishing warehouse covered in ivy. She studied the steel frames with the translucent squares of glass and counted the ones which had been punched out, thirteen in all. The entire space reeked of rotted fish. Above the windows, on the eve of a rusty red roof sat seven crows with their necks tucked into their feathers, looking over at the crowd of onlookers gathering around someone on the concrete dock.

Pushing through the solid gaggle of people, they forced their way into an open area to assess the situation. Before them lay a man in a moth-eaten navy sweater and gray skull cap sprawled on the dock, his head resting in a congealing pool of blood. His face was streaked in deep burgundy, and an empty eye socket glanced up at the sky. Beside him lay a small arrow-shaped spear with a gelatinous, deformed eyeball attached to it. The optic never dangled from the meaty casing in tangled red threads, and a milky pupil glared out at the crowd.

"That's just not right." Charles turned away from the body with his fist pressed over his lips.

"You gonna be okay?" Charlotte patted him on the shoulder.

"Yeah, just give me a minute."

"Sure thing" She nodded. "Take your time. Hey," she turned and glanced about the crowed. "Who called this in?"

"I did."

A man with a bushy salt and pepper beard stepped forward. He was wearing a juniper Shetland sweater, and a charcoal-gray ensemble composed of waders, raincoat, and leather bucket cap. With a scowl on his face, he put his arms across his chest as he continued to chew on some tobacco. Behind him, a small group of anglers gathered, and Charlotte couldn't help but think that he looked like a demented Gordon Fisherman with a ruthless gang of thugs ready to wage war. Something about him made the hairs stand up on the back of her neck and her feet were urging her to retreat from him.

"You want to tell us what happened here?"

"He shot himself with a spear gun," the man spit out the green goop he was working on at her feet, "what it look like to you, kitten?"

"No need to be so rude, sir." Charlotte stormed past him to the body. "I think we both know what I meant. Like what led up to him shooting himself. Did he say anything? Was he acting different today? Was he depressed over the last few days? Any changes in his life which might have caused him to take his own life?"

"No different, no changes. Just took his life."

"No one just up and takes their life like that. What did the man say before he did this?"

"Ma'am," a younger man stepped forward despite the old salt trying to stop him, "old Frank here, he was saying something about how it's that time again. He wasn't making much sense with his babbling, and then he said he would not go out on her terms. He was not going to let her steal his essence. There was also some talk about how he'd rather the devil have his soul and that we'd all leave if we knew what was good for us. Then, he picked up that there gun, aimed it at his head, and fired."

"I see..." Charlotte knelt by the man to check his pulse, but no sign of life were to be found. "Who ripped the spear from his head?"

"Why, he did before he dropped where he is now. We haven't touched the body, just called it in to you guys."

"All right, I've heard enough. Chuck, there is nothing we can do for him. Call it in to the hospital and then I will help you load him on the stretcher, and we'll transport him to the morgue."

Nodding his head, Charles walked away to relay the information to the hospital staff who would enter the death in their logs and instruct them which cooler to put the body in when they got there. Normally, such jobs were reserved for the corner, but on a small island like this, a medical examiner with a van was a luxury. Instead, the transportation of bodies fell to the ambulance staff, and the autopsy was the job of a doctor at the hospital who also doubled as a pathologist.

Dispersing the crowd, and instructing the fishermen to return to work, Charlotte covered the body up in a white sheet and waited for her partner to complete his call. Having finished his conversation with the examiner, Charles wheeled the stretcher over, and they lifted the dead man up, not bothering to strap him in. Charlotte leaned over to grab the spear with the eyeball on it and placed it next to the body. She would leave the gruesome task of sliding it off to someone else. Rolling the corpse over to the ambulance, they loaded him inside and shut the door. Grabbing the keys from Chuck, Charlotte got in the front of the cab and started it up, ready to make their five-minute journey to the hospital.

CHAPTER EIGHTEEN

"Death was a living creature. Death was a man tormented by his past. Death was once a human."—S.K.N. **Hammerstone**

T*hey* drove in perfect silence, and the world outside appeared to be more somber as even the trees seemed to weep. There were no words to describe what they both felt, nothing to express the horror and agony of something as tragic as a suicide. It wasn't her first, and it sure would not be her last, but Charlotte's heart bled for the anguish the man's family would feel once word got to them about his death. And it was during this solemn time of reflection which had come over the cab that a strange sound coming from the back caught their attention. The ambulance seemed to be alive with the commotion of rattling and banging coming from the cabin. Their patient was still alive in the back and in need of aid. Charlotte scanned her partner's ashen face, suspecting he thought the same thing, and swallowed the lump in her throat.

"What the hell is that?"

"I have no idea. But let me pull over so we can check. Perhaps he isn't as dead as we suspected."

Wishing to avoid sitting in traffic, Charlotte had taken a shortcut. It was an overgrown dirt road which hadn't seen traffic in over half a century, and she was looking for a place to stop. Spotting a small dirt lot with a cracked, ivy-clad stucco building, and rusted gas pumps which served no customers since the fifties, she turned off and parked by the boarded-up garage bay. Above, faint ghosts of letters indicated this was once *Gus' Grub &Gas*. She had no clue who Gus was, or what happened to him, but something told her a dark fate had befallen him like so many others.

Keeping the engine running, Charlotte and Chuck hopped out and headed to the back of their ambulance. Half expecting to find the dead man walking around, they pulled open the doors and peeked inside, but the cab was deathly silent, nothing moved, and everything appeared to be in order. Scratching their heads, puzzled over what they heard, they were about to lock it up again when the body on the stretcher sat up. The white sheet slowly slipped off to reveal the man's blood-streaked face, and he sat motionless, staring at them with his hollow eye socket.

"Sir?" A hoarse whisper escaped Charlotte's parched throat. "Are... are you, all right?"

"Get off the island." The man belted. "Get off if you know what's good for you. Before she can steal your soul."

With that warning, the body collapsed back down, and death

fell over the cab again with only the squawking of crows to remind the two medics that they themselves were still alive. With racing hearts and sweating palms, they slammed the doors shut and leaned against them, hoping to keep the dead man from getting out. With stagnant air sitting in their lungs, they looked over at each other, finally able to catch a breath. Charlotte noticed her partner was as pale as a corpse himself, and she worried about his well-being.

"W-what..." he gasped. "What was that? Did you see that Char? Please tell me you saw what I saw. Tell me I'm not going crazy."

"You are not going crazy." She reassured him. "I saw the same thing you did. Do you think he might still be alive?"

"What? After he yanked his eyeball and half his brain out? No way. No fucking way."

"We should go in and check just to make sure."

"Absolutely not. There is no way in hell I am getting in the back of that ambulance with him. If you really want to make sure, then you can go back and check it out yourself."

"Fine. Chicken."

With a jackhammering heart, Charlotte turned, and pried open one of the doors to steal a glance inside. Silence greeted her from the cab, and she handed the steel panel over to Chuck to hold as she climbed in. The body lay still on the stretcher, the white sheet draped over his lap where it fell. Picking up his wrist, she felt for a pulse, but found nothing. Fishing round behind her, she found a stethoscope and reached under the man's shirt for a listen. Static from the diaphragm crinkled through the earbuds—no thumping of the heart, no hiss of lungs filling with air—the man was as dead as the moment they found him. Putting the stethoscope down, Charlotte covered the body back up with the sheet and backed out of the ambulance for the fear he'd come back to life and attack her.

"Well? He dead?"

"As a door nail."

"What is going on here? What's happening on this cursed island."

"I don't know man, but let's just transport him to the morgue and go back to the station. I don't want to stay here longer than need be."

"I'm with you there, sister. But no more pulling over, no matter what we hear."

"Deal."

Getting back in her seat, Charlotte gripped the steering wheel with shaking hands. Even as she drove, her rational brain kept trying to explain what they saw, but no such explanation came to mind. There was only one explanation left—something supernatural was happening on the island—but it was so improbable she dared not consider it. To her side, the new hospital loomed over them, and she could finally breathe easy again.

Realizing they didn't hear a single sound from the back, she stepped on the gas until she pulled into a small bay at the back of the hospital.

CHAPTER NINETEEN

"It's the silence that scares me. It's the blank page on which I can write my own fears. The spirits of the dead have nothing on it. The dead one tried to show me hell, but it was a pale imitation of the horror I can paint on the darkness in a quiet moment."—**Mark Lawrence, Prince of Thorns**

S tanding in the deserted service entrance of the hospital, Charlotte and her partner waited for the elevator with the dead man between them. There was still something odd about the place, she thought, something unsettling. It was almost noon, one would expect the hospital staff to be moving about the building and hear talking and phones ringing, but once more, there was none of that there. The place was as deserted and silent as an abandoned building in an ancient ghost town lost to civilization. To make matters worse, the builders covered the glass on the doors with a dark tint, making the world outside appear as if night had fallen.

The ding of the elevator coming to a spot sounded like cannon fire, causing both medics to jump back. Sliding open, the metal doors revealed a dim interior with two flickering light bulbs overhead. Glancing at Chuck, Charlotte thought he seemed a bit nervous as small beads of sweat glistened on his brow. She didn't like the idea of going into a tiny, enclosed space either, but they had no other choice of getting the body down to the morgue. Gripping the sides of the gurney, she motioned her head for the elevator, and they cautiously wheeled the man in. With them safely inside the meal box, the doors shut, trapping them with a corpse who moments earlier was talking to them from the back of the ambulance.

Expecting the body to reanimate at any moment, they gripped the sides of the stretcher until their knuckles turned white. The ride down to the bottom level seemed to take an eternity and Charlotte held her breath until the basement light turned white and the door released them from their trap. Partially relieved to be out of the elevator, Charlotte glanced about the deathly quiet space and was instantly reminded how much she hated hospital basements. Fluorescent lights hummed above the concrete walls painted in mint green, casting haunting sulfur shadows on the floor, and the exposed metal pipes running over their heads creaked and moaned from the internal pressure, while a faint, damp scent of mildew covered up by a sharp smell of antiseptic surrounding them in a cramped, tube-like hallway.

"Let's drop this guy off and get out of here." Charlotte stared down the elongated hall. "I don't wish to be here any longer than need be."

"Well, better get moving then. Meat locker is all the way at the end, just past the room where they keep the drugs."

Pushing the stretcher down the hall, the echoes of the squeaky wheels bouncing off the wall sounded deafening. Charlotte could hear the pounding of her heart inside her chest as the hall seemed to stretch without an end. They passed several closed doors with no soul in sight until they reached the black metal door plastered with signs: morgue, staff only, keep door closed.

Turning the handle, they found the door to be unlocked, and stepped inside the hollow room with cold lockers on one side and two autopsy tables in the middle. Light bounced and glimmered off the polished stainless-steel surfaces. The place was organized and cleaned at an almost neurotic level. If it were not for the strange jug of blood in the room's corner, Charlotte would have said the place was never in use. As she looked around, an icy blast of air hit her, causing her to shiver, but tried as she might, she could not figure out where it came from.

"You spoke to the staff. Which cabinet do we put him in?"

"They said someone would have come put his last name on the tag for us. So, we are looking for a Moore."

"Well..." Charlotte spotted the only tag with writing on it, "I guess that would be the one. They were even nice enough to put him at stretcher level, so all we have to do is slide him in."

"What are we waiting for then? Let's go put him in the freezer and go back to the station. I don't like it here one bit."

Nodding in agreement, Charlotte pushed the stretcher forward and pulled on the latch of the small box to pull out the tray. Lifting the dead man, they slid him in and shut the door behind them. In the time it took them to transfer the body, the air inside the morgue got colder and staler. Wishing to return into the warm sunshine and fresh air of the outside, the two of them went for the door which suddenly slammed shut in front of them before a distinct sound rooted them in their spots.

Bang. Bang. Bang.

"What. Was. That?"

"I... I don't know." Charlotte cocked her head. "But it sounded like it came from the body locker behind us."

Bang. Bang. Bang.

"S-s-should we go check it out?"

"Oh, hell no! I'm not sure about you, but I have had enough of that guy coming back to life to taunt us. Plus, you already checked him over twice, you said he is as dead as dead can be. Let's just forget about him and skedaddle on out of here. We can go hang out at the station house with Iris the rest of the day. Grab an ice cream at the creamery. Anything but deal with *him* again."

"Fair enough, lets move."

With one hand still firmly on their stretcher, Charlotte went to take a step forward when she caught something out of the corner of her eye, a dark shadow sliding along the wall. Suddenly the lights flickered. The stroboscopic effect caused the shadows to pulse on the walls, and she could have sworn one had a vaguely human shape to it. Around them, the dense air grew colder, and she could see the vapor of breath before the lights turned off, turned on, flickered, and stayed on. Holding her breath, her eyes darted around the morgue, waiting for something else to happen, but it never did.

Spurred on by fear, the two medics sprinted for the door, flinging it open and running out into the hall. Still holding on to the gurney, they wheeled it down as fast as it would go until they reached the other end. Cursing, Charles mashed the elevator button while Charlotte continually glanced over her shoulder. She thought she saw something lingering amongst the shadows as the lights went out one by one, darkening the hall gradually in black cells. The thought of taking the stairs crossed her mind more than once when the elevator doors opened, and they ran inside. The hall on the other end continued to grow darker, one square at a time, and the murmuring shadows almost reached them when the doors shut, and one loud bang on the door startled them before the elevator nudged upwards.

Exiting the hospital, they dared not look back, fearing the thing from the morgue had taken the stairs to pursue them. Instead, they shoved the gurney into the back of their ambulance, slammed the doors shut, and peeled out of the parking lot, heading for the station. Neither one of them dared to speak, and they sat inside the cab panting, trying to catch their breath. Charlotte didn't dare to relax until the brick building, and paneled garage doors of the station greeted them, signaling what they thought to be a safe haven. Little did either of them know that their nightmare was only beginning.

CHAPTER TWENTY

"I felt myself on the edge of the world; peering over the rim into a fathomless chaos of eternal night."—**H.P. Lovecraft**

The first thing Charlotte noticed before pulling up to the station was the seven crows sitting on a window ledge, glancing into the distance. Pulling into the bay, another thing struck her, the eerie graveyard silence. Once the engine of the ambulance cut off, nothing stirred in the background, the building appeared abandoned. Exchanging worried glances, Charlotte and Chuck went for the stairs.

Walking up one step at a time, their footsteps sounded thunderous inside the hollowness of the stairwell. They checked the second floor, but no one was there, not even Iris at her desk. Frowning, they continued to the third floor where they were relieved to see a fireman sitting in one of the recliners, his face buried in the morning paper. The man paid no attention to them, and they both went for the doors when the lights above their heads began to pulsate as they did back at the hospital.

With each flicker of lights, Charlotte thought she could see something in the shadows as the room beyond the glass filled up with thick, black smoke. The mist continued to swirl on the other side, but the man sitting in the chair seemed to be oblivious to it. He continued to page through his paper as if there was no light show going on in the building, and no smoke gathering around him. Then, the lights finally blew out, leaving them in the gloom, for even the windows darkened, blocking out any light from the outside. A dank draft flowed past them, filling the small hall between the medics and the break room with an unnatural chill which reeked of sulfur and decay. In the darkness, a bleat from a wounded animal pierced the deafening silence, filling Charlotte with soul-searing panic. She sensed *it* was in the room with them, and she couldn't begin to surmise what it wanted.

Suddenly, the lights flickered back on, and through the dark strips of vapor, she spotted the pigman standing behind the fireman. Beside her, Charles let out a gasp and grabbed hold of her wrist, pulling her back. She didn't move, she stood paralyzed in place as she looked at the creature looming over the unsuspecting man, its broad snout huffing out plumes of light mist that churned and joined the blackness. Pulling away from her partner, she went over and slapped her hand on the glass, shouting for the man to move. The fireman turned to regard her with a frown, and the pigman tilted his head to her, letting out an ear-splitting roar. Turning behind him, the man let out a blood-curdling scream and darted for the door, but he did not make it. The creature grabbed hold of him and dragged him down into the mist as his victim clung to the glass, sliding down into the abyss as he vanished from sight.

"W-what was that?" Charles' voice was shrill with panic. "You saw that too, right? Tell me you saw that too."

"Yes. I've been seeing it since I got on this island."

"What? You have?"

"Yes. It's been following me, but I have no clue as to why."

Charlotte was getting ready to tell Charles to get out of the building when the lights flickered out again, leaving them trapped in a blinding darkness. She felt the chill in the air, it was the icy grip of death, grabbing hold of her. Then, she smelled it, the acrid scent of a rotting corpse, putrid and sickening. Knowing what was coming, she backed up against the wall, trying to find the door, and pushing Chuck with her. He did not protest, he was shaking, she knew he felt it too, and he was trying to find the door to escape. She heard the handle jiggle, and the lights came back on, revealing the head of the pig right in front of her.

"Run," she screamed, "let's get out of here."

Charles was the first to run out the door, and Charlotte was close behind him. Her sweaty palms gripped the railing as she jumped down three to four steps at a time, too scared to look back. She had reached the second-floor landing before the lights started to oscillate and a low, deep groan came from behind her. Finally, daring to steal a glance over her shoulder, her heart sank into her ankles as she spotted the black-cloaked creature slithering down the stairs after her. Letting a soft scream escape her throat, she turned and ran even faster as her heart leaped painfully in her chest and her lungs burned from exhaustion.

On the last stretch of stairs, when she had the rear door in sight, she tripped over her own two feet and flew down to the bottom landing, slapping the concrete loud enough to make a whispering echo around her. Her body screamed in agony from hitting the ground, but she pushed herself up and ran for the door, pushing on the metal bar which would not budge. Defeat crept over her, the creature was going to kill her, but she pushed and pulled on the handle regardless, trying to pry her way out.

"Let me out." She hollered and pounded on the door, hoping that Charles or someone else would hear her plea. "Someone let me out. Please. I don't want to die."

Her voice grew hoarse, and she could barely talk through the sobs. Hearing a clatter behind her, she turned to see the pig creature slink down the last set of stairs, he was almost upon her. No, she thought, please don't let me go out like this, not yet, not now. Above her, the lights flashed, went out, and blinked back on, revealing the creature standing nose to nose with her. Its elongated snout snorted at her, and she gagged from the putrid air coming from it. Tears streamed down her face, and she turned her head away from it, squeezing her eyes shut.

"Please," she murmured, "don't kill me."

To her surprise, the pigman did not take her. Instead, an icy hand reach out to wipe the tears from her face and lift her chin back to face it. Forcing open one of her eyes, she saw the dead eye sockets looking at her. The pigman's breaths were gentle, she realized it meant her no harm. Straightening up, she glanced at the creature. She wished to ask it what it wanted, when it lifted its hand and pointed to his left, as if reading her thoughts. It was pointing towards the old hospital, and she wanted to know why. But before she had a chance to ask it, the pigman nodded and vanished in a plume of black smoke, leaving her standing alone in a deserted stairwell with eyes full of tears. Turning, she tried the door again, and to her surprise, it opened, letting her stumble out into the fresh afternoon air.

CHAPTER TWENTY-ONE

"Hearts can break. Yes, hearts can break. Sometimes I think it would be better if we died when they did, but we don't."—
Stephen King, Hearts in Atlantis

L eaning bent over on her knees, Charlotte heaved to remove the staleness the creature seemed to produce. She did not know why he let her go, but deep down she knew it wanted to help her somehow. It was one of the good guys despite its gruesome appearance. Her knees and elbows still ached from her fall, but the warm rays of the sun were quickly making the pain a distant memory. From the corner of the building, she saw something move and glanced up, only to see old Cyrus approaching her with a warm smile on his face. Seeing the man made her forget all about her encounter from a moment prior, and she lifted her hand to wave at him.

"You feeling all right, young lady? You look like you just seen a ghost."

"No, no ghost. Darn door just jammed, and I got stuck inside. I yelled for someone to help, but I guess no one heard me, so I had a mild panic attack at the thought of being stuck in the stairwell all night. Why is the station empty anyway? Where did everyone go?"

"Oh, that." He continued to smile. "Well, we seem to have a special guest here in town. I genuine celebrity. Everyone was so eager to meet him they all rushed out of the station, much to Miss. Owen's chagrin. Speaking of the boss, she said she wants you upfront, stat. I think she got a special job just for you."

"Oh, all right. I'll go to her right away. Where is she?"

"Everyone is back out front of the station house. I'd hurry. I think she's about to lose the war with her staff."

Giggling, Charlotte gave Cyrus a wink and jogged around to the front of the station. She was curious who this celebrity guest was, or what Victoria wanted with her, not expecting to see the man who was drawing the crowd. Her feet screeched to a halt and her heart leaped into her throat. Suddenly she wanted to turn back and run away, as far away from *him* as possible. Men and women alike surrounded him, all vying for his attention while he signed whatever they happen to shove at him, including a few bare chests. She didn't know what he was doing there, she didn't care to find out, she just wanted him to leave without catching a glimpse of her. Turning her head back to the parking lot, she thought about slinking away when Chuck called her name, making her freeze, and she cursed him under her breath.

"Ah, there you are, Miss. Briggs," Victoria turned to her with a frown that etched harsh lines on her otherwise delicate face. "As you can see, we have a special guest here. You might be aware of who Mr. Campbell is. Apparently, *everyone* here knows who he is. Anyhow, he says wants to poke around the station and learn our spooky history for a new book he's writing. And as you can imagine, I need some help..." she glared at the crowd with an ice-cold gaze, "containing him."

"Cherry berry?" Zack turned upon hearing her name and a broad grin spread across his face, lighting up the surrounding space. "Is that really you?"

"Hey, Zack." Charlotte pressed her lips together and gave him an awkward wave. "Long time no see."

"Ah," Victoria let out a sigh, "so you two are familiar with each other then?"

"We uh, well, we used to date in high school. It's ancient history now though."

"Well, even better. Guess that means you won't mind giving him a tour then."

"What, me?" Charlotte gasped and shook her head. "Why?"

"For one, I doubt any more calls will come in. Plus, I figured you'd be the least celebrity crazy person here, but now that I know you are familiar with Mr. Campbell, I know I can trust you to not be distracted by his fame, and boyish good looks. I'll leave the two of you to it, while I go contain my staff. And Miss Briggs, "Violet hissed, "I don't think I need to stress this to you; I want his visit to be brief. He has interrupted me enough already."

"Yes, ma'am. I'll be as quick as possible."

Huffing, Victoria gathered the first responders and ushered everyone inside, leaving Charlotte alone with Zack. Silence fell between them, and she looked up to study him. She hated seeing him so perfectly unchanged—his muscles were huge, his hair styled, his clothing neatly pressed, and his chin as clean-shaven as always—he looked even better than he did in high school. Familiar, long-forgotten emotions stirred in Charlotte, and she hated herself for it. It's been ten years since they parted, she thought she moved on, but apparently, her heart thought otherwise.

"Hey Cherry, I can't believe I found you here." Zack approached her with his infections smile. "You look amazing. Why, you haven't changed one bit."

"Thanks." She rubbed her arm, being all too self-conscious of the small pouch she retained from having a baby, the one that made her resemble a burst biscuit can with her medic pants on. "You look great too."

"So, what are you doing here? Last time I checked, you moved to Seattle with some douchebag."

"I could ask you the same thing. Autumn Falls is the last place on earth I'd expect to run into you."

"Right? It's actually the darnedest thing." He put his hands in the pockets of his black cargo pants and smirked. "Truth be told, I got a strange phone call the other day telling me that if I want an original ghost story for my next book, this is the place to go. I was told the island had a colorful history of witches, demons, and ghouls alike. I couldn't resist. How about you?"

"Well, I split up from the guy I was dating, since he turned out to be rotter to the core. I was a bit down on my luck for a bit when I got a strange call offering me a job here. After a year of living in shady no-tell-motels, I couldn't resist either."

"So, you work as a paramedic now? I thought you wanted to be a doctor. Whatever happened to that idea?"

"What can I say," she shrugged, "shit happens. You know how it goes. After all, you wanted to be a journalist, and now you write books about ghosts and little green men from outer space."

"I guess you're right." Zack laughed and looked around. He reached up and rubbed the back of his head with his hand like he always did when he was nervous, and cleared his throat. "So, uh... you seeing anyone?"

"Nope. Been single ever since I left Bret."

"Does this mean you want to grab dinner after you show me around?"

"How about I show you around first, and we'll talk later."

"Playing hard to get, are you? Fine, I can wait. Give me a tour of your station, and I will see if I can sweep you off your feet again."

Charlotte rolled her eyes; she didn't care to tell him there was no need to sweep her off her feet because she still pined for him even after all those years. She wanted him to leave, but she was stuck with him until she did her job, so she led him inside the building and showed him around. He kept asking her questions about hauntings, and she wanted desperately to tell him about the pigman from earlier, but she didn't dare reveal herself to be crazy, especially not to him. Instead, she shrugged off his questions and told him she knew nothing until they got to the picture of the four medics.

She relayed the story of how two of the men died in a freak accident twenty-five years ago, and how she and her co-workers all saw the echo of the ambulance speeding down the street. Zack seemed fascinated by this and asked her to show him where it was, so he could check it out. Guiding him outside, Charlotte motioned to the intersection where it passed, hoping it would be enough to get him away from her. Much to her dismay though, he wrote down where to go and stood in place, looking down at her with his soft blue-gray eyes, and that darn smile that she just wanted to slap off his face.

"So." He rocked on his heels with his hands in his pockets. "How about that dinner? We can do Italian; it was always your favorite."

"How about a rain check? I have other plans tonight, and this is all last minute."

"Promise?"

"Yeah. Sure. We'll grab dinner and catch up soon."

"I'll hold you to that Cherry, you know me."

"I know, now go hunt your ghosts, or demons, or aliens, or whatever else you think you'll find here. I need to go home, so I can change out of this uniform, it reeks of death."

"All right. I'll see you around. And," he smirked at her, "I look forward to our date."

Leaning against the brick of the building, Charlotte waved to Zack and watched him walk across the street, and climb inside a forest green Range Rover. He always did like to show off, she thought, now he had the means to do so. She thought that seeing him leave would provide her with some relief, but instead, it left an empty void inside her, and a lump formed in her throat. Thinking this was the last she'd see him, she swallowed down her sadness, and went to the parking lot where Cyrus was waiting to take her back home, to the one person in her life who she could always count on, Kevin.

CHAPTER TWENTY-TWO

"There is something at work in my soul, which I do not understand."—Mary Shelley, Frankenstein

The ride in the Jeep was awkward. Charles and Iris kept staring at her with eager eyes, and Charlotte knew they had questions they were dying to ask her, ones they dared not ask with Cyrus in the car with them. Not wishing to discuss Zack at any point in the evening, she asked the old man to drop her off at the local burger joint. It was only half-a-mile downhill from the hotel, and she figured she could walk after picking up dinner for her and Kevin. Cyrus was more than happy to accommodate, and having grabbed their meals, she started up towards the hotel, noting the six crows hopping along behind her.

Arriving at the side door, she glanced back, frowning as her six feathery companions sat a suitable distance away from her, watching in silence. Grumbling under her breath, she went inside and headed for her room, thankful for the lack of activity from the other side, and for her co-workers not ambushing her in the hallway. Walking inside her room, Charlotte spotted Kevin sitting on the bed, playing with his iPad, and looking glum. Hearing the door shut, the boy looked up from the screen and waved at her as she lifted the bags of burgers and fries to signal dinner time. Placing the iPad down, he hopped off the bed and ran for the table as she sat their bags down and pulled out a couple of sodas from the mini-fridge by the television. Sitting down to eat, she handed Kevin his food before she looked over at him and forced a smile.

"So, how was your day?"

"Boring, like last time." The boy groaned. "I just sat around and did more busy work at school, while the teacher read her book. At lunch, I ate the food I got from here at my desk in silence with everyone else. Then I came home and played with my iPad until you got home. What about you? Anything exciting happened?"

"Not really. Just transported a dead guy to the morgue and went back to the station house until it was time to leave."

"Sounds so exciting," Kevin rolled his eyes and bit into his burger. "Do we have to keep living here?"

"Yes, of course. Where else are we supposed to go?"

"Grandma's house, she'd love to have us back. You can find a job in Boston. Or we could move to Florida, or Georgia, or Louisiana. Surely any place is better than here."

"Look," Charlotte looked up from her food with a sigh, "I know this place is not ideal, I actually don't like it much either. But let's give it at least a year before we decide to turn tail and run. I'd like to settle down at some point in my life."

"Are we looking to settle down or die of boredom? Because I think I can bet on which one will happen first."

"Very funny, young man. You know I'd like to find a good father figure for you, buy a house, and a large dog, and live a normal life. I want your life to be stable, and not this living on the run business we have gotten used to."

"Yeah, okay. Like you'd actually find a man here. They are all either too old, too young, or are brain-dead zombies. Plus, what's wrong with my *real* father anyway? Why can't you call my dad up and see if you guys can work things out?"

"Kev, we've been over this a million times. Your father, your real father, well... he's just not someone you can meet. And, as much as I would love to have things work out between us, I don't think they ever will. That ship has sailed a long time ago."

"How would you know, you're not even willing to give it a try? I mean, you still won't even tell me his name. I think I have the right to know who he is, don't you?"

Charlotte looked over at her son who had tears forming in his eyes, and guilt ate away at her. He was right, he had a right to know, and so did Zack, and she could easily tell them both now that he was in the same place, but she couldn't bring herself to do it. Fear kept its grip on her. She was terrified of how Zack would react, he would probably hate her, and Kevin would be so excited for his idol be his father, but he would most likely get his heart broken when his dream turned out to be nothing like he expected.

No, she thought, now is definitely not the right time to be honest. One day she would be ready to tell Kevin the truth, but tonight was not the night for honesty.

"Perhaps one day." She looked up at him with a sad face. "One day I'll be ready to tell you. I promise. But for now, how about we watch a movie or something to get your mind off things?"

"Can we watch Zack Campbell's new show instead? It's called *Scare Share*."

"That guy has a new show? What's this one about? Chasing UFOs?"

"No mom. He takes people to spend the night in famous haunted locations and films them. It's fantastic, and today they are going to Leap Castle in Ireland. I *really* want to watch it."

"Oh fine... I guess it won't hurt. Go put it on."

Sitting down with Kevin, she watched the man she talked to earlier appear on her television screen. He was as dynamic in the show as he was in real life and nostalgia washed over her again. No matter how much she hated to admit it, she still missed him, and now he was everywhere, including the one place she didn't want him to be, on the same small island with her. She wondered how long she could avoid him for. Surely, he would not stay on the island long. But then again, she could be wrong. Mulling over her thoughts, she watched one entire episode of his show and part of another before she realized Kevin had fallen asleep in her lap. Tucking the boy in bed, she sat back on the couch and continued to watch Zack on the television until she too passed out on the sofa.

CHAPTER TWENTY-THREE

"Night was a very different matter. It was dense, thicker than the very walls, and it was empty, so black, so immense that within it you could brush against appalling things and feel roaming and prowling around a strange, mysterious horror."—Guy de Maupassant, The Complete Short Stories of Guy de Maupassant

Waking up coughing, Charlotte strained to see through the thick clouds of black smoke. She knew she was no longer in her room; she was in the *other* world. Heat pricked her skin, and she rolled over, realizing she was lying on the grass outside the hotel. Looking up, she saw an unfamiliar structure burning beside her in a world leached of all colors. This must be the great hotel fire, she thought, I am witnessing another event in the past.

Getting up to her feet, she waved her hand in front of her face and stumbled into the smoke-filled street where people were rushing around with buckets to keep back the scalding flames. She noticed their faces. They were still human faces, but they warped and melted like the guy in *The Scream* painting, and their skin seemed to be dissolving away from them like wax from a candle.

She stumbled down the sidewalk, away from the section of the hotel that was on fire, and made her way slowly down the hill as people passed through her. Stopping at the end of the gates, she looked about, searching for *him,* the creature who brought her there. The darkness was blinding, and she could barely see in front of her. She was beginning to lose all hope when she finally caught a glimpse of shadows moving in the tree line. It was him; it had to be, and she ran forward until she spotted a hem of the black robe sliding along the ground, barely lit by the light of the ashen moon.

"You." She screamed as she sprinted after him. "You brought me here, didn't you?"

The figure stopped moving and turned around, its empty eyes glaring over at her, still weeping blood from their wounds. The snout twitched and arched back as the creature inhaled the smoke. He said nothing to her, he simply approached, belted out a groan, and nodded his head. For the first time since seeing him, Charlotte was not afraid of him, instead, curiosity to know why it kept trying to communicate with her overcame her, and permeated her thoughts.

"What do you want from me? Why do you keep stalking me?"

Silently, the pigman raised his hand and pointed up to a small hill where the old hospital stood. *There, go there.* She couldn't explain what she heard. The creature's lips did not move, but his voice clearly resonated in her head, the voice of a young man. It must be able to communicate telepathically when it wanted to, she thought, and the pigman nodded its head as if he could hear her.

"The old hospital?" She glanced back over her shoulder to where it stood lurking in the distance. "You want me to go to the hospital, right?"

Once again, the figure grunted and gave her a slight nod with his hand still pointing to the place Victoria warned her not to go.

"But why? What's there? What do you want me to find?"

Go there. Find answers. Or die.

The pigman's mouth did not move, but she heard his message in her head, and wondered if he meant it as a warning, or a threat. There was still so much she wanted to ask him, but she would not get the chance. Silently, he walked over to her and put his hand over her eyes. *Sleep now.*

The command took hold instantaneously, causing her to fall asleep and flop over into his arms. When she awoke again, she found herself still on the couch. Across from her, the television hissed with snowy static and the alarm clock on her nightstand blinked out three in the morning. Shaking the dread from the message she received in her dream, Charlotte crawled into her bed and fell asleep, pondering what she should do next.

CHAPTER TWENTY-FOUR

"Which is the true nightmare, the horrific dream that you have in your sleep or the dissatisfied reality that awaits you when you awake?"—**Justin Alcala**

The following morning, Charlotte was sitting behind the wheel of the ambulance, staring at the seven crows sitting perched on the park bench. Beside her, Chuck was sipping his coffee, gazing at her. She knew what was on his mind. He and Iris would not stop scrutinizing her with the same curiosity-filled eyes since they learned Zack was her high school sweetheart. Not that she blamed them for wanting to know, she would be curious too if the tabled were turned, she just wished he would come out and ask her instead of staring at her as if the answers he wanted would simply fall out of her head. Heaving out a frustrated sigh, she turned to regard her partner, who quickly averted her gaze.

"Okay. You've been gawking at me since last night. What is it you want to ask?"

"I... well, I wanted to..." Chuck fumbled around with his cup and side-glanced at her, "I was just wondering if we were ever going to talk about the elephant in the room?"

"Like?"

"Uh," he finally looked up to meet her eyes, "like the fact that Zack Campbell, *the* Zack Campbell, is your baby daddy. I mean, he is like *the* paranormal expert of our time."

"Expert?" Charlotte snorted. "I would hardly call him an expert. He wrote some popular books about *other* people's accounts of ghostly and alien encounters. That makes him lucky, but not an expert."

"Still, he's famous. And the dude has got to be loaded from hitting the New York Times Best Seller list four times in a row. Not to mention he has three shows out now."

"Why are you so shocked? I told you he was kind of rich and famous now."

"Yeah, but I was thinking he was a singer for some local hair band that hangs around in bars and has a few groupies."

"Seriously, man?" Charlotte leaned forward on the steering wheel and frowned. "Do I strike you as someone who would date one of them emo punks?"

"Hey, we all do strange shit while in high school. I once dated a goth girl who was into cutting herself and drinking blood. She was a strange one, but she was freaky, you know, in a good way. We had lots of fun together until she ended up slitting her wrists in the tub one night. She passed away on her way to the hospital."

"Jeez, man. I'm sorry, that had to have been hard on you."

"It was. But all I was saying is, you never know what someone does when they are younger, or what their tastes were. So, how did you end up having a kid with Campbell, anyway? Was he like some big-time nerd back then, or what?"

"If you really must know, Zack was a jock, and I was the school nerd. He was the captain of the football team, and I was president of the debate team. We met one day at the library when he was looking for a book. He asked me to help him study for a test the next day. I still don't know why he asked me. I was a freshman, and he was a junior when we met, but I had a huge crush on him, so I eagerly agreed. We started dating not long after, and I got pregnant at the end of my sophomore year, during prom night. I found out a week after he dumped me, so he could run off to UCLA to live his dream. I haven't spoken to him again until yesterday."

"Shit, girl. It's no wonder you kept the kid a secret." Charles put his cup down and leaned back in his seat. "You plan to tell him now that he's here?"

"Hell no."

"Oh, come on Char, I understand the guy was a dick when he dumped you, but he still deserves to know. Let the past be in the past, that's what my mama always said. And you know, he's here, so why not give it a try?"

"Oh yeah, I can picture it now. I'm just going to walk up to him and say: 'Hey Zack, how have you been? Want to go on that date you asked about? Oh, and by the way you have a nine-year-old son you didn't know existed.' Yup, that should go over as well as a fart in an elevator. I mean, I'd be lucky if he doesn't file a restraining order against me."

"Okay, okay. I get it, you're scared of his reaction, I would be too. But all I'm saying is, don't completely discount him. It may not be as bad as you think. He might want to step up and be a dad, you know. Plus, I saw the way he looked at you. He still holds a flame for you."

"Yeah, sure." Charlotte rolled her eyes at the thought of Zack still having the same feelings for her that she held for him. "But, fine, you win, I'll give it some thought later, and *maybe* I will let both of them know about one another."

"What? Your kid doesn't know who his father is either?"

"No, and I don't wish to explain myself on that matter." Charlotte started up the engine and began to drive with Chuck going back to sipping his coffee silently. She hated to snap at him as she did, but she wanted to conversation to end, and decided it was best to change the subject. "By the way. I saw it again. The pigman we saw at the station house."

"What? When?"

"Last night. I woke up, but I was not in my room, I was on the grass outside the hotel when it was burning."

"Say what now?"

"It's happened to me before. Like the day I went to grab my

bag, that's why I was so frazzled when I came back. I know it sounds crazy, but almost every time I meet him, I'm transported to another period in the island's history. I can tell I'm in the past because the colors are different, and the people pass through me as if they were ghosts. I'm there, but not really. Just a silent observer of a time gone by. I can see and smell the world around me, but I can't interact with anyone. I'm like a traveler in a virtual reality game. The time is always different, but the pigman is always there, waiting for me."

"What does *it* want with you?"

"The last few times I've seen it, it has pointed in the old hospital's direction. Last night I asked it if it wanted me to go there, and it nodded a yes to me and said I have to go there to find answers, or die."

"Die? Was that a threat?"

"I don't have a clue. I think it was more of a warning. Like, maybe the hospital has information that would help save my life if I had it or something. Not to mention," she subconsciously lowered her voice, "don't you find it a tad strange how adamant Victoria was about us not going to that place?"

"Yeah. Almost like she's hiding something in the building or on the grounds."

"Exactly. I bet that place holds something she doesn't want us to see, because I sure as hell am not believing the story that people just stay away from that place. We really need to check it out at some point if we ever get the chance."

"We? When did you drag me into this?"

"Sorry. I figured you'd want to know, and I don't want to go there by myself."

"You can always ask your boyfriend to help. After all, he's here investigating paranormal claims, and I bet he'd jump at the chance to spend some time with you exploring an old spooky hospital."

"He's not my boyfriend."

"Not yet."

Chuck laughed at his remark even as Charlotte swatted at him for having fun at her expanse. The two of them continued joking and having a great time until the radio clicked on, putting a damper on their mood.

"EMS thirty-six fifty-five, please respond to the three-hundred block of Spruce Avenue for a hit-and-run. I got reports of a seventy-year-old female in critical condition."

"Ten-four, we are on our way." Chuck hung up the receiver and glanced over at Charlotte with a scowl. "Well, lets get going, partner. Looks like the island has struck again."

Turning on the sirens and emergency lights, Charlotte stepped on the gas and sped up the hill towards their destination. She knew where they were going. There was a small French bakery on that block where she and Charles had grabbed some pain Au chocolate the day they first started out as partners. It was hard to believe anyone would be involved in a hit-and-run there as residents of the island were overly cautious and the speed limit was only twenty-five miles per hour. Recalling what Chuck said after he reported to Iris, Charlotte thought that no words could have best described what was happening. The island seemed to be thirsty for blood, human blood, and these strange accidents were becoming all too routine.

CHAPTER TWENTY-FIVE

"Everybody is a book of blood; wherever we're opened, we're red."—**Clive Barker, Books of Blood: Volumes One to Three**

The siren whooped as the ambulance came to a stop before a hoard of people gathered in a circle at the street corner outside the bakery. Hopping out from the cab, Charlotte stole a glance at the six crows sitting huddled on the striped, blue awning, looking down at the cobblestone pavement in silence. Pushing through the crowd of emotionless onlookers, she spots her patient, lying propped up in the baker's lap in a pool of gummy blood that snaked through the gaps in the stone. Flesh had been completely stripped off her leg from the impact, Charlotte could see her blood-specked tibia amongst the curtains of flesh, muscle, and yellow fat. The woman's skin was raised up past her thigh like a stalking, with everything else stripped clean below the knee. Her ankle had been snapped at her shinbone and lay at a ninety-degree angle from her leg, dangling precariously by a stretched-out tendon. Layers of crimson and yellow tissue spread out on the stones in heaps, some still oozing blood which had stained the stones. This was the worst survivable hit-and-run she had ever seen.

"Holy shit."

Charlotte glanced over at Chuck, who was bent over with his fist pressed to his mouth. His face was ashen, and his hands trembled despite him trying to keep it together. He looked like he was about to lose his breakfast. That's when she noticed something else, something strange. The people who gathered around did not act normal. Usually with trauma this bad they were either desperately trying to help, or they were looking the way Charles did. Yet these ones didn't have a shred of emotion on their faces, they seemed numb, and some even continued to eat their bagels as if a woman was not bleeding to death in front of them. The revelation sent a shiver through Charlotte as her skin prickled with cold heat, and she had to turn to her partner before she did something she would regret.

"Hey," she put a hand on his shoulder, "you going to be all right?"

"Yeah, just give me a minute. I wasn't prepared to see this."

"Don't worry about it. Go call it in and grab the spine board and stretcher while I make sure she is stable."

"All right, thanks, partner."

"Don't mention it."

Kneeling beside the elderly lady, Charlotte reached into her bag, and pulled out a cervical collar which she put on as she laid her patient flat to assess her. Despite being dazed from the accident, the woman appeared to be breathing fine, and otherwise in good health, aside from her mangled leg. Giving her a shot of pain killers, Charlotte began trying to assemble the bits of flesh and bone on the pavement, so she could wrap them up the best she could for transport to the hospital. By the time Charles got to them with the back board and stretcher, she had collected as much of the woman off the pavement as she could, leaving bits of fatty tissue that were lodged in the crevices of the stone, glued in by drying blood.

Turning the patient enough for Charles to slip the spine board under her, they covered her with sheets and loaded her on the stretcher. The crowd parted in unison, still unemotional at what was happening, and allowed them to put the elderly woman into the back of their ambulance. Charlotte hopped in with her and waited for the door to shut behind her, and for the siren to kick back on as they raced for the hospital.

In the back, she continued to monitor her patient, bending over the cardiac monitor with a frown. Something was not right, the patient's heart rate was eighty beats per minute, it was normal and did not indicate the woman had suffered severe trauma. Reaching for the blood cuff, she measured the woman's blood pressure and found it to be normal as well. Perplexed by the unusual readings, Charlotte was about to call it in to the hospital when the woman reached out her blood-strained hand and took hold of Charlotte's wrist. Turning to tend to her patient, she noted her glossy eyes were sincere and warm, yet she continued to tremble despite knowing the woman was not about to turn like the last guy had.

"They are coming for you, sweetie." The woman mumbled. "You have to leave, or they'll get you like they got me. The Feast of Shadows is fast approaching."

Closing her eyes, the elderly woman let go of Charlotte and fell back onto the stretcher. The heart monitor whined as the heart line went flat, then it bounced and beeped while the pulse restarted itself. Swallowing hard, she looked at the monitor, the number appeared to be more normal now, reaching almost one-hundred beats per minute. She waited for her patient to regain consciousness as she continued to work on her, but she never did, not even when the trauma team at the hospital took possession of her. Charlotte knew her prognosis was grim, but she hoped for the best, regardless.

Driving away from the hospital, the two medics opted to go sit on a bench by the ocean and discuss the island's blood-lust. Both agreed that the number of traumatic calls was unusual for such a small place, but neither could come up with a good explanation. They knew that to find answers, one, or both of them would have to go poke around the old hospital, but neither one dared to volunteer. Not to mention neither one of them wished to go back to the station house and deal with Victoria, so they sat in their seat overlooking the ocean and pondered what else the island had in store for them until it was time to leave and wait for the next day to show its hand.

CHAPTER TWENTY-SIX

"The truth will set you free, but first it will make you miserable." — James A. Garfield

After a long day of avoiding her boss, Charlotte had to go back to the station to take a shower and change out of her blood-stained uniform. Having sent the others on their way, she walked back to the hotel while she went over the events of the previous three days in her head. Lost in her thoughts, she opened the door to her room, expecting to find Kevin playing with his games or watching television, and not the least bit prepared for what actually awaited her on the other side. Letting out a yelp, she fumbled with her phone, almost dropping it on the floor as she spotted Zack sitting at the corner table, chatting with their son. Her heart raced as she wondered what they were discussing, and crippling fear of how much they figured out on their own consumed her.

"Kevin," her voice came out shriller than she expected, "what is going on here?"

"Oh, hey mom." The boy leaped up, knocking over a chair.

"Why didn't you tell me you and Zack Campbell went to high school together? Or that you used to date him?"

"Hmm, guess it must have just slipped my mind. But that still doesn't explain what he is doing in our hotel room. I thought I taught you not to talk to strangers, and not to let them into our home, no matter how famous they may be."

"Don't be mad at him, Cherry. I came by to insist on that dinner you promised me, and he opened the door. I told him I knew you from high school, and he told me he was my biggest fan before he let me in to wait for you. Neither one of us realized you'd be an hour late."

"It was a rough day." She grumbled. "How did you find me, anyway?"

"I called up the station looking for you. That nice girl, Iris, told me you were on a call, but that if I wanted to catch you, I could find you here, in this room."

"Figures she had a hand in this. Bet Chuck put her up to it." Charlotte cursed herself for ever telling the two of them anything. "So, what do you want?"

"Well, I came by to ask you on a date, but now I want to have a talk with you on a different matter. Is there a place where we can chat, in private?" He shot a glance at Kevin. "If you don't mind, that is."

"Fine. Let's step out into the hall then, since that's the only privacy we will get around here."

Motioning for Kevin to sit in the chair and wait for her, she led Zack out into the hallway and shut the door firmly behind them. At first, she did not care who would spot them together like that, but as she glanced at his face, she saw in his eyes the words that remained unsaid between them for far too long, and suddenly, she hesitated. Regret took hold of her and instead of confronting him, all she wanted to do was run. There was no longer a way to avoid him, or the truth that was about to come to light, yet she was not ready to face any of it, even as she stared defiantly up into his face.

"All right, Zack, talk. What is it you want?"

"How about we start with you telling me if that is my son in there?"

His question hit her like a speeding freight train, knocking the wind out of her and making her dizzy. She knew he had to have figured it out, it should have been obvious to both of them given the timeline, and she guessed that much when she walked into the room, but she was not prepared for him to confront her about it. Trailing her eyes down to the paisley carpet, she bit her bottom lip while rubbing her shoulder. Could she lie to him, she thought. Would he believe her if she told him Kevin wasn't his? She knew he wouldn't, she realized he already knew the truth, even if she still entertained the possibility of being able to fool him.

"Oh no you don't." Zack lifted her face back up to his. "I know you well enough Cherry to know that means you are thinking about lying to me. So, the next words out of your mouth better be the truth."

"Fine." Charlotte took a deep breath and briefly closed her eyes. "Kevin is your son, so what of it?"

"What?" Zack grabbed hold of his head and ran his fingers through his thick black hair. "Why... why didn't you tell me?"

"What if I did?" Charlotte demanded as the lid on the anger she held for him finally came off. "What then? Would you have abandoned your dream of UCLA, stayed behind in Boston, and played house with me?"

"I don't know." Zack snapped and threw his hands up in the air. "But I would have liked the option to make that decision."

"Yeah, well, your mother didn't want you to make that choice, and neither did your sister, or your friends. They all bullied and harassed me into keeping my mouth shut. Called me a worthless whore who was out to ruin your life. Spray painted 'slut' on my locker and even threw a brick through my bedroom window with a note warning me to stay away from you. So, this is what I did, Zack, I let you go like they wanted me to. I let you go live your dream while I had Kevin, and raised him by myself, even if it meant giving up everything I wanted."

"Wait, hold up, my *mother* knows about this?"

"Oh yes, she was livid when my mother told her. Said to keep me away from you, and I think she was the one to turn your sister against me too. She's seen her grandson once, at the hospital when she threw an envelope of cash at me to support him for the first year. These days she sends him a birthday card every year with a check for five-hundred dollars in it, but we never cash it, we don't do handouts, especially not from people who hate us."

"This is absurd." Zack slammed his fist on the wall. "Everyone knew, and yet not one person cared to tell me I had a son? Not one? Not even you?"

"I wanted to Zack; I really did." Charlotte reached out and grabbed his hand. A flood of emotions battled for prime position inside of her making it hard to find the right words. "I thought of telling you after you graduated, but by then I had moved on, and when he turned out to be nothing more than a jerk, Kevin was already eight and you were famous. I thought it would be absurd to tell you at that point. It would seem like I was just after your money or something."

"I'd never think that Cherry, you should have known that. Or, do you really think that poorly of me?"

"No, of course not, it's just—"

"Is it true?" The door to the room creaked open and Kevin poked his face through the crack. "Is Zack Campbell my real dad?"

"Didn't I teach you it's not nice to eavesdrop?"

"I didn't," Kevin rolled his eyes and opened the door further, "I could hear you two arguing all the way at the table. With the way you were yelling at one another, I think the whole hotel heard you. Plus, I sort of put two and two together when he told me you used to be a couple. So, is it true?"

"Yes, I'm afraid Zack is your real father. But I'm sure you're just heartbroken over it."

"Sweet! I can't believe my idol turned out to be my dad! Does this mean he can stay for dinner, mom? After all, he did come to ask you on a date."

"Well, I don't know, I mean..."

"Oh, come on Cherry. You've kept him from me for nine years, let me at least get to know my son, and catch up with you. You did promise me a date."

"Fine, I give, you can stay for dinner. You both all right with subs? I can go pick them up while you two catch up."

"Sure. Are you fine with that kid?"

"Yes! I love subs. Meatball for me, mom."

"I know, I know, with extra sauce and provolone. How about you, Zack, still an Italian guy with ranch dressing and Swiss?"

"You still know me so well; I have to admit that makes me happy." Zack reached into his pocket to grab his wallet and pulled out a crisp fifty-dollar bill. "Here, I'll pay."

"There is no need, I can more than cover it, plus, my food here is free."

"Would you stop that?" He frowned at her. "I get it, you're a strong independent woman who survived this long without me, but I still like to pay for our dates."

"Who said anything about this being a date?"

"Me, I'm counting this as a family date whether you like it or not."

"Fine." Charlotte snatched the cash out from his hand, and turned with a huff. "I'll be back in a jiffy. Don't do anything I wouldn't approve of."

"I won't. Grab chips and drinks too."

"And don't forget the cookies, mom."

Rolling her eyes, Charlotte strolled down the hallway. An enormous weight had been lifted off her chest. Charles was right after all. She was exaggerating the exchange that would take place, and now she felt less guilty about the secret she kept for so many years. Walking out of the hotel with a smile, she scattered the six crows which were sitting on the sidewalk waiting for her and continued to the small sub shop a five-minute walk away to pick up their orders.

CHAPTER TWENTY-SEVEN

"You know how sometimes you tell yourself that you have a choice, but really you don't have a choice? Just because there are alternatives doesn't mean they apply to you."—**Rick Yancey, The 5th Wave**

Returning to the room, Charlotte found Zack and Kevin sitting at the table having a grand old time chatting. They seemed to be discussing Zack's time in high school and how he had met her, which did little to amuse her. She was glad to see they got along so well together, almost as if they had known each other this whole time, but she didn't want her son to learn much about her life prior to having him. Sitting down in a chair between the two of them, she distributed their meals, unwrapped her sandwich, and bit into it as she continued to observe their conversation. Laughing, Kevin went for his food while Zack grabbed hold of his drink, leaned back in his chair, and looked over at her while playing with his straw.

"So, our son tells me you guys have been living in hotels for well over a year now."

"Yes, unfortunately." Charlotte put down her food, and leaned back into her chair. "That's what happens when you leave an abusive relationship on a medic's salary in Seattle. But now that we are here, I can find a place to rent once I finally get a day off."

"Why not come stay with me instead? I have two extra bedrooms at the house I'm renting, and I will be here for a while. This place is full of secrets waiting to be discovered, so I'd say I'll be here at least a month, if not longer. It will get you out of the hotel and give me time to bond with my son. And you never know, you might convince me to stay here, or I might convince you to move."

"I don't know about that..." she glanced over at Zack and her heart panged. New possibilities were open to her now that the truth had come out, but caution still lingered in the back of her mind. "I'm not sure that would be the best idea given our past and everything."

"Come on mom, don't be like this. Think about me. I'm so bored with no homework while I wait for you, and dad can show me around and teach me things instead of me sitting here playing video games all day. Plus," Kevin poked at his sandwich, "we can finally stop living on takeout. You'd have a kitchen, and you can start cooking again. I miss your cooking, and I bet dad has never tasted how good it is."

"Actually, I have on many occasions, but that's a story for another day. What do you say, Cherry? It's not like I bite."

"Pretty please." Kevin glanced up at her with pleading eyes and brought his hands together up to his face. "With a cherry on top."

"Oh fine, I guess it will get me to stop worrying about you, and with separate rooms, nothing should be an issue. We can pack our bags after dinner, and I'll go check us out, so we can go live with your dad for a bit. After all, I guess there is no harm in giving it a try."

"Yes! You're the best mom ever."

"You won't regret it, babe, I promise you."

"Yeah... I sure hope I won't."

Sitting at the table, looking over the two men in her life, the surrounding air grow heavier. A nagging foreboding stirred deep in her gut, like an itch she could not scratch, making her squirm in her seat. Somehow, and she didn't know how, she knew that Kevin and Zack were in danger, and she recalled the words the pigman spoke to her: go there, find answers, *or die.* In the dream she was not sure what it meant, but now the warning felt more pungent, resonating deep in her soul as she finally deciphered its urgency. If they stayed on the island without figuring out its secrets, they would all perish in a few days' time. Choking down her food, Charlotte excused herself to go check out of the hotel while her stomach continued to twist with this new revelation.

CHAPTER TWENTY-EIGHT

"The past beats inside me like a second heart."—John Banville, The Sea

The drive over to Zack's rental was not long. The two-story, navy-blue Gambrel house was a short distance away from the station. As the Land Rover pulled into the gravel driveway Charlotte's eyes trailed past the enclosed porch with the white latticed windows and landed on the balcony above. On the navy, Chippendale railing sat six crows, one for each of the posts. She paid no attention to them, instead her eyes focused on the red door leading out onto the platform. Beyond the door lay long-forgotten memories which were now being dredged up, swirling like murky waters in her mind. Happiness came over her, followed by dread, and the pang of sadness. Startled by this strange cocktail of emotions the house elicited from her, she let out a small gasp.

"What's wrong?"

"This will sound strange, but..." she turned to glance at Zack, "I remember this place. It's hazy, almost like a distant memory which I locked up tight and tucked away in the corners of my mind, but it's becoming clear with me being here."

"Is this *your* memory or an ancestral memory?"

"Mine, I think. Maybe my family vacationed here one time or something."

"That could be it," Zack shut off the engine of his SUV, "although I find it unlikely given how much your mother hates the state of Maine. I mean, she pitched a fit when I asked you to come to Bar Harbor with me and my family the summer after we met. Remember, I thought it was because she didn't want us doing things together and didn't trust my folks, but then you assured me it was because she didn't want you setting foot in the state for some unknown reason."

"Of course, I almost forgot," Charlotte giggled at the memory of Zack's horror-stricken face when he thought her mother figured out their secret. "It's the reason I am yet to tell her Kevin, and I moved here. I'm afraid I'll give her a heart attack. She always turned white as a sheet whenever Maine was brought up, almost like some horrible thing happened to her here, one she did not wish to recall. And you want to know something else that's strange?"

"What?"

"For some odd reason, I picture this place a lighter color, a silvery-gray I want to say."

"Well, anything is possible, after all, the new owner recently redone it. I was told this place had sat abandoned for twenty-five years before someone bought it. So, if you visited it at some point, you would have had to be a year old, or younger."

"Really, that's fascinating, I didn't think babies could have memories."

"Why not? It's more like we have memories from when we were little, we just can't recall them because there are few feelings attached to them."

"I guess you're right." Charlotte hopped out of the car and looked over her shoulder at the enclosed porch at the back. "Why do you think someone would abandon this place? It's gorgeous."

"No clue. Maybe it was bankruptcy, storm damage, death of the owner. The possibilities are limitless." Zack got out, shut the door, and put his arm around Kevin. "You guys want to go have a look around? I know you always had an affinity for Dutch Colonials, Cherry."

"Why, Zack, did you rent this place because it reminded you of me?"

"Maybe... let's just go in, so I can give you a tour of the place."

"Fine. Lead the way."

Showing them through the front door of the house, Zack pointed to his study with all his equipment thrown about to the left. His notes and maps sprawled out along the stately mahogany desk, almost burying the paper-thin silver laptop glowing under the mound of paperwork. Straight ahead, beyond the modern interpretation of colonial furniture, nestled in the yellow walls sat a white fireplace, with a painting of a Fluyt caught in a raging storm. Charlotte always loved naval history, ever since reading *Moby Dick*, and she guessed the painting was of the ill-fated *Sophie Schreur,* which was thought to be lost at sea with all one-hundred souls on board. Still admiring the picture, she barely heard what Zack said until Kevin grabbed hold of her hand and pulled her along towards the stairs beyond which lay a modern kitchen and an attached dining room.

The boy pulled her up the steps to a narrow hallway on the second floor. Behind her, another set of stairs led to the attic. More nautical paintings of sailing vessels falling victim to giant squids or other sea monsters decorated the Oxford blue walls. Before her were three steps leading to an elevated platform with double doors, she guessed lead to the master bedroom. Another two doors were on either side of her, and all of them were closed. She wanted to ask which room she should put her stuff in, and Zack, who always seemed to read her mind, smiled, and looked down at her before he guided her to the left.

"All right, so my room is straight ahead. It has the door which leads out onto the balcony. Cherry, you can take the one right next to it on the left. The door to the right has the bathroom you will share with Kevin, unless of course, you'd rather use the one in the master bedroom."

"No, no, I'm fine with the one on the right."

"Where is my room?"

"Yours is right down that small hallway, it's called the bunk room."

"Bunk room?"

"Come on, I'll show you. Something tells me you're going to love it."

Zack guided Kevin to a door hidden in the small alcove, and Charlotte followed behind them into a generously sized room. It had two closets with a white desk and chair on the left and to the right was a white twin over queen bunk bed. Straight ahead, raised slightly above the rest of the room, was a sitting area with two powder blue chairs, a white coffee table, and two matching bookshelves on either side. A large picture window behind the chairs looked over onto the gravel driveway where the Land Rover was parked, and two more windows flanked the bed, glancing over the back yard. Kevin's eyes lit up, and he ran around inspecting the room, eventually dropping his bag in the sitting area, and running over to the bed.

"Sweet! I always wanted a bunk bed."

"Well, now you got one. At least while you live here. And you know what else?"

"What?"

"You can sleep in any bunk you want."

"Yes..." Kevin jumped up and down. "I'll sleep on the top."

"I figured that much." Charlotte smiled at his excitement, knowing full well that now the only bed he'd ever want would be a bunk bed like this one. "Why not get ready for bed so you can test it out?"

"Do I have to, mom? I was hoping I could talk to dad more."

"No, your mother is right. You can settle down and read a book or play your games. I think she and I need some time to catch up and discuss things further. I promise you that tomorrow I will be all yours as soon as you return home from school."

"Oh fine." The boy ran over and hugged his father. "I guess maybe it will give you guys a chance to work things out, so I don't have to live with another Bret." Kevin shuddered at the thought of the man before muttering to himself. "I doubt you could get much worse than that guy."

Zack said good night to his son and said he was going downstairs to prepare tea because he knew how much Charlotte enjoyed a cup at the end of the day. She watched her son run into the bathroom before she made her way into her room to put down her bags. The room with its full-sized bed and two latticed windows overlooking the street held a familiarity to it, triggering in her the strange slew of emotions. Setting her bag down by the striped chair near the window, she glanced through the sheet of white curtains and a strange sense of dread set in deep in her stomach, and her heart twisted in her chest. She was suddenly afraid—afraid of losing Kevin and Zack—and no matter how hard she tried, she could not shake the feeling that she may never see them again.

CHAPTER TWENTY-NINE

"I know that's what people say—you'll get over it. I'd say it, too. But I know it's not true. Oh, you'll be happy again, never fear. But you won't forget. Every time you fall in love it will be because something in the man reminds you of him."—
Betty Smith, A Tree Grows in Brooklyn

Putting away her things and saying goodnight to Kevin, Charlotte made her way down the stairs to sit on the porch swing overlooking a small row of shops. The still air outside was calm, yet oppressive, and the chirruping of crickets in a nearby hedge sounded threatening. Deep in her gut, something told her terrible things were coming her way. Shivering despite the warm evening, she folded her arms around herself as Zack came out to join her. Placing the two steaming cups of tea on a nearby table, he sat down beside her, putting his arm across the back of the swing.

"So," he looked at her with a serene expression and a soft smile, "did you name him Kevin because I always said that's what I wanted to call my son if I ever had one?"

"Yes. I guess a part of me always dreamed things would return to normal between us and that we would be a family. And also, another part of me just wanted to hang on to you in any way it could, even if reality told me I'd never see you again."

"Yeah, I guess I know what that's like." Zack went silent for a moment and glanced down into his lap before he spoke again. "Kevin told me all about Bret and how he treated you. I'm sorry."

"Don't be, it's not your fault."

"Maybe it is. I was the one who left you, so I can't help but feel responsible for what you've been through."

"You were not responsible for the choices I made; those are on me. I don't need you blaming yourself for my poor decisions."

"All right, fine, I'll let you be the martyr of this story, but just this once." He looked up at her with an infectious smirk. "So, aside from having my kid and giving up your dreams, how else have you been the last ten years."

"I've been surviving, I guess, but when you make as many mistakes as I do, that's about all you can do." Charlotte continued to gaze into his eyes, and her heart fluttered again. "And what of you? How did you go from wanting to be a journalist to being a so-called paranormal expert?"

"Funny story, really. After I graduated UCLA with honors, I moved to New York with this stupid idea that I was going to land a job working for the Times, but they laughed me out of there and told me to gain more experience first. I spent the next year looking for a job with no luck, all the while working odd jobs to pay for a little shit hole apartment in Brooklyn I lived in. And it was in that apartment that I had a creepy experience of stumbling on a ghost of a young woman in white, watching me while I slept. At first, it freaked me out, but then I decided to figure out why she was haunting the place. Turns out they used my place as a sick house during the typhoid outbreak in eighteen ninety-nine, and she was one of the people who died from it. It intrigued me so much that I tracked down other people who had an encounter with her and wrote a book about it."

"Ah, yes, *White Lady of Crown Heights*."

"You read it?"

"I couldn't resist after seeing your name on it. I didn't think it was real though."

"Well, now you know it was." He glanced back down at the folded hands in his lap. "The rest is history, I guess. I realized I found my calling and went on to track down more stories of the paranormal and published more and more books. Then I got a few TV show deals, and my career really took off."

"Yes, you've done well for yourself. I'm proud of you, Zack." Charlotte looked out onto the empty street before turning back to him. "And is it true what they say, do you really own that famous haunted house on Ocean Drive now?"

"Yeah, it's true." Zack chucked. "Though it's anything but little, or haunted. You should come check it out. Both you and

Kevin can come live with me, you know, we can be a family like you always wanted."

"I don't know Zack," Charlotte's heart leaped into her throat, "I'm not sure that's a good idea."

"Why not Cherry? I missed you, you know." Zack leaned in closer to her face, making her body grow hot. "I've never stopped loving you. And despite all my success, I have never felt emptier in my life because you were not in it."

"And I feel the same, I do. But it's just... Kevin has only now got you in his life, and I know he dreams of having his parents together. I don't want to get his hopes up if things don't work out between us. Not to mention we are different people from who we were in high school. We need to spend some time getting reacquainted before we decide to jump into things."

"All right. We'll take it slow then. We still have at least a month to spend together, and I'll leave my offer on the table. Just know that I am not leaving this island without the two of you. I'll stay here for the rest of my life if I have to."

"Thank you... I think."

"Don't mention it. Although I want you to know I never did date anyone after you."

"Really?"

"Yes." He glanced over at her with his sparkling grayish-blue eyes. "I mean, I tried, but no girl, no matter how gorgeous or smart she was, could ever compare to you. After a semester of failed dates, I focused on school and promised myself I'd get you back as soon as you graduated. I even tried calling you up a few times beforehand, but I could never bring myself to speak to you."

"You were behind all those prank calls?"

"Yup, I was a fool, I know. If I spoke to you sooner, maybe I would have known about my son a long time ago, and maybe I would have had you in my life. But by the time I got the courage to speak, you had moved on, and I was left alone. Guess that's part of the reason I worked so hard to become famous. I wanted you to notice me again."

"Oh, Zack... I wish I knew..."

Taking hold of Zack's hand, Charlotte felt conflicted by the surge of emotions she was experiencing: guilt, love, pain, and fear. She never knew the whole time he was hurting as much as she was, and it overcame her with compassion for him, and with a longing of wanting to be with him again. At the same time, she was afraid of getting close to him. She was afraid of losing him, not to another person, but to death, and on this island, something evil was looking to take him away from her. Leaning in to kiss him, a thunderous sound of twisting metal and shattering glass pulled her back, interrupting the mood between them. Jumping in their seat, they turned their heads to see a car wrapped around a telephone pole with a body lying motionless across what remained of the hood. There was no sound of breaks squealing beforehand to warn them of the tragedy, and Charlotte knew the driver didn't try to stop.

He drove into that pole head-on, on purpose.

"What the hell?"

"Go inside and call an ambulance, then go grab my bag. I left it by the chair in my room."

"What are you going to do?"

"I'm a medic, I have to go offer aid before the ambulance arrives." Charlotte jumped off the bench and headed for the stairs. "Now go, hurry, there may still be time to save them."

Scattering the murder of seven crows which had gathered on the front lawn, Charlotte dashed across the street to the mangled car. The acrid scent of gasoline filled the air and as she looked over the body, she knew the man it belonged to was dead. A lifeless heap of flesh lay sprawled over the curled white metal of the hood. Blood dripped from the car, pooling by her feet as she attempted to figure what was what in the malformed blob of human tissue and glass. She found a piece of the face with the eyeball still attached a few feet away from her, next to what remained of the man's brain, at least she thought it was a man, but it was hard to tell from what little of him remained intact. Swallowing the bile coming up, she leaned inside the car and let out a sigh of relief as there was no one else with him. She was thinking of running inside the house to grab a sheet to cover the body up when the sound of bones cracking and snapping grabbed her attention. Turning around, she saw the mangled flesh twitching and turning until a crushed skull looked at her with a skeletal grin and one remaining eye.

"A deal was made," it gurgled, "now someone has to pay. Will you pay, Charlotte?"

Screaming, Charlotte leaped back onto the curb as the body collapse again, showing no further signs of life. Disturbed, she turned to run back to the house but stopped dead in her tracks when she collided with Zack's broad chest. Still shaking, she glanced up at him and noticed he was frowning and holding up her med bag. Seeing her distraught expression, his face softened, and he put his free arm around her, drawing her in for a hug and melting her fears away.

"Everything all right?"

"No."

"Is he going to make it?"

"No, he's dead, he died from the impact." She glanced back over her shoulder, trying to guess how fast he was going when he hit, knowing he had to more than triple the speed limit to sustain those injuries. "Did you call the ambulance?"

"Yeah, they are on their way. Should be here in a minute. Are you okay Cherry, you look like you have just seen a ghost?"

"No, I'm terrified." She wrapped her arms around his waist and buried her face in his chest, hoping desperately to block out the memory of the corpse's face. "I want to get out of here, go back inside, but we have to stay here until the guys arrive."

"All right, well, we can back away from the body and wait by the flower shop if it's bothering you."

"It's not the body," Charlotte cocked her head to the wreck behind her, feeling a sinister presence nearby, "it's something else."

"Like what?"

"I don't know, I can't begin to explain it to you."

"Hey, it's okay." Zack rubbed her back while backing away from the car. "Take your time. You can tell me whenever you are ready. I'm always here to listen, and I'm not going anywhere this time, I promise."

"I know." She wrapped her arms tighter around him. "That's what scares me."

They stood on the corner of the street for what seemed like an eternity until the night shift paramedics arrived. The two men from the original crew did not seem phased by what happened as they bagged up the remains and got their statements. One of the men, a stout guy in his late forties with salt and pepper hair, kept glancing in their direction glaring. Thinking how peculiar this was, Charlotte was sure to steal a glance at his tag with J. Jones written on it. Thanking them, she walked away with Zack, back to the house, thinking how she would ask Chuck or Iris to investigate him further. It may have well been her imagination and frayed nerves, but something about the man did not sit right with her. Zack had offered to reheat their tea, but she declined the offer, opting to take a hot shower instead.

Standing in her room, dressed in her pink pajamas, she pulled back the curtain and glanced out the window. A tow truck was loading what was left of the car onto its flatbed, and a firetruck was washing away the glass and blood into a nearby drain. Thinking how strange it was that everyone seemed so calm despite the circumstances, she shook her head and caught sight of something in the trees. Looking closer, she spotted the pigman in the front yard, looking up at her with his finger pointed towards the old hospital.

Once again, the voice of a young man spoke to her in her head, it was the creature communicating telepathically. *Beware the Feast of Shadows.* Spooked by the warning, she yelped and let the curtain drop. When she regained her composure long enough to steal another glance out the window, the mysterious being was gone, and so was the car wreck. Unsettled by how the night played out, she crawled into bed, pulling the covers up over her head and forced herself to fall asleep while images of the man's grotesque skeletal smile continued to permeate her thoughts.

CHAPTER THIRTY

"Your nightmares follow you like a shadow, forever."—
Aleksandar Hemon, The Lazarus Project

W*ondering* through a dense fog, darkness blindfolded Charlotte like a damp rag. She felt something cold and wet under her bare feet; leaves still drenched from the rain. She realized she was lost in the forest, still dressed in her pajamas. Thinking how strange it was that she could have wandered out this far, she remembered it had not rained on the island since she got there. The ground should not be wet. Wondering what was happening to her, she continued to explore the area when someone's crying coming from deeper in the forest glued her feet to the soggy soil. Straining her ears, her heart grew ice-cold as the sounds of crying turned to screaming and wailing, which turned into blood-curdling shrieks of agony. It sounded like a man was being tortured and torn apart. She thought of going for help when the sounds suddenly stopped.

Paralyzed by fear, she took an uneasy step forward, heading in the direction the screams came from. A light flickered from somewhere in the dense foliage and once again she was cemented in place, but this time by another horrifying sound. Squealing saturated the dark space around her. All she could hear in her bones were the horrible, agonizing howls of an animal in distress. Tears stung the corners of her eyes. She loved animals, especially pigs, and knowing one was suffering nearby caused her gut-wrenching pain. Moving for the light, she hoped to save it from its fate, but the screaming stopped, and the air grew thin and frigid.

She did not know how long she stood there, a minute, maybe more, when a bleat pierced the silence followed by a woman's scream. Glancing about her, a rustling in the nearby bush drew her attention. Squinting her eyes in the noise's direction, she spotted shadows moving in the distance and something rushed past her, knocking her off her feet. Wet soil broke her fall, and as she stood up, she caught sight of a cloaked figure chasing after whatever had taken her down. The robed person stopped and turned to look at her. This stranger bore a striking resemblance to Victoria, except this woman was wrinkled with a crooked nose, a hairy mole on her chin, and long white hair tangled in knots.

"You," the woman sneered, "you're not supposed to be here."

Reaching for her belt, she yanked something out, and as the sharp edge of the knife glistened in the blood-red light of the moon above, Charlotte knew her life was in danger. The woman swiped the blade for her neck, and she fell back, feeling the razor edge nick the skin of her throat. Falling to the soggy ground once more, she scurried away from another blow, backing herself up against a tree. Her attacker approached, holding the weapon up, ready to strike her down. Charlotte thought that was the end of her when the sound of her name in the distance pulled her back to her own time, and the world around her started to disintegrate.

"Cherry." Someone was shaking her shoulders, and she opened her eyes to see Zack kneeling by her bed, his face full of worry. "Cherry, are you all right? I heard you screaming all the way in my room and rushed in."

"Just a bad dream, I guess."

"You want to talk about it?"

"I was lost in a forest, and I heard a man and an animal being tortured. I wanted to see what it was when something knocked me over. Then this crazy woman attacked me. She had a knife, and she..." instinctively Charlotte reached for her throat and gasped at the stinging of her raw skin and the fresh blood on her fingertips, "... oh god, this can't be?"

"What's wrong?"

"Zack," she stuttered, "turn on the light."

"Okay." Reaching over, he pulled the chain on the bedside lamp and drew a sharp breath. Looking over at his ashen, wide-eyed face, Charlotte knew she hadn't imagined things, even before he spoke to confirm her fears. "What... what on earth happened to you? You are bleeding and covered in mud!"

"I don't know how to tell you this without making myself

sound crazy."

"I would never think you to be crazy." Zack sat down on the bed beside her and wrapped his warm arms around her fidget, wet body. "Just tell me what is happening to you, Cherry."

"The woman, she cut my neck, and now I'm bleeding where she cut. And I'm wet and dirty from falling onto the forest floor. I can't begin to understand how this is possible, but I think I was somehow transported into my dream, and what happened to me there, happened to my physical body here." She looked up at him still holding her, and he gave her a nod to go on. "And that's not even the strangest thing that happened to me here. I've been noticing all sorts of odd things on this island."

"Like what?"

"Well, for one, have you noticed the crows on this island? They only sit in flocks of six or seven."

"Yeah, like that old nursery rhyme. I guess it makes sense considering my informer told the natives believed a demonic being lived on this rock."

"Cyrus, my driver, told me the same thing."

"I was also told that no other birds dare come here."

"You know, Chuck pointed that out too. And the seagulls circling my ferry turned back when we got close."

"I noticed that too. So, what else have you seen?"

"Promise you won't think I'm nuts?"

"I promise." Zack pressed his lips on her forehead. "After all, you are talking to the guy who was terrorized by a dead woman in his apartment and wrote several books on ghosts, goblins, and UFOs."

"Well," she snuggled up against him, "for one, the dead people don't stay dead. They come back to life briefly and talk to me. And not just me, Chuck has witnessed it too once when a dead man caused a ruckus in the back of our ambulance."

"What do they say?"

"Strange things. Mostly warnings to get off the island and that someone has to pay. But it's not just the dead, the injured people do and say strange things too."

"Like?"

"Like they turn into something that isn't human. The first time I saw it, it freaked me out. It was my first patient here. He cut off his foot with a saw. I was tending to him when he grabbed hold of me, his eyes black as coal, and his mouth filled with needle-like teeth. He told me time was running out. And then, a woman who was hit by a car today told me to get off the island, or they will get me like they got her."

"Odd." Zack frowned. "Anything else?"

"I also see this creature around all the time. Chuck has seen it too, at the station the day you got here. It's a figure wearing a black robe with the head of a pig and a body of a man. It appears out of nowhere, and sometimes when I see him, I'm transported to another time, a time I can experience but not interact with. He always points to the old hospital, and he talks to me telepathically. He tells me to find answers there and warns me I will die if I don't."

"Do you know what's there?"

"No. But, I was told by my boss that I should never go to the hospital and to stay away from it. At first, I thought it was because of the dark history surrounding it, but now, I'm not so sure."

"I thought they were hiding something there too, especially given that no one dared talk about the place. It's as if it doesn't exist to these people."

"That's not all. I saw the pigman again outside the window tonight, in your yard. He told me to beware of the Feast of Shadows."

"What the hell is that? Some odd local holiday?"

"I don't know. If it is, it's not one I have heard of. But I know that it has something to do with that old hospital on the hill.

"We will have to explore it then. But I need more information first, I will not put you at risk if I don't have to. I already have one of my guys working on it now, but I will relay to him what you told me, and maybe he can find more answers for us."

Sitting with him in silence, the floorboards creaked above their heads in the attic and dust rain downed on them from the ceiling causing Charlotte to twitch. Someone, or something up there, listened to their plans, and she got a sick filling in the pit of her stomach. Kissing her forehead, Zack got up to leave, but she grabbed hold of his hand, knowing she couldn't let him go back into his room. She knew something was lingering on the top of the stairs, waiting for them to separate so it could hurt him, stop him from finding their secret, and she was not about to let them have him.

"Please don't leave, Zack. I'm still scared to fall asleep again." She looked at him with pleading eyes, tightening her grip on his wrist and pulling him down in bed beside her. "Could you maybe stay with me, for a bit?"

"Of course." He smiled and curled up beside her. "I'll stay with you for as long as you need."

She pressed her body closer to him, scared to let go. Warm memories of better times replayed themselves in her mind, but pure terror continued to replace them. A strange melancholy washed over her, and she was afraid for her son sleeping in another room. The thing breathing heavily outside her room didn't care for the boy though, not tonight. It wanted Zack, but it would not be long before Kevin's life was in danger too. Somehow, deep in her bones, she felt the island wanted her, and it wanted her son, and that the man next to her stood in the way. Zack was not supposed to be there, he was not part of the plan, and his arrival had thrown a wrench into things. Pressing herself closer, she hoped she could figure out the island's secret before it was too late for all of them, and waited for Zack to fall asleep.

CHAPTER THIRTY-ONE

"If we were always conscious of the fact that people precious to us are frighteningly mortal, hanging not even by a thread, but by a wisp of gossamer, perhaps we would be kinder to them and more grateful for the love and friendship they give to us. "—**Dean Koontz, Seize the Night**

Waking up to the warm rays of sun caressing her skin, Charlotte found herself still wrapped around Zack. During the night she had waited for him to fall asleep before she allowed herself to doze off. The thing that was sitting on the landing at night continued to snarl and pace around the hall, as if it dared not show itself to her, for the moment. She also knew that if she let Zack go, he would meet with an unfortunate accident, like so many other people on the island, and she did not want to risk losing him. Stirring in bed, she turned to see Kevin leaning on the door jamb with crossed arms and a mischievous smirk on his face.

"So... what are you guys doing?"

"Nothing." Charlotte sat up and stretched out. "I had a bad

dream and I guess we just fell asleep together. Nothing more."

"Uh huh." Kevin rolled his eyes; he knew she was lying. "Well, as much as I'd love for you and dad to work things out, you're going to be late for work if you don't get going in the next five minutes. It's sort of becoming a thing for you here."

"Shit." Charlotte jumped out of bed and ran for the bathroom. "Wake your dad up."

Throwing on her uniform, she ran out of the bathroom and was instantly hit in the face by a wall of oppressive air in the hallway. She felt something in there with her, watching, waiting. For what, she could not say. A knot twisted itself in her stomach, her palms started to sweat, and she got short of breath. A sudden premonition told her something was going to happen to Kevin, not that day, but at some point, in the near future. Taking a quick, shallow breath, she watched Zack walk out of her room, smile, put his hands in his pockets, and lean on the door frame.

"So, Kevin tells me we fell asleep together." He winked. "I could get used to this, Cherry."

"We did, and we can talk about it later. I got to get to work. Think you can drive Kevin to school? I don't want him walking today."

"Sure. I'll even pick him up to make you feel better."

"That would be great. Thank you, Zack." She came over to him and kissed him on the cheek. "I'll see you guys later. Stay safe."

"Hey." Charlotte turned to Zack rubbing the back of his head behind her. "You need a ride over to the station? We can drop you off if you give me like five minutes to throw some clothe on."

"No, it's only a mile away. I'll walk, it's good for me. Plus, something tells me Victoria wants you to stay as far away from it as possible."

"Oh, okay." Zack looked mildly disappointed as he glanced down on the floor. "What time will you be home then?"

"My shift ends at four. With any luck, I'll be back by four-thirty. Now seriously, stay safe, Zack. I don't want any calls coming in about you or Kevin."

"You still worry too much." He shook his head smirking. "But I promise you, I will stay out of trouble. You take care too, don't want any more patients assaulting you."

Assuring Zack she would stay safe, Charlotte ran out the door and paused to look at the spot where the grisly accident took place. The firemen meticulously cleaned up the corner and the utility company promptly repaired the pole overnight, as if nothing ever took place there. People were going about their daily lives, oblivious to the death of a man who they probably knew well. The entire town seemed strange, much like Kevin mentioned the other day, with the citizens acting like robots, devoid of any human emotions. Not even a single flower was left in the spot where the accident happened. In Seattle, there would be a memorial erected on the spot within the hour and stay up for weeks until someone finally cleaned it up, but there was no such momento here.

Unsettled from the events of the previous night, and the behavior of the people outside, she looked at the island differently as she walked to the station, making note of anything out of the ordinary. Besides the seven crows following her, Charlotte noticed that Autumn Falls citizens were not as friendly as they appeared at first glance. This was a small island, and like any small town, everyone knew each other, but here, although they smiled and waved at one another, no one appeared to be on friendly terms.

Their greetings seemed rehearsed, more like those of strangers than old friends, and that made her uneasy. Everyone behaved perfectly, like they were reading from a script—unless they were cutting their feet off or shooting themselves with a speargun—every person on the island appeared to be a model citizen who dared not stray from the ordinary. Disturbed, she noticed something else, their hungry stares when she was near, they knew who she was and why she was on the island, and that made her nervous enough to pick up her pace.

CHAPTER THIRTY-TWO

"I swear from the bottom of my heart I want to be healed. I want to be like other men, not this outcast whom nobody wants."—E.M. Forster, Maurice

J*ogging* to the station house to escape from the looks of the people outside, Charlotte went in and found it to be unusually quiet. Thinking back to her first day, she recalled it was always a bit odd. The building had a calmness to it, not the friendly calmness of the employees hanging around, talking with each other until a call came in. No, this was the still calmness of a funeral parlor, somber and heavy. Footfalls of firemen rumbled above her head, but there was no perkiness in their steps. They were not enjoying the company they were in, they were waiting for something, almost like they *knew* another accident would take place soon.

Walking up the stairs to the third floor, she found Charles right where she expected him to be, in the break room, sitting with his feet on the coffee table, sipping coffee from a blue mug. Spotting her through the glass, he smiled and waved her over to join him. Something told her she had a bit of time to kill before the next call came in, and she went inside to wait. Grabbing a white mug from the pantry, she filled it up with the fresh coffee, which got done brewing a moment earlier, and went over to the sofa to sit beside Chuck.

"I see you got my message."

"Well, good morning to you too sunshine." Chuck regarded her with a smirk, removed his feet from the table, and slid over to allow her room to sit down. "I take it things are going great between you and Mr. Paranormal. After all, you moved out of the hotel to be with him."

"Just for now, to see where things go. He and Kevin want to bond with one another, and I can't stand in their way. Although," she glanced down at her distorted reflection in the coffee, "I don't want to get Kevin's hopes up. You know, in case things don't work out."

"Yeah... something tells me that won't be an issue. You still care a lot about the guy, and from what I've seen of the way he looked at you the other day, he feels the same. So why not be honest with me Char, what's *really* stopping you from getting back together with him?"

"I..." she paused to reflect on the nagging sensation eating away at her, "I don't want to be background noise again."

"Background noise?"

"Yes." Charlotte continued to peer at the coffee in her mug.

"When I found out I was pregnant with Kevin, many people shunned me and lashed out at me. They said I was being selfish by keeping him, and that I should consider Zack's future. His sister even told me how it would be rude of me to ruin what he had going for him and to stay away from him if I knew what was good for me. I had people physically assault me, throw things at me, break windows at my house, and I even had the word 'slut' spray-painted on my locker. And you know what the worst part of all that was?"

"What?"

"Not one person, aside from my mother, not one goddamned person stood up for up. All these friends I thought I had vanished without a trace. They left me to fend for myself, and some of the people I considered friends even joined in on the bullying. That was when I realized that no one care about Charlotte as a person. I was just an extension of Zack. The only reason any of those people were nice to me was because they wanted to get on his good side and spend time with *him,* not me. And with him finally out of the picture, no one felt the need to be nice to *me* anymore, I became a nobody overnight. And—"

"You are afraid that if you gave him a second chance, things would go back to being how they were in high school, especially now that he's famous. You think you would lose your identity and become just a tumor growing off his side again."

"Yes. A tumor..." Charlotte snickered at the accuracy of the reference. "I'd also be the heartless bitch who hid his kid from him for nine years. The same people who made me keep my mouth shut will be the same ones who will slander me for being a selfish bitch for not telling him he had a son."

"But none of them matter Char, especially not to Campbell. You are the only person whose approval he wishes to earn. So, I say fuck them all to hell and go be happy for once. You actually think *that* many people will buy into the bullshit rumors those idiots he doesn't even talk to anymore would spread? And, even if they do, you have enough people who will stand up and fight for you this time, including Zack."

"Him and who else?"

"Me and Iris for one. We consider you our friend, and we won't let anyone talk shit about you. And what of all the people you helped save in your years as a medic? You have touched so many lives, and those people will not listen to the rumors of the feeble mined because they know better. Do what makes *you* happy and screw the rest of the world and what they think."

"I suppose you have a point." She smiled at him. "But there is no reason to not be cautious."

"True, just know I got your back when you do finally decide to go back to him."

"You say that like it's a sure-fire thing."

"Oh, it is, even if you don't want to admit it yet. And I want an invitation to the wedding by the way."

"Fine. I promise to invite you if I ever get married." Charlotte pushed Chuck over, causing him to laugh. "So. Anything new today?"

"Nope, but I hear you had one hell of a night. Cyrus mentioned something about a nasty accident outside the house Campbell is renting."

"Oh... that. Yeah, some guy drove into a telephone pole and went through the windshield of his car. He had to have been doing at least sixty, he was dead before I even got to him."

"Did he do that thing..." Chuck lowered his voice. "You know, like the rest of them."

"Yes."

"What this one say?"

"Something about some deal and how someone *had* to pay."

"That sounds a bit... ominous." Chuck put down his coffee mug. "Do you have any idea what he was talking about?"

"Not a clue. But Zack says he plans on investigating the old hospital soon. The one pigman wants me to go to. I figured I'd go with him, and maybe I can uncover the mystery of this place before it's too late."

Charlotte looked over at Chuck, who looked ashen. She knew what was going through his mind because it was going through hers too. The feeling she got from the place, the magnetic pull of it, he must have felt it too. She wanted to ask him if it wanted him the way it wanted her, but she never got the chance as the door opened and Iris stepped inside to join them. The girl shook and fiddled with her thumbs, and her eyes filled with worry as they darted between Charlotte and her partner.

"Iris, is everything all right?"

"No, I... I don't know how to say this, but there has been an accident at the school."

"What?" Charlotte jumped to her feet, her heart dropping into her stomach. "What kind of accident?"

"I... I don't know. It's not any of the kids, I know that. The only thing I know is that someone fell and got seriously hurt, and that the ambulance should get there right away. I know your son goes to the school and I don't know if they are keeping the kids away or anything, but you may want to have his father pick him up."

"Thanks, I'll consider that." A breath of relief escaped her. At least Kevin was not hurt. "All right, Chuck, your turn to drive."

"Let's roll and see how bad *this* one is."

Grabbing the keys from the table, Charles ran out the door and Charlotte followed him down the stairs. Hopping in their ambulance they raced towards the scene of the accident, wondering what they would find. Neither one of them said it, but they wondered if this one would be dead or alive, all while trying to imagine what horrible things it would say to them. Rounding the corner onto School Street, Charlotte's heart once again sank, and her stomach twisted as she saw a crowd of children gathering in the street. Iris was right in her concern. The school seemed to be letting the children take in the grisly scene instead of keeping them inside, where it was safe.

CHAPTER THIRTY-THREE

"There are horrors beyond life's edge that we do not suspect, and once in a while man's evil prying calls them just within our range."—H.P. Lovecraft, **The Thing on the Doorstep**

*C*huck honked the horn and Charlotte watched the children move aside in two perfectly straight lines, revealing the horror they concealed. Hanging from the spires of the wrought-iron fence was a young man in a black leather jacket with his jeans hanging loosely over his hips. A dark spire stuck out from the top of his head, parting his green mohawk caked in dark purple stains. A stream of fresh blood steadily flowed down the metal bar, pooling beneath his body.

"Good Lord." Chuck gasped. "How the hell do you think that happened?"

"I don't even want to guess. That fence has to be at least six feet tall. Let's jump out and assess him before we try to figure out what we should do. I'll try to find Kevin as well. He must be terrified. I don't know why they are letting the kids just stand there and soak up the sight."

Jumping out from the ambulance, Charlotte walked past the children who were still looking at the man impaled on the fence with amazement. Upon closer inspection, the spire poked through the skin of his lower jaw and out the top of his skull as if someone slammed him straight down onto it. She figured there was no way of surviving a brain injury like that, but his fingers twitched, and she reached out for a pulse which simply was not there. The body on the fence was ice-cold and turning a shade of blue. He was also no longer breathing and judging by the stickiness of the blood under her feet and the dark stains on his lime-green hair, he'd been hanging around for a while before the call to assist him came in.

"Mom! Thank God you're finally here."

Pushing through the crowd of other children who seemed intent on keeping him back, Kevin ran up and flung his arms around her. The boy trembled, his backpack still on. The accident, if you could call it that happened shortly after he got to school. A woman in a long, powder-pink dress with a high collar glanced over at the two of them with a scowl. Her gray hair was rolled up tight in a perfect donut on top of her head without so much as a hair out of place. Watching her thin lips form a sinister smile, Charlotte trailed her eyes past her long, hooked nose to the two beady eyes that were as cold as ice, making her shudder.

"All right, children," the woman's voice was sharp and harsh as she pushed the kids past the gate, "in you go. Let the paramedics do their job now. Come on, Kevin, let's go inside, you have work to do."

"No." Charlotte snapped and drew her son behind her back. "Kevin is going home with his dad."

"I was not aware the boy *had* a father. At least not one who chose to be in the picture."

"Well, he does, and I'm calling him to come pick him up."

"Really Miss, there is no need to overreact. He'll be fine, it's just a dead body, he has to get used to the idea of death, eventually."

"I don't care what you think. You letting the kids stand, and look at a scene like this is unacceptable. I'm calling his father to come grab him, and I'm unenrolling him from school."

"Is that so?" The woman scowled at Charlotte as she continued to sneer. "I will have a talk with your supervisor about this. What do you say to that?"

"Go ahead. She has no say in how I raise my son, and frankly, neither do you."

"We shall see about that, Miss. Briggs."

The teacher snorted, turned, and walked back into the building. Standing in her spot shaking and growing hot from the confrontation, Charlotte wondered if she looked as terrified as she felt. She always hated getting in scuffles with people. Even if it was a mild disagreement, she preferred to not rock the boat, but this time she could not avoid it, and to make matters worse, she did it in front of her son, which made her even more self-conscious.

"Meeeooow," Chuck approached them, "look at them claws coming out. I didn't think you had it in you, partner."

"Guess I lost my cool when it came down to protecting my son."

"Hey, I ain't blaming you. I like this new side of you." Looking over at the body, he muttered something under his breath. "Is he?"

"Yup, he is no longer part of the living. You'll have to call it in to the hospital, and then you'll need to call the fireman. We need someone to come cut the fence, so we can get him down, and they are the only ones with the tools. Can you go do that, so I can call Zack to come grab Kevin?"

"Sure thing, not like our patient is going anywhere."

Chuck walked off, talking on his radio, leaving Charlotte alone with her son to dial the phone. Zack picked up after the first ring, his voice filled with worry, wondering if something happened to her.

"I'm fine, but you need to come to the school, and pick up Kevin... I'd rather not say it over the phone, you'll see when you come here... all right, I'll see you in a bit, just hurry."

Hanging up the phone, she got the odd sensation of someone watching her. The eyes seemed to burn a hole in her skull, and she cranked her head over her shoulder to steal a look. Behind her, through a slightly drawn back curtain, was the teacher, glaring at her with her dark, hateful eyes. Something about the woman made Charlotte agitated, and she swallowed hard, knowing she was watching her, even as the curtain fell closed. She could tell the teacher was still glaring at her, her faint outline observed them through the sheer panel. Pushing Kevin away from the building, she spotted Zack's Range Rover approaching, taking an unseen burden off her shoulders. She watched as he pulled up beside the ambulance, hopped out, and ran over to her, his eyes still filled with worry.

"Damn..." he froze and glanced over at the body with revulsion, "that just isn't right. What the hell happened here?"

"It happened a minute after you left dad. I was walking into the building when that guy was skateboarding past on the sidewalk," Kevin pointed to a broken board leaning against a fence, "he was just approaching the school when he hit something no one could see. Then, he flew through the air as if someone was holding him and landed like that."

"And you witnessed all this?" Charlotte gasped.

"Yes..." Kevin nodded and turned away from his mother. "I wanted to go inside mom, I really did, but the teacher insisted we watch the miracle of death. I think we stood staring at him twitch for a good twenty minutes before she finally went inside to call you. I'm sorry mom, I know I should have called you the second it happened."

"Don't be sorry, Kev, you had no idea what these people were going to do. You go home with dad now and try to forget what you saw. I'll deal with the rest."

"Yeah, you can help me do some research, and after we can hang out and watch movies and stuff."

"Really? You'd let me help you do book research?"

"Absolutely kid. I could use a partner in crime while I'm here." Zack smiled. "We'll hit up the local library first and see what we can dig up. Go hop in the truck, we'll even grab some snacks on the way."

Squealing with excitement, Kevin ran and clambered into the car, forgetting all about the dead man in the prospect of spending time helping his father. Walking around the ambulance, Charles gave them a nod of his head, turning to the back and giving Charlotte some time alone with Zack. Looking over at him, his silence hit her hard. Knowing what was on his mind, she smiled and did her best to maintain her composure despite how scared she was.

"Thanks for coming to grab him."

"No problem, I'm actually glad I'll be able to spend more time with him. You sure you'll be all right here?"

"Yeah, I can handle this, just a normal day on the job." She forced a laugh, trying to downplay the severity of the situation. "I'll see you tonight for that dinner you promised to cook me. You just stay safe and keep our boy out of trouble." Charlotte stole a glance behind her shoulder where the crack in the curtain hid the beak nose of the woman still staring at her. "There is something not right with the people on this island."

"Yeah, I got that much a while ago. All right, I'll keep an eye on Kevin. You just take care of yourself. I don't want to see anything bad happen to you, Cherry."

Placing a kiss on her forehead, Zack walked to his car and pulled out of his spot, leaving Charlotte alone with the dead body. Walking behind the back of the ambulance, she saw Chuck sitting on the bumper with a stretcher out and ready to go. Sitting down beside him, she looked out at the crows sitting next to the body— three to either side— and frowned.

"We all set?"

"Yes, ma'am, the firemen are on their way, and I got the stretcher ready, so we can get the hell out of here the moment he's down."

"Great, I don't want to stay here a minute longer than we have to."

"I bet," Chuck nodded his head towards the window, "You sure pissed her off, considering she's still watching us."

"Yeah, did you hear the way she threatened me when I said I'll raise my kid the way I see fit?"

"Uh huh, makes me overly worried about you. These teachers, they are not to be trusted. I don't think anyone on this island is."

"Right? And get this, Kevin told me she waited twenty minutes before calling us because she wanted to teach the kids about the miracle of death."

"Now *that* is messed up. Maybe we should all just leave this damn hunk of rock before it claims us too."

"If we can."

"You sense it too, don't you? The way the island pulls you, lulls you, and makes you want to stay just a little longer?"

"Yes, and I also feel like it wants me. It desires me. It needs me. And it's hiding things from me, things that someone else wants me to figure out."

"I feel it too, deep in my bones, this insatiable lust, and it scares the shit out of me."

Nodding her head, Charlotte continued to ponder the perception they both got from the island. Something was compelling them to stick around while their entire body was telling them to run. An ancient memory was flashing warning signs at her, telling her she was in danger, but she got the impression that she was under a spell, making her never want to leave. She wanted to be part of the island, be one with it, even if she knew that meant death. But no matter the hold it had on her, she suddenly wanted to fight it, Zack gave her a reason to want to leave, and as she chatted with Chuck, she realized that was what made him so dangerous, and why this place wanted to get rid of him.

CHAPTER THIRTY-FOUR

"Humanity is a parade of fools, and I am at the front of it, twirling a baton."—**Dean Koontz**

S itting on the back bumper of the ambulance, Charlotte and Chuck continued to wait for the firemen to arrive, carrying on their conversation. She relayed to him her concerns about the island wanting to dispose of Zack, and he agreed, claiming he sensed it too. Zack was an outsider who was not like them, he was never supposed to come to this sacred place. An unearthly chill filled the air as they mentioned his name. The cool breeze coming off the ocean was stiff and suffocating, growing heavier by the second. Suppressing a shiver raking down her spine, Charlotts stole a glance at her watch and frowned.

"What the hell is taking them so long? The station is three minutes away, yet we've been waiting here for over twenty-minutes with a dead guy on display behind us."

"No clue." Charles glanced over at his own watch. "I'd say maybe they had another call, but in *this* town, I doubt that's the case."

"Yes, strange how only one call ever happens per shift, isn't it? We don't have days with no calls, and we don't have days when we are swamped, we just receive one call every day. No more, no less."

"And they are all accidents. Not fires, not natural causes, but horrible, brutal accidents. If you can call them that since they all seem to be self-inflicted."

"What do you suppose it all means?"

"No idea, but maybe we should keep our mouth shut for now." Chuck motioned his head to the red fire truck slowly climbing down the hill. "I have this perception that our friends are not on our side."

The firemen pulled up beside them and got out of their truck without saying a word to either of the two medics. Charlotte exchanged glances with her partner as they got up and watched the men cut the fence and haul the body down. There was no reaction from them, not even a flinch of emotion on their stony brows. Giving them a friendly smile as they laid their patient on the ground, she sent them off with a nod and waited for them to leave before she wheeled the stretcher closer. Coming around the corner of the ambulance, she thought she saw an eyeball move in its socket, making her freeze with a gasp. But upon further inspection, she concluded that her mind was playing tricks on her and went to collect the body.

Having put the man on the stretcher, they wheeled him into the back of their ambulance. Getting ready to leave, Charlotte walked past the gurney when a stiff, cold hand grabbed a hold of her wrist. With a startled yelp, she whipped around to the man with the iron spire still sticking out of his head sitting up, looking at her. His eyeballs twitched and jerk around in different directions until they rolled all the way into the back of his head, getting replaced by black, inky pools. Red foam bubbled out of his mouth as she witnessed his teethe getting replaced by jagged, snarled fangs. Letting out a hiss, the corpse tightened his grip on her, pulled her closer, and spoke.

"We're coming for you."

Screaming, Charlotte pulled on her arm attempting to free herself but the thing beside her held tighter, pulling her even closer, snapping its jaws at her. Shoving the stretcher aside, Chuck covered the short distance between them, prying the hand off her and pulling her out the back. The thing sat up at a crouch, getting ready to strike, and they shut the doors behind them just in time to hear the thud of it hitting the metal. It clawed and banged on the doors, trying to breakout. Not daring to stay and see if it could liberate itself, the two of them scrambled for the cab, locking their doors, and peeling out of their spot. Panting heavily as they sped down the road, they looked at each other's blood drained faces, with Chuck being the first one to speak.

"You know, I am getting tired of the dead coming back to life and threatening us."

"You and me both. And just think, we have to go drop him

off at that creepy morgue."

"Oh, I sure am looking forward to this one. Think it will be as bad as it was last time?"

"I sure hope not. But here, you never know."

Silently, the two continued to the hospital where their second trip to the morgue was mostly uneventful. Aside from the elevator door refusing to open and another stroboscopic light show, nothing seemed to pursue them. Opting out of going back to the station, the two of them sat and talked outside a café until it was time to leave. Getting home shaken and exhausted, Charlotte found Kevin dead asleep and Zack waiting for her in the kitchen with two hot cups of chamomile tea and a bowl full of pasta primavera.

"Hey, how was the rest of your day?"

"The usual for here, I guess. I see Kevin is already in bed."

"He was tuckered out by the time we got home. I think the events of the morning really got to him. He was seriously worried about you the whole time. He said he felt something odd on this island, something that wanted to murder you."

"He's not the only one who feels it, you know." Charlotte sat down in a chair across from Zack and wrapped her hands around the warm porcelain mug. "I feel it too, and so does Chuck. And we all know that you are not supposed to be here. You are not welcome, and this island is coming for you."

"Is..." Zack swallowed his tea and glanced up to pierce her

with his gaze, "is that why you let me sleep next to you last night? Because you were afraid something would happen to me?"

"That was part of the reason." She avoided his gaze. "I heard something lurking in the hallway last night, waiting for you, and my gut told me that if I let you go, I'd never see you alive again."

"What was the other reason?"

"I think you know." She stared at her cup with a sly smirk "I think I could get used to sleeping next to you again. I enjoy having you close."

"So, you admit that I'm irresistible?"

"Oh, I don't know..." Charlotte rolled her eyes, "I guess I am."

"Does this mean you'll keep me company again tonight?" He looked at her with his puppy-eyes and a pout. "In my room, perhaps?"

"Only if it keeps you safe. I don't want to be telling Kevin his father died just as he got to know him."

"Ouch. Why must you be so cruel?"

"Because I think you earned it."

Laughing, the two of them stayed up talking until late into the night. Charlotte had agreed to spend the night with Zack, as long as he respected her boundaries. Unable to sleep, she lay awake, watching his chest rise and waited for something to come. Straining her ears, she attempted to pick up signs of the shadowy creature from the other night, but aside from the creaking of the house, the hiss of the radiator, and the rustling in the trees outside, the house remained silent. Getting up, she threw on a robe and strolled outside to the balcony, tightening the pink terrycloth as the wind picked up, whispering in her ear. The cold autumn's breath carried a voice on it, one she was familiar with, and, despite not being able to see him, she heard his warning loud and clear. *Beware, the time is almost up.*

CHAPTER THIRTY-FIVE

"Thank God you are still alive for many have died and are dying as I speak. You still have the opportunity to change and make things right whilst those that have died wish for that second chance."—**Aleksandr Sebryakov**

Eventually, Charlotte fell into an uneasy sleep, filled with horrifying dreams of slaughter and death. Tossing and turning half the night, she woke up at the crack of dawn, just as the crimson sun was cracking the skyline with its vermilion presence. Opting not to go back to sleep, she got up and made her way into the kitchen where she began making breakfast. Lost in the fresh scent of brewed coffee and the delightful aroma of the pumpkin pancakes, she didn't hear Zack come down, not until he wrapped his arm around her waist and nuzzled his face into her hair.

"What are you doing?" She turned to face him. "I thought we agreed to not give Kevin the wrong idea?"

"And what idea is that?" Kevin who had bounced down the stairs pulled out a chair and flopped into it, looking at the two of them with a huge grin. "That my parents may actually get back together, and we can be a normal family?"

"Precisely." Charlotte pushed Zack away and looked at her son. "You know there is a chance it won't happen, right? Sometimes, no matter how much we want, things just don't work out."

"Yeah, I know... but there is no harm in you guys trying, is there?" Kevin stared back at her with a scowl. "I mean, dad is willing to try, but you keep resisting. And it's dad after all, not Bret, he won't do the same things that loser did."

"See, Cherry," Zack pulled her back into his embrace, "even our son sees we belong together. Why can't you just give it a chance?"

"Our son," Charlotte pulled away from him and returned to the stove, "is thrilled to have his idol be his father, and he wants to see us together because he wants to be like all his friends. But fine, I relent. Seeing as I'm outnumbered on this, we can talk later, *after* we go to the beach. Now," she turned around with a plate full of food, "who wants pancakes?"

"Me!" Kevin jumped up in his chair, nearly spilling the milk in his glass. "It's been a long time since you made pancakes."

"I know." Charlotte's heart leaped at the memory of what happened last time Kevin spilled milk. But to her relief, Zack steadied the glass and ruffled the kid's hair instead of raising his hand. Smiling, she placed the dish in the center of the table and sat down. "I am amazed I remembered how to make the batter. I was afraid I would have to look it up, but it looks like I still got it."

Sitting down to breakfast, Charlotte got lost in the aroma of her coffee while looking over Zack interacting with Kevin. They looked so natural together and her spirits lifted at the thought of having a family. This was exactly what she wanted, ever since they met all those years ago, and with his offer on the table, it was a real possibility. Only thing standing in her way was the island. She knew she would have to leave to be with Zack, she'd have to move to New York, but she was afraid the island would not let her go. Unless she figured out how to break the spell it had on her, she would be trapped on it, until it was her turn to die, and that was the scariest realization of all.

CHAPTER THIRTY-SIX

"Who knows the end? What has risen may sink, and what has sunk may rise. Loathsomeness waits and dreams in the deep, and decay spreads over the tottering cities of men."—**H.P. Lovecraft**

Strolling along the beach after breakfast, Charlotte watched as Kevin ran ahead, playing in the sand and surf. The sun was warming the stiff air, glistening on the foam-laced waves crashing to the shore, carrying with them seaweed and sticks. Inhaling the salty sea air, she closed her eyes and a warm hand envelop hers as Zack laced his fingers through hers. Once more pleasant memories of better days suffocated her, and she looked up at him. He looked down on her with a shy smirk on his face and rubbed the back of his head.

"So, Cherry, I know you didn't want to talk about it now, but... what do you say we give this another go? You know—you, me, Kevin—a family?"

"What if it doesn't work out?" Her eyes fell to the wet sand under her feet absorbing their footprints. "What then?"

"Then I'll still be in Kevin's life. No matter what happens, I'll always be a father to him. Now that I know I have a son, I am never letting him go, and the two of us would figure out how to make it work. But what if it does work out?" He glanced at her, the sun shimmering in the blues of his irises. "Have you ever thought that both of us ending up here was fate giving us a second chance?"

"Maybe..." she paused to study a ship bobbing on the horizon, "it sure is strange isn't it, how we both wound up here?"

"I'm telling you; it was fate." He squeezed her hand, and it forced her to peer back over at his earnest face. "Remember what I told you before I left for UCLA?"

"You broke my heart that day, Zack, how could I ever forget? Those words are seared into my memory. You said, if we are meant to be together, then we will find a way back to each other, and then, we would know."

"Exactly, and what a fool I was when I said them, because for the next ten years, I would be eating those words every damn day of my life."

"What do you mean?"

"Well, I told you how I figured out I couldn't date because no one compared to you, right? What I neglected to tell you was how I spent every night afterward praying that we would get another chance meeting. Actually, I was starting to give up hope when I got the call to come here. I figured I'd come here, write my story and dedicate my next book to you, so maybe, just maybe, you would see it and come find me. What I didn't expect was to find you here. That's when I knew that fate had finally smiled upon me. It was giving me a second chance to be with you, and this time I intend not to fuck it up. So, what do you say, give this fool another chance, please?"

"Tell you what," Charlotte stopped, wrapped her hands around his waist, and looked at him, "I'll give you a *very* tentative yes. If you can keep showing me you are sincere in your efforts to be with Kevin and me, then when you are done with your work here, we'll pack up and go with you to New York."

"You serious?"

"As a heart attack."

Laughing, Zack brought her in closer, kissing her on the top of her head as she buried her face in his chest. Listening to the sound of his heartbeat, and the motion of the waves, Charlotte felt a strange disturbance in the surrounding air. The island was angry with her now that she had voiced her decision to leave, and something told her it would not give her up without a fight. Clinging to Zack, she continued to listen to the rumbling of the ocean as an offshore breeze picked up and brought with it a strange scent and the distant sound of shouting.

"Hey, you smell that Zack?"

"Yes. A faint scent of rum and teak wood."

"Isn't it strange? Where do you think it's coming from?"

"I have no clue, but do you hear the voices too?"

"Yes. They're speaking Dutch."

"Dare I ask how you know that?"

She was about to reply when Kevin's shouting drew their attention to where he was playing in the sand. He was jumping around, screaming, and her heart dropped thinking he possibly hurt himself. Turning to run to him, Charlotte spotted the smile on his face and heaved out a heavy breath, relieved the boy was only excited. Continuing to spin around in a circle, the boy was holding something in his hand and waving for his parent to join him.

"Mom! Dad! Come see what I found."

Rushing over to meet them halfway, Kevin thrust a rough disk up into the air. Furrowing his brow, Zack took hold of it and ran his finger to remove the sand from its tarnished surface. On the blackened coin was a coat of arms with two lions raising their right paws in the air, enclosed in a wreath of what looked like ivy. On the outer edge, Charlotte could make out *SI 1628* and *Ordin West*. Flipping it over in his hand, Zack brushed more sand off and lifted it to study the ornamental cross with the rose at the center. Outside the dotted circle, the writing on this end was almost ineligible, having been washed away by its time in the elements.

"What is it, dad?"

"An old Dutch Schilling." Zack scowled. "But I have no idea

how it got here. I am not aware of any Dutch ships going down around here, and this island wasn't settled until 1699."

"The Sophie Schreur."

"Is that a ship?"

"Yes. It was a Fluyt bound for the new world in 1628, but it never made it here. No remains were ever found, and they assumed it to be lost at sea with all one-hundred people on board."

"How do you know so much about Maritime History?"

"I took an interest in it after reading Moby Dick."

"Why am I not surprised?"

"Wow, do you really think this coin is from that ship mom?"

"Maybe. That's the best explanation I can come up with."

"Awesome! What should we do with it then?"

"Why don't you keep it, for good luck?" Zack handed him the coin. "Once we return to the mainland, I'll have one of my guys look into it and see if we can confirm your mom's suspicions?"

"That would be so cool! What should we do now?"

"What do you want to do?"

"What you do. I want to hunt spooky things and do research."

"In that case..." Zack smiled and winked at Charlotte. "Do you two want to go explore that old lighthouse and search for hidden ghosts?"

"Yes!"

"What?" Charlotte shook her head. "No, we really shouldn't. What if someone is there?"

"Then I'll just tell them we want to poke around and do some ghost hunting and research for my book. At worst, I'll give them some money, and they'll let us in. Come on, where is your sense of adventure, Cherry."

"It left when I had a baby."

"Well, Kevin is a big kid now, time to get it back."

"Come on mom, let's go have a peek. There is no harm in that, plus you always said how much you love lighthouses, this is your chance to explore a really old one without a guided tour."

"Fine." She folded her arms over her chest. "But I am not responsible for what happens to you two."

Strolling back up to the Range Rover, Charlotte sensed someone looking at her from the tree line. She turned, but despite feeling several sets of eyes on her, she could see no one peeking out from the small patch of forest. There was something else about those eyes, unlike the eyes at the house at night, these weren't threatening, they were more inquisitive, pleading even. Something about the way the forest looked at her caused her to grow sad, as if the longing of countless souls radiated through her. Some force on the island wanted to kill her, but something else pleaded with her to be saved. Turning her back to the tress, she walked to the car, while her unseen company continued to trail behind her.

CHAPTER THIRTY-SEVEN

"Chasing ghosts while pursued by daemons..."—**Gail Carriger, Blameless**

riving up the winding wooded path, Charlotte caught glimpses of the lighthouse whenever the Range Rover slowed down for a sharp turn. The forty-one-foot ivory tower constructed of brick peeked its way above the trees even before they pulled up to the small, dirt lot next to it. Some of the paint had faded away, revealing splotches of red beneath. A small brick house was attached to the wide base, boarded up without a need for a keeper to live in it. Jumping out from the car, Zack went to try the black iron door pitted with rust, but the heavy slab refused to open.

"Dang. It's locked. Let me see if I can find another way in. There should be an entry point from the keeper's cottage, maybe I can find my way inside."

Wondering around looking at the small red house, Zack left Charlotte and Kevin alone by the main entrance. The structure had a somber energy about it, as if the building itself was in mourning.

Below the hill they were on sat the old hospital encased in the forest and the light ocean breeze floating past it carried up the scent of sulfur and a pained, unintelligible voice. The hairs on Charlotte's arm stood up. She was aware of someone else there with them and listened to muffled clangs on the other side of the door. Silence followed the commotion, and after a brief pause, the metal creaked, groaned, and swung open, welcoming them inside. Blinking, she stared into the abyss of the tower and a strange pull begging her to explore urged her inside.

"Hey Zack," she darted her head around, looking for him, "the door just opened."

"What?" Zack rounded the base of the tower and looked at her with a crinkled brow. "How?"

"How would I know? Maybe you loosened it up or something."

"I guess so. Shall we go up and explore?"

"Last one up is a rotten egg."

Kevin darted past the two of them and ran into the mouth of the building. Charlotte tried to grab hold of him while shouting for him to wait, but he slipped past her fingers and clambered up the metal stairs. Muttering at himself, Zack ran in behind him, leaving her alone outside. Peeking her head through the frame, she stepped into the cold interior and glanced up with a shudder. While all lighthouses employed the nautilus stairs design, which she was not fond of, she hated this style in particular. Browned, rickety metal steps spiraled upwards with nothing between them to catch her if the steps broke, and she fell. Gripping the railing on both sides, she slowly made her way up, counting the steps along the way, one-hundred and twenty-five in all. At the top, the site of Zack and Kevin, standing frozen in fear next to the lens greeted her.

"What's wrong you two?" Charlotte huffed and wiped her sweaty palms on her jeans. "You both look like you have seen a ghost."

"Mom... there is no light here."

"What do you mean? The bulb is right in front of you and I see the light from here all the time."

"See for yourself." Zack stepped aside. "There is nothing here. Just an empty house and some brass tube looking thing. It looks more like a museum piece than a working lighthouse."

"Oh my," Charlotte walked over to them and glanced at the lighthouse component with sparkling eyes, "this *has* to be one of the original Fresnel Bull's Eye Lenses. Why, I have never seen one outside a display before. And this," she pointed to the two oxidized brass tubes "this is a Funck Constant Level Fountain Lamp. They stopped using them in nineteen-ten, and they are extremely rare."

"Like I said. This thing is not operational."

"But..." Kevin took hold of Zack's hand. "If this thing doesn't work, then where does the light come from."

"A ghost light."

"Really, Zack? Have all the ghost stories you've researched gone to your head? You seriously expect me to believe that the light coming from this lighthouse is not real?"

"Oh, it's real, it's just not made by that thing you mentioned, the Fluke something or other."

"Funck Constant Level Fountain Lamp. And if the lighthouse doesn't use it, then how can there be a light coming from it?"

"I don't know, but it's not unheard of. This phenomenon has never been explained, but it happens in lighthouses all over the world, even ones that have officially retired. Almost as if the dead keepers continue to do their job despite the building being decommissioned."

"Or a more logical explanation would be that *this* lighthouse never went automatic and continues to use the fountain lamp."

"Then *who* do you suggest operates it? The keeper's hut is boarded up and falling apart. No one has lived in this place for close to a century."

"Perhaps a local volunteer. Why jump to supernatural conclusions when we have plenty of normal explanations?"

She continued to stare at Zack, who didn't seem to have a rebuttal, and as much as she wanted to say it was odd that a lighthouse would not get automated, she was not about to admit to the possibility of ghosts. Despite everything she encountered on the island, Charlotte wanted to cling to the rational, for admitting to the existence of the supernatural would send her over the edge.

Suddenly, she had the urge to leave, but as she turned to head down the stairs, a tolling of a bell in the distance pulled her back. Walking outside to the railing, she glanced over at the horizon and saw a three-decked, wood ship bobbing in the waves with raised, white sails. Impossible, she thought, but as the vessel drew closer to the jagged rocks beyond, her jaw dropped, and she had to accept the only explanation left available.

"Is..." she dared not say it, the words refused to leave her lips. "Is that what I think it is?"

"A ghost ship." Zack put a hand around her. "Do you believe me now, Cherry?"

"I don't know." She shook her head with her voice dropping to a whisper. "I don't know what to believe anymore."

"Wow, I can't believe I had my first ghost sighting today. This is so cool. Do you think it's the ship you mentioned mom, the Sophia Schrodinger?"

"The Sophie Schreur. And no, this can't be her. This is a nineteenth-century British warship. But I have no idea which one it could be."

"Another lost ship? This is amazing. I can't wait to go home and help dad figure out which one it is. I want to be just like him when I grow up."

"Gee. Thanks."

"Sorry mom, but your job creeps me out a bit. I don't like blood or dead people and... I always wanted to be like him, even before I knew he was my dad."

Charlotte smiled at his remark and nodded as she continued to scrutinize the ship as it speared itself on the jagged rocks and vanish from view. She wondered what happened to the people on board. The rocks were close to shore, some of the men could have survived. Then again, if they survived, why was there no record of the wreckage. Surely a shipwreck this close to land would be a prime location for researchers and treasure hunters. And yet, this was the first time she was learning of a ship going down in this part of the ocean.

Staring out at the fog on the horizon creeping closer to shore, she continued to ponder the fate of the doomed vessel when the door downstairs slammed shut, the clang echoing up through the tower. She turned and listened to the footsteps jangle on the metal steps, bouncing off the brick walls, and coming closer. A volunteer must have come to light the lantern, and Zack would have to talk his way out of this one when they were discovered trespassing. Charlotte hoped this trip would not cost her job and was preparing an explanation in her head when the footfalls suddenly stopped. The hairs stood up on her arms as the flame flickered to life before the invisible keeper started back down the stairs. Paralyzed by shock, she looked at the beam of light cutting through the fog engulfing them until the squeaking of the metal hinges let her know they were alone.

"Okay, I've had enough of this." Charlotte grabbed hold of

Zack's arm. "Can we please just get the hell out of here and go back home?"

"Yeah dad, I think this is enough spooky stuff for one day."

"I concur. Let's go home."

Forgetting her fear of heights and the metal steps, Charlotte bound her way down the stairs behind Zack and Kevin. Rushing out into the creamy blanket of fog, she slammed the door shut behind her. Stumbling to find the car in the thick vapor, she didn't turn to look back, not even as someone called her name from the forest. Finally spotting the outline of the Range Rover, she ran for it, tripping over rocks as she went until she was safely inside the cabin. They drove down the hill as fast as they could, with neither of them mentioning the lighthouse until they were safely back at the house.

Having finished dinner and shaken off the events from earlier, Charlotte put Kevin to bed and snuggled in besides Zack. It did not take him long to fall asleep, and he lay next to her snoring while she stayed awake and looked into the shadows lurking past the doorway. Once more her arm hairs stood up, and she spotted something moving in the darkness, lingering, and waiting for a chance to strike. Occasionally the creature would mew and snarl, getting closer to the room, but quickly retreating into the hallway. She didn't know what was keeping it away, but it would not be long until she had to confront it, her time was slipping away like sand in an hourglass.

CHAPTER THIRTY-EIGHT

"The world outside had its own rules, and those rules were not human. — **Michel Houellebecq, The Elementary Particles**

After two sleepless nights at the house watching the shadowy figure lurking in the hallway, Charlotte went into work exhausted. She joined Chuck, who sat in the break room, waiting for her. Ever since the day the pigman dragged away the fireman, no other first responder dared to go up to the third floor except for them. Neither of them cared though, they had both concluded the creature was not after them, and they enjoyed the peaceful mornings all to themselves. Having brewed a fresh pot of coffee, Charlotte handed a mug to her partner and sat down next to him.

"So, I'm thinking about taking up Zack on his offer and leaving the island to be with him in New York."

"What?" Charles laughed, nearly spitting out his coffee. "Does this mean the ice queen has a heart after all?"

"Haha, very funny. You're a real comedian, you know that?"

"I'm just teasing you, Char. I'm glad you decided to give the poor schmuck a second chance. With the way he looked at you when he first saw you, I thought my own heart was going to break. He really does care for you; I hope you realize that."

"I know, that's why I'm willing to give him another try. And..." she rolled her eyes, "I never could resist his charms, even when I'd rather punch him in the face."

"Ouch, I hope the poor guy remembers what he's getting into." Winking at her, Chuck put his mug down and leaned back. "Does this mean you'll be seeking another job in the Big Apple?"

"Absolutely, I still love this job, even if it's not the one I originally wanted."

"Would you still consider having me as a partner?"

"Well, yes, but..."

"Don't worry, Iris and I were thinking of leaving his cursed place as well, and with you moving to New York it works out great. My uncle works for the mayor there, and he can pull some strings and keep us working as a team, and Iris would go work for him. As long as you want to still be my partner."

"Oddly enough, I'd actually enjoy that. You are the first partner I've opened up to, and I would love to continue our friendship."

"I'm honored you think so highly of me, especially since I feel this odd connection to you."

"Strange, I feel it too." Charlotte looked over at him. "What made the two of you decide to bail?"

"Everything. Aside from the alien nature of the place, neither of us feels welcome here. Iris always thinks someone is watching her, and me, well I get goosebumps at night because something is calling to me out of the gloom. There is always this sense of danger here too, and neither of us likes it. I'm sure you understand it better than anyone."

"Yes, but I don't think this place is going to let us leave, at least not without a fight."

Glancing over at her, Chuck nodded his head. She knew he had the sense of being wanted too, and not in a good way. The island hungered for them the same way a wolf hungers for a meal after a long winter. She wondered what was in store for them, and then Iris came into the room, looking ashen and fiddling with the hem of her yellow sweater. Her eyes were moist with tears and her lower lip quivered as she looked over at the two of them. Chuck must have noticed too, for his face suddenly went blank, and he was up to his feet before the words even left his mouth.

"What's wrong, Iris? You look as white as a sheet, love?"

"There has been a boating accident at the pier." Iris's voice cracked and broke as she tried to keep herself from crying. "A little girl is involved, she's seriously hurt, and her father is dead."

"Say no more." Charlotte jumped up to her feet and snatched the ambulance keys off the table. "We are on our way."

Rushing down the stairs to the ambulance, Charlotte spotted

a firefighter in the corner, leaning against the wall, staring at them with a smirk. A police officer who was talking to him gave her a side glance, and the corners of his lips curled into a sickening grin. The hairs stood up on her arms again, something was not right about the two of them, about the entire department actually, but she paid little attention to the nauseating feeling forming in her gut, she had an injured child to save. Hopping in the ambulance's cab, she turned on her sirens and drove out of the bay. Stealing a glance into her rear view mirror as she turned the corner, she spotted the two men standing side by side, arms crossed, watching them.

CHAPTER THIRTY-NINE

"That was the thing. You never got used to it, the idea of someone being gone. Just when you think it's reconciled, accepted, someone points it out to you, and it just hits you all over again, that shocking. "—**Sarah Dessen, The Truth About Forever**

Pulling up to the beach where Kevin found his coin, they spotted a small group of people standing around a pair of bodies. In the ocean, a few feet from the shore, a speed boat dangled off a smaller vessel. It must have hit the victims as they were out on a pleasure cruise. Walking out towards the scene, the first thing she noticed was the sand, its golden grains stained a deep crimson. A man lay to the side, facing up to the sun, the skin on his face hanging open to reveal the skull beneath. The propeller sheered the nose clean off his face, and in the bone-rimmed sockets a pair of golden eyes stared out into the sky. He didn't flinch, and he was not breathing; he was clearly beyond their help. A short distance away a small, blonde girl, about five or six, reached her hand out to Charlotte, her pale green eyes begging for help.

"You go cover up the guy and call it in. I'll see what I can do for the kid."

Leaving Chuck alone with the dead man, she ran over to the child who did not appear to be in any pain. Glancing down the girl's leg, she spotted three deep gouges slicing through layers of tissue, and fat to the muscle beneath. That must have been where the propeller hit her, but aside from steadily oozing blood, it did not appear to be life-threatening. Relieved, Charlotte put down her bag and knelt beside the girl to inspect the injuries closer.

"Hey, there." Charlotte assessed the cuts which missed any major arteries, "what's your name?"

"Hailey."

"Hi, Hailey. I'm Charlotte."

"I know. You are Mr. Campbell's girlfriend."

"How... how did you know that?"

"Clarence told me."

"Who's Clarence?"

"A friend."

"I see." Charlotte reached for her bag. "Well, your friend sure knows an awful lot, don't he?"

"He knows everything, about everyone here. That's his job, you know, so he can keep people safe." The girl paused and looked up with a tear glistening in the corner of her eye. "Miss. Charlotte... can you keep a secret?"

"Of course, I'm a pro at keeping secrets."

"I don't *really* want to die today, Miss. Charlotte."

"You won't die, sweetie; your injury is not bad. I will patch you up and take you to the hospital where they will give you a few stiches. You will be as good as new in a few weeks."

"You don't understand, I have to die, we all do. I have already been marked for death, there is nothing you can do. And don't you know, no one ever survives on this island?"

"What?"

"Everyone dies here. That's why she brings us to the island, so we can provide her with blood, and then there are those like you, those whose souls keep the beast at bay."

"That must be the pain talking dear," Charlotte forced a smile despite the hairs standing up on the back of her neck and the gooseflesh forming on her arms, "let me give you shot, and you will forget any of this ever happened."

"But I have no pain, Miss. Charlotte. Clarence made sure there wouldn't be any when he laid claim to my soul. He *always* makes sure the innocent here don't suffer, and saves as many souls as he can from the soul eaters. He's the one trying to save you from the witch who brought you here, and he wants to save Mr. Campbell too. He is in grave danger you know."

"Who? Zack?"

"Yes. He shouldn't be here. He was never meant to be here, and he is the key to breaking the spell. She wants to kill him before the Feast of Shadows. You *must* leave this island, all of you, before it's too late."

Taking hold of Charlotte's hand, the girl took a deep breath and closed her eyes. The little hand she was holding on with grew limp and fell to the ground. The child was no longer breathing. Shocked, Charlotte realized what happened and began to perform CPR, but as she looked up, she saw the girl standing across from her, holding her father's hand before they both faded from view. Falling backward with shaking hands, she began to cry as the reality set in. The child was dead, and she had warned her to not stay in Autumn Falls, or she too would meet a similar fate, along with Zack, and Kevin.

"Char, you okay?" Charles ran up to her and knelt by the child. "I got the defibrillator; we can still save her."

"No, we can't Chuck. She's dead, I just saw her ghost."

"Her ghost," he came over and put his hand around her, "how can that be?"

"I don't know, but before she died, she told me that no one gets to live around here."

"Come again?"

"She said that everyone dies here."

"She was probably delusional from the blood loss, surely not everyone dies."

"But what if they do? I mean, have you seen any of the people we transported alive around the island? Have we even checked up on them?"

"Would you like me to? Would that make you feel better?"

"Yes, and if she was right, maybe it will tell us more about this place."

"All right, I will have Iris investigate it tonight." Charles offered her a hand up and she took it. "Why don't you go take a breather and let me call this in. We can load them up and transport them when you're ready."

Agreeing with Chuck, Charlotte went to sit on the curb while he went to deal with the hospital staff for the second time. Her stomach twisted and churned painfully. A dreadful feeling that the girl was telling her the truth gnawed at her, and she was overwhelmed with worry for Kevin and Zack. She had left them alone, unprepared for the dangers lurking on the island, and she regretted not asking Zack to leave sooner. She knew something was out to hurt him; she felt it for days, and now her worst fears were confirmed. The urge to leave suffocated her. It was impossible to get a breath in, but she knew she'd have to wait until her shift was over before she could make her move. Feeling her arm hairs stand up, she turned and saw the pigman standing in the distance. It gave her a nod of its head as if reading her thoughts again, and instantly she was at peace. Her family was safe, at least for the time being, the creature would make sure of it.

CHAPTER FORTY

"I must not fear. Fear is the mind-killer. Fear is the little-death that brings total obliteration. I will face my fear. I will permit it to pass over me and through me. And when it has gone past I will turn the inner eye to see its path. Where the fear has gone there will be nothing. Only I will remain."—
Frank Herbert, Dune

That night Charlotte told Zack everything, from the way the island wanted her, to the way a dying child confirmed her fears of all of them being in danger. Much to her dismay though, he insisted on staying on the island just a little longer, so he could finish compiling his research. It was irrational to want to leave; she needed at least two weeks to let the station house know, but something deep down inside warned her that the time to leave was growing increasingly shorter. Going to bed that night, she listened to a mournful bell tolling somewhere in the distance. What it signaled, she did not yet know, but it was bad, and this Feast of Shadows was almost upon them.

Sleeping curled up in bed, a loud noise coming from the attic startled Charlotte awake. Amongst the rustling and the banging, she heard guttural moans and snarls, along with something raking across the floor. The thing that had been watching them the last few nights was upstairs, and it was tearing the place apart in search of something. Hearing muffled footsteps in the hall, she turned over and looked into the darkness of the doorway where to her shock she found a man standing in the jamb, looking straight at them. He was not an islander, at least, not anymore as he wore an old British naval uniform. The man continued to look at her with a blank stare, pointing his finger up to the ruckus coming from above their heads.

"Zack," she reached over and shook his shoulder, not daring to break her gaze from the stranger, "wake up."

"What?" Zack mumbled groggily while stirring beside her. "What's wrong, babe?"

"There is a man standing in our door, and someone is rummaging in the attic."

Bolting up in bed, Zack grabbed hold of her, and they both looked at the officer in the hallway while holding their breath. Harsh, stale air stung Charlotte's lungs as the man tilted his head to the ceiling. From the attic, something let out a shriek which bounced off the walls and pierced her to the marrow. An icy chill ran down her arms and the hairs stood up as she listed to something big hit a wall, and then the scampering of footsteps rushing for the stairs. The man in the doorway turned and motioned for her to follow as he glided towards the last room at the end of the hallway.

"Kevin."

The air finally escaped her lungs. Jumping out of bed, she dashed after the stranger with Zack close behind her. To her surprise, the officer did not go far. He stood outside the boy's room and pointed his fingers at the door. Her heart raced as she wondered what this man wanted, or if he was even friendly. Standing with Zack behind her, she reached to open the door, stopping when a clatter came from somewhere behind her. Something was trying to open the attic door. A pause, then another bang and the splintering of wood. The door to Kevin's room suddenly opened on its own, silently swinging in inward. The British officer walked around them and drew his sword.

"Get in." He commanded. "Now."

Hearing another long crash and the upstairs door shattering, Charlotte grabbed hold of Zack's arm and pulled him inside. Slamming the door shut, she turned the lock and pressed her ear to the wood. At first, there was nothing. The house on the other side was still with only the hum of the radiator to break the silence. Then came something that made her blood run cold and her heart to leap into her throat, the ear-piercing yowl of a large animal. It sounded sickly, or injured, like a creature who no longer had anything to lose. Holding her breath, she pressed even closer to see what would happen next and caught the sound of metal hitting metal, followed by a tumultuous scuffle. The battle continued to rage for a few minutes with wood splintering, pained screeching, and pictures falling off the wall, when suddenly, it stopped.

Backing away from the door, she waited with her heart throbbing in her throat. From the other side, whimpering and snarling drifted into the room, until suddenly, the doorknob moved. Twisting slowly at first, then jingling harder, until it was being rattled and pulled as if the thing on the other side was trying to take the door from its hinges. Unable to get in, the creature on the other side bellowed and slammed against the door, shaking it in the frame and clawed at the wood. The door continued to bend and bulge, and Charlotte feared it would give way at any moment. Zack called her name out beside her and she turned to him, motioning for her to move out of the way. She stepped back as she was told, and he slid a dresser over to keep the door secure.

Knowing this barricade would do little if the creature shredded the wood, she backed up and sat on the bottom bunk of the bed. Staring at the only thing standing between them and the monster in the hallway, she began to sob. Sitting down beside her, Zack put his arms around her and buried his face in her hair, shaking while the wood continued to shatter and crack. She thought they were going to die for sure when the banging stopped and the creature in the hall snarled, screeched, and vanished as there was no more struggle coming from the other side. They waited, holding each other until they were sure it had gone, and when they felt safe, they finally went to sleep.

CHAPTER FORTY-ONE

"Do not be afraid; our fate cannot be taken from us; it is a gift."—Dante Alighieri, Inferno

Charlotte woke up to the wind whispering through the trees outside. Opening her eyes, she noted the world beyond the window was lifeless and gray. A storm was approaching. The stark bleakness outside reminded her of the night before, and she cringed as she rolled over to steal a glance at the door. The lacquered mahogany slab, with the white-washed dresser pushed up against it, spit down the middle from where the creature almost made its way in. The gaping wound in the wood spit splinters out onto the rug beyond, and she could almost see into the hallway. Hearing something stirring in the room with her, she froze in fear until her son's voice caused her to let out a soft gasp.

"Mom? Dad?" She glanced up at Kevin leaning over the bunk railing, looking at them. "What are you two doing in my room? And why is there a dresser in front of my door?"

"Sorry." She mumbled sleepily. "Some scary things went down

last night, and we slept here to keep an eye on you?"

"Scary things? Oh, man, what did I miss?"

"Not much bud." Zack sat up and stretched. "Just some creepy noises and stuff, nothing to worry about."

"Well, if that's the case," the boy hopped off the top bunk, "wake me up next time, I want to see. And can you free up my door? I *really* have to pee."

"Sure thing, wait here with your mom while I go make sure it's safe."

Getting up from the bed, Zack plodded to the door, leaning over to peer into the crack. Breathing slowly, Charlotte watched him as he pulled away from the door and pushed the dresser aside, slowly opening it barely enough to stick his head out and glance into the hall. All she could hear was her heart hammering in her chest as she waited for something to pounce on him, but it never did. The creature was gone. Pulling his head back into the room, Zack looked over at her and Kevin, nodding his head and leaving the door open.

"Seems like the coast is clear. Go on, Kev."

Kevin, who was dancing in place beside Charlotte dashed for the door, fling it open and let out a high-pitched yelp. The boy stood in place, trembling, and Charlotte got out of bed to see what had her son paralyzed. Strolling over to him, she placed a hand on his shoulder and opened the door all the way to reveal a message left for them which made every bone in her body shudder. There, scratched into the wood, was a single word, but its warning came as no surprise, even if it was now staring at her from a door and not simply reverberating in her head.

BEWARE

"What is that?" Kevin stood in the doorway shaking, pointing to the letters gouged in the shiny surface. "Was that written for... us?"

"I don't know." Charlotte rubbed his back and put on her best smile. "Go use the bathroom, love. Your dad and I will figure it out in the meantime." Watching the boy run into the room next door, she turned to Zack who was still staring at the message, and wrapped her hands around his waist, pressing her head into his back. "What are we going to do now?"

"I haven't figured that out yet, but I want you to call your mom and get Kevin off this damned island today."

"I... I can't do that."

"Why not?" Zack turned around, shouting. "Why do you want to keep putting our son in danger?"

"I don't. But he won't leave unless we do. I know him. God knows I tried to get him to go stay with my mom for a while now, ever since I left Bret, actually."

"Damn it. He gets his stubbornness from your side of the family, you know."

"I suppose there were worst traits he could have inherited."

"All right, fine. If he won't leave alone, then we will all leave this cursed place, together, today."

"That's crazy, Zack. What about my job? What about your research?"

"I don't care about your job, or my research. I care about you, and Kevin, and this thing is after the both of you, so we are getting out of this place right now. I know this is sudden, and I realize I'm rushing things, so you can go stay with your mom instead of coming with me to New York. I don't care either way, but I am not putting you or Kevin in any more danger."

"Okay, we'll leave today, and Kevin and I will go with you like I promised we would. Although," she glanced over her shoulder at the wind howling in the trees and stripping the branches of leaves, "shouldn't we at least tell someone we're leaving?"

"Fine, you can make that phone call now, go inform your partner or something. I'm going to go get us packed."

"What's going on mom?" Kevin walked up to the door glancing between the two of them. "Why are you guys talking about packing?"

"Oh, we are just going to stay with your dad in New York, give this whole family thing a try."

"Okay, that's a bit sudden." The boy bit his lip and shifted his weight. "When do you plan to leave?"

"As soon as possible." Zack replied. "Go pack your stuff, both of you."

Watching Zack run for his room, Charlotte shrugged at Kevin and told him to go pack his bag while she grabbed hers. Fortunately for her, she owned little, and she quickly transferred her limited wardrobe from the drawers of the dresser into her suitcase. Stealing a glimpse at the clock by her bed, she noted it was almost seven o'clock. The station would expect her to show up to work in an hour.

Deciding she would call in sick before letting Charles know what she was up to, she picked up the phone and gulped. The line was dead. Only thing greeting her from the receiver was the hissing of static somewhere in the distance. Placing the phone back in the cradle, she picked up her cell phone, and found that she suddenly had no bars, all means of communication had been cut off. Collapsing onto the bed, she listened to the trees creaking outside with the blustery gale, and realized escape would not be so easy.

CHAPTER FORTY-TWO

"There are things known and there are things unknown, and in between are the doors of perception." —**Aldous Huxley**

*S*he had no idea how long she sat on her bed, looking at the wind-swept landscape beyond her large picture window when a rapping on the downstairs door made her jump up to her feet. Listening closely with a raspy breath, she heard the knock again, louder, more determined this time. Concern welled up inside her. Perhaps someone had figured out what they were up to and came to stop them. Her heart pounded erratically in her chest even as she forced her feet to move forward, rushing down the stairs for the front door. Peering through the squares of lead-glass at the top, she heaved out a sigh; it was only Charles and Iris standing on the stoop, getting misted by the drizzle and battered by the wind. Flinging open the door, she ushered them inside and motioned for them to sit down on the sofa.

"You caught us just in time, guys. We are leaving on the next ferry to head to New York. We've had enough of this forsaken place."

"No, Char, you're not." Chuck muttered and hung his head between his knees. "None of us are. Seems like we're stuck here."

"What... what do you mean?"

"The ferry terminal..." Iris's voice broke with the tears forming in her eyes, "it's gone."

"What do you mean gone?" Zack barged into the room. "How is that possible?"

"I don't know, man." Charles looked up, shaking his head. "All I can tell you is that Iris and I went to buy tickets ourselves for this afternoon and the damned place was gone. Seems to have vanished overnight, as if it was never even there."

"That's right, then we tried to call you, but all the phone lines are dead, and our cell phones have no signal."

"Yes, I tried calling the station, and you, but I found the same thing."

"No." Zack pulled out his phone for the first time. "No, it can't be. Damn it! We're trapped here like rats."

"Relax pretty boy, there is more than one way off this island. I was going to go find us a boat, but we needed to talk to you guys first and warn you. Iris found something unsettling about this place, so unsettling it made us want to leave, and I was not going to go without dragging you three with us."

"This can't possibly be good. And we don't have much good news either. How about I go make us some coffee while Zack fills you in on the night we had and you can tell us what you've discovered?"

"Can you make it an Irish coffee? I could use something to steady my nerves after what Iris told me."

"All right," Charlotte winked, "four Irish coffees coming right up."

Walking into the adjoining kitchen, Charlotte listened to Zack recount their night as she got the coffee brewing. The bitter aroma instantly filled the air, and she stole a glance at the distorted world outside the rain-beaded windows before going to the pantry to fetch a bottle of whiskey. Zack didn't drink much, so the only alcohol in the house had been from the previous owners, and she had to search to pull out a dust-filmed bottle of Jameson. Adding the whiskey to the coffee, she placed the mugs on the tray and stole one last glance at the rain streaking down the glass beyond the sink, pondering why the world outside appeared to be sleeping, and walked back to the living room.

"So..." she placed the tray down on the small table between them, "what did you uncover, Iris?"

"I... I don't know how to say this, but," Iris paused, and glanced into her coffee mug, "the little girl was right. Everyone does die around here."

"Well of course everyone dies, we all die."

"No, Mr. Campbell, I mean the hospital here has a one-hundred percent mortality rate."

"No way." Charlotte picked up her mug and stared at the rain picking up outside, rapping on the windows with the wind. "That's impossible, even for an inner city."

"I know, but that's how it is here. Anyone who goes into the emergency room at that hospital, or for surgery, or anything... well, let's just say they don't leave. That man you transported on your first call here, Luke McGuire, dead. I looked him up like you asked, and he died an hour after arriving at the hospital from blood loss."

"Okay, that's bullshit. I stabilized him. He was fine when we dropped him off. I mean sure, they may not have been able to save his foot, but there is no way he would have died from that unless they left him to bleed to death in that room."

"That's what I told her, but then she showed me his death certificate. That old lady who was hit by the car, she's dead as well. Oh, and here is the kicker, the hospital records show her as being dead on arrival when we both know she was still alive when we brought her in."

"And these are just the ones we know of personally, but the list goes on and on. In the last ten years, people have died from things like appendicitis and the common cold there."

"How is that even possible?"

"No idea." Iris placed down her mug and glanced over her shoulder before dropping her voice to a whisper. "I only found the records from when the new hospital was built, there is nothing from the old one, and I'm willing to bet they are still buried in that place and if we were to look we'd discover the same thing."

"Guess we know what we have to do next." Zack leaned back with a scowl. "After last night, I was hoping to avoid this, but we are left with no choice now. We have to break into the old hospital and see for ourselves what these people are hiding."

"No way, man. You can go do all the ghost hunting on your own. Iris and I will stay here, where it's safe."

"It's all right, Chuck. I'll go with him; you guy can watch Kevin and keep him safe. These things are after him too. But..." Charlotte looked at the clock behind her, "what are we going to do about work, all three of us are late, don't you think they will notice and come looking for us."

"Doubt it. Autumn Falls is a ghost town, there is not a soul in sight. Not to mention Iris and I have already been to the station, it's deserted, not even Victoria Owns is anywhere to be found."

"That's a bit peculiar, where do you think everyone is?"

"How should I know? Maybe they are all bracing for the incoming storm, and they couldn't reach us because all the lines are down."

"Maybe, or," Zack darted his eyes around the room, "maybe something is going on here that they don't want us to know about. We should go check out the old hospital right now."

"No, we will go tomorrow, after we all come up with a plan to return to the mainland. Right now though, I want to check out the attic. That thing was up there last night, looking for something, and I want to know what it was."

"Fine, you have a point, getting the hell out of here is a priority. You two want to join us upstairs or will you stay down here?"

"I'll stay here and keep an eye on Kevin if that's okay with you. I don't much like attics, never have since I was a kid."

"Of course, Iris, just ask Kev to show you his latest drawings or something." Charlotte placed her mug on the tray and go up. "Chuck, want to come with?"

"Sure, why the hell not? Partners till the bitter end, sister."

Walking up the stairs to the second floor, Charlotte instructed Kevin to go downstairs and keep Iris company while they fetched something from the attic. For the first time since they got up, she took in the sights of the aftermath of the fight between the Naval Officer and the creature. They had slashed the blue floral wallpaper in several places. Some marks were from a sword, and some from a four clawed animal. Picture frames lay on the floor, shattered or with faint ribbons snaking down the glass. The banister to the attic had been gouged and splintered. Walking up the creaking steps to the third-floor landing, she had to step over chunks of wood of the door split in two, half of it still swaying on the hinges. Fearful that whatever burst through was still inside waiting for them, Charlotte swallowed the rock in her throat and stepped into the musty, dim space beyond.

CHAPTER FORTY-THREE

"Some people think that the truth can be hidden with a little cover-up and decoration. But as time goes by, what is true is revealed, and what is fake fades away."–Ismail Haniyeh

The room lay in shambles. Scattered boxes littered the floor, spilling the papers and knickknacks they once contained onto the unfinished boards beneath her feet. One of the two dormer windows burst inward, letting in the rain which specked the papers and shattered glass. A stiff wind picked up outside and whistled through the jagged edges of the frame, causing Charlotte to hold tight to her sweater. Surveying the mess, she strolled over to the far corner and picked up a box of mildewed baby toys, setting them aside.

"Okay, let's see if we can figure out what that thing was after."

Agreeing, Zack joined her at the opposite end while Charles went to scour the middle, coughing as he brushed aside the dust and the cobwebs dangling from the ceiling. Shifting through the rubble, all Charlotte discovered was some stuffed animals and baby clothes, nothing that would be worth tearing the place apart over.

Aside from kitchen utensils, holiday decorations, and winter clothing, no one found anything of value until Chuck stumbled upon a small door hidden in the wall behind some boxes. Prying it open, he pulled out a wood chest and blew the dust off, digging through the contents while Charlotte and Zack continued to sort through the rest of the attic.

"Hey... Char," Chuck called out to her as she was repacking a split open box of china. "Does your mom's first name happen to be Eleanor?"

"Yes, why?"

"And where did you say you were born?"

"Boston." She turned, rubbing her arm with a frown. "What's this all about?"

"Well, this here birth certificate says otherwise. Come, take a look."

Dashing for Chuck, she snatched the paper out of his hands and reread the lines over and over, unwilling to believe what she was seeing. At first, she attempted to rationalize what she saw by trying to convince herself it belonged to a different girl named Charlotte. But it was her birth date on the paper, the exact time she was born, her weight, her mother's name, and hers, although her last name was different. Unable to deny what she saw, her hands trembled, and a lump formed in her throat. Sick to her stomach, her knees wobbled as she cried, unable to stop the tears from falling.

"Hey..." Zack came over, putting an arm around her, warming her up. "What is it, babe? What's wrong?"

"It..." she sobbed, "it says that I was born here—in this very house—to an Eleanor Briggs and a Cyrus Sinclair. This is my home, and the paramedic who died twenty-five years ago was my father. My actual name is Charlotte Mary Sinclair, and I belong in Autumn Falls. That's why the island wants me."

"Wait a sec." Chuck rubbed his stubbly chin. "You don't think C. Sinclair, is the same Cyrus as the guy who's been driving us around the island this whole time, do you?"

"Well, I mean, if my father lived, he would be around the same age as Cyrus… but my father is dead, and Cyrus is very much alive. I'm sure it's a strange coincidence. Not like Cyrus is an uncommon name or anything, right?"

"I guess. But I wonder if our Cyrus knew who you were, and if he did, why did he not say anything?"

"I'm sure he had his reasons, just like how my mother had reasons for lying to me all these years."

"Hmm." Zack blew a layer of dust from a photo album sitting in the box by Chuck's feet. "Maybe we can find some answers in here."

Opening the water-logged album, they flipped through the surviving photos. First few pages were filled with Cyrus and Eleanor as a young couple, their engagement, their wedding and the house in Autumn Falls. Towards the back were pictures of baby Charlotte and the last photo was of the three of them, smiling as they looked at the camera. Grabbing the sepia picture from the album, Charlotte flipped it over and read the writing on the back. Her mother dated it three weeks before Cyrus Sinclair died in the accident. Sliding it into her pocket, she looked over at Zack who was still scratching his head.

"I don't understand. Why did mom leave all this behind? Why didn't she take any of these with her? Why did she hide this behind the wall?"

"No clue. I'd tell you to ask her, but the phones are dead. Maybe she did not want to be reminded of it all after your dad passed."

"But what about my birth certificate? My real name is Charlotte Sinclair. Why would she change it? Why wouldn't she tell me who my dad was and how he passed away? Why did she tell me never to go to Maine? Even you mentioned how strange that was."

"I don't know, babe. I am guessing she was trying to protect you from someone, or something."

"Like what? Was it this island she was trying to keep me away from, and if so, why not just come out and say it?"

"Look, Cherry, I'm just as bewildered as you. I can't even imagine what went through your mom's head, but I promise you, we will sort this out."

"Here." Chuck folded up the certificate, handing it to her. "At least you can have your real identity back if you want."

"Thank you." She smiled and put the paper into the pocket with the photo. Outside the window the rain picked up, dousing them in cold water. "Let's get out of here, we can figure out what to do next downstairs, where it's dry."

"Sure thing. After we are done here, Iris and I will return to the hotel and meet you back here in the morning."

"No. You go grab your things and come here. You two can have the spare room since Cherry sleeps with me."

"Oh, what's this Char? You are sharing your bed with him already? Well, that was quick."

"Oh, shut up Chuck. Enough joking around. Zack is right. You and Iris will be safer here, with us, where they can't pick us off one at a time. Plus, once we figure out how to get out of here, it is best if we didn't have to meet up. Now let's go, I'm freezing."

Leaving the attic behind them, the three rushed to the living room where Iris was playing cards with Kevin. Sending the boy into the family room to watch television, they set off to figure out a plan to retreat to the mainland. Getting a boat was the only way off, and the island had plenty around. Problem was, Charles would have to steal one since the rental store vanished with the ferry terminal. They agreed he would sneak over to the fishing docks in the morning and see what he could find while Zack and Charlotte broke into the old hospital to look for clues before meeting at the house for their trip back to shore.

CHAPTER FORTY-FOUR

"Sometimes human places, create inhuman monsters."—
Stephen King, The Shining

L ightning split the sky, shaking the windows, and
illuminating the living room as everyone sat around
talking. The storm had gotten worse. Rain battered the
windows, filling the house with a dull drumming. The gale outside
howled, and the trees groaned as they bowed with its prowess.
Charlotte curled up next to Zack on the couch, glancing outside
with a shiver as Chuck continued to formulate his plan. Even the
crackling fire, and hot chocolate did little to keep the unearthly
chill away, which seemed to have come from the underworld itself.
More so than ever she wanted off the island and back into the safe
arms of the mainland, but she knew it would not happen, at least
not until the weather let up.

Another blaze of lighting burned the sky and thunder
followed on its heels, causing Charlotte to jump up and stare out
the rain-streaked windows. The gale had stopped, and aside from
the rain hammering the pavement outside, all was silent. It seemed

as if the weather had eased for a moment before the sky unleashed and hail poured out, slamming against the glass, filling the room with a clatter. She thought the brief reprieve was strange and sat still, drowning out everyone's voices, listening to the faint rustling coming from upstairs. At first, it sounded like a mouse scurrying down the hall, and then the soft creaking of a door, followed by a scream.

"Kevin!"

Leaping off the sofa, Charlotte nearly knocked over the coffee table as she bound her way up the stairs, rushing for the room her son was sleeping in. Gripping the frame of the door, she stood and peered into the dark, hearing only the raspy rhythm of Kevin's breathing. He was sleeping on the bottom bunk, and she could see he was sitting up with an inky outline crouched on the mattress beside him. A flash of lightning illuminated the room, revealing an ashen, hunched over Gollum sitting at the edge of the bed. Skin clung to its bone; the bumps of its spine arched as it reached a clawed hand for the boy's face.

Jolting from her spot, she made a dash for the bed to snatch her son away from the creature before it had the chance to hurt him. Once more the room lit up and the thing turned to her with a primitive, spine-snapping hiss. Charlotte stood in front of it and looked at its black, hate-filled eyes as shiny as glass beads. It opened its mouth again, revealing rows of snarled and jagged fangs, and with a roar, it reached out and raked its razor-sharp claws across her arm. Staggering back with a pained yelp, she gripped the torn sleeve of her sweater as warm blood seeped between her fingers. Undeterred, she stepped back towards her son and the creature lunged at her, swiping for her throat. Leaning away from the claws, she heard heavy footsteps clamoring up the stairs and motioned for Kevin to back away while the thing was distracted.

"Stand back." Zack shouted.

Taking a step back, she watched him flick on the lights, causing the creature to cover its eyes, giving him a chance to run into the room holding a fireplace poker. The creature leaped off the bed and scuttled toward Zack with a gurgling growl. Ignoring the monster, he lunged and pierced its chest with the tip of the brass poker. With a shrill howl, the creature thrashed and clawed at the air as he pushed it against the floor, pinning it to the wood boards. Black ooze seeped from its body, getting absorbed by the planks, singeing their surface. It let out another bleat, swiped at Zack, and vanished in a cloud of dark smoke, leaving everyone baffled.

Yanking his half-melted weapon out of the floorboards, Zack looked at Charlotte's mangled arm and back over to Chuck and Iris, who were standing in the doorway, their faces frozen in a silent scream. Below the window, more creatures yelped and bellowed as their claws scratched against the outer walls. A glass pane exploded in the kitchen, and yips akin to a pack of hyenas out on a hunt drifted up past the stairs.

"Quick, everyone, in my room. Help me board it up. We'll be safer in together."

Yanking Kevin off the bed, Charlotte wrapped the shaking boy safely in her arms as she dashed out of the room behind Zack. Spotting more things climbing up the stairs, sprinting after her, she picked up her pace and made it to the room in time to shut the door on one of them, chopping off its fingers which vanished in a plume of smoke before they hit the floor. Zack latched the door shut and pushed a dresser against it while Charles and Iris secured the shutters on the windows. Setting Kevin down on the bed, Charlotte winced and collapsed to the floor. The room spun around her; she held back the bile as she lay against the cool wood, clutching her throbbing arm.

Grabbing her med bag off the floor, Chuck knelt by her side and cut away the remainder of her sleeve, revealing the strips of raw flesh pulsating blood beneath. Pulling out a suture kit she insisted on having, he did his best to stitch up her arm, before wrapping it tight with the bandages on hand. Lifting her into his arms, Zack held her tight, and carried her to bed, laying her down next to Kevin before settling down on the other side. Lifting her heavy lids, she wrapped her arm around her son and took hold of Zack's hand. Confined safely in the room, she listened to the storm batter the house, and the creatures slashing at their door until sleep took hold of her, and she drifted away until morning.

CHAPTER FORTY-FIVE

"People are supposed to fear the unknown, but ignorance is bliss when knowledge is so damn frightening."—**Laurell K. Hamilton, The Laughing Corpse**

D espite it being noon, the island was painted in mute colors with the rain continuing to pour down. The sky was an ominous gray blanket, snuffing out the sun and with it any hope of getting off the island before twilight fell. Sitting in the passenger seat of the Range Rover, Charlotte glanced out the rain-washed windshield at the mist of the headlights refracting in the fog as they idled behind an abandoned building a short track from the hospital. It was a brick building with a rain-worn sign, two windows filmed with dust and barren metal shelves. Ivy crept up the walls, and as she stepped out of the car, Charlotte got a chill as voices whispered from inside the building, turning into inaudible mumbles in the rain sizzling on the pavement. She didn't need to hear what they were saying; she knew they wanted her to turn back. Ignoring their warning, she tightened her windbreaker around herself and set off down the narrow gravel path after Zack.

Lighting rippled through the sky as they arrived at the wrought-iron gates of the old hospital. Intricate designs of ivy swirled and intertwined under the pointed spikes that alternated in height. Beyond the fence lay a field of rain-flattened grass collecting pools of water, plopping with the drops of rain. A metallic scent of ozone intermingling with something Charlotte couldn't place filled the air; something old, stale, with a hint of sulfur that burned skin. Zack gave the gate a push and the rusted latch groaned as it swung open to let them in. Slipping through the crack behind him, she crouched as they snuck their way to the side of the building closest to the woods. Away from the sight of prying eyes, they located an open window not glued down by years of neglect and layers of paint and quietly slipped inside.

Turning on her flashlight, Charlotte surveyed the mildew-scented room while the hollow rain continued to batter the building. A single gurney with pitted white legs, crusty green cushions, and a head strap sat in the middle of the room beside a table with a gutted metal box on it. The antiquated device only had two nobs left on it, one for dosage minutes, the other for intensity. Old electroshock room, she thought while her beam of light continued a steady path around the room. Mint-green tile went halfway up the wall, and to the left, above it was a message written in dripping red letters. *And I looked, and behold a pale horse: and his name that sat upon him was Death and Hell followed with him.* Shuddering, she traced her light to the door, above which hung an upside-down crucifix, tittering on a single screw.

An inkling of dread stirred in her stomach, and as they opened the door and stepped out into the deserted hallway a wave of sour air hit her face. Paint peeled and hung from the ceiling, white specs occasionally raining down on them. Parts of the wall were missing plaster, revealing the skeletal wood beams beneath. Bits of paper floated down the tile floor with its patterns of flowers laid out in white and Sienna. The beams of their flashlight splashed back from the floor, washing over the tattered walls and glittered on the metal doorknobs. There were only two ways to go from there, left down to the central room of the hospital, or down the ever-stretching dim hall to the right.

"Where to now, Cherry?"

"We need locate the basement, that's where they would store the paperwork we need. Iris said that according to Cyrus, they kept all the medical examiner's notes and paperwork in the morgue. Which means," Charlotte looked around, swinging her light from side to side. "We have to find a set of doors which lead to the stairwell. Normally they have at least one in each wing since they are used as a fire escape, so let's head right."

"Why not left?" Zack stole a longing glance at the open space a few feet away from them. "Wouldn't the main part of the building have a stairwell as well?"

"I don't know. Something is pulling me to the right. Plus, we have less chance of someone spotting us if we stay away from the central hub."

"Fine, we'll go down the long creepy hall, which makes my skin crawl. You check the doors on the right, I'll try the ones on the left."

Walking down the corridor, they opened the doors one by one, looking into the various rooms without finding a stairwell. Their muffled footfalls echoed through the hollow space, bouncing off the walls to sound like waterfalls. Somewhere in the darkness a rustling of papers and clanging of chairs, along with a monotonous patter of dripping water called to them. Turning off their torches, a faint light flickering on the wall, pouring out from a room with an opened door, beckoned them to investigate. Shuffling forward, they leaned around the doorjamb to peer inside.

Along the wall, on the opposite side of the melting candles, stood a metal tub, filled to the brim with a dark crimson, coagulating liquid. A green-slicked faucet protruding from the tiled wall dripped burgundy drops down, which splashed and splattered in the dark waters below. Above the popping flames of candles and wax pooling on the floor, hung metal chains with hooks clacking against one another with a metallic din. The air inside was hot and suffocating, causing Charlotte's lungs to burn as she stepped around the door to inspect the room beyond. Beside her, Zack turned on his light, the beam of which bounced in his shaking hands as he turned to look at her, his face as pale as the tile on the walls.

"What's that?"

"Old hydrotherapy tub, I think."

"What's with the meat hooks?"

"I have no clue, but I don't think they are meat hooks, or at least I hope they are not."

"So, what's in the tub then?"

"Blood from the looks of it?"

"Think it's human?"

"Hard to say." Charlotte took a step into the doorway. "Sure is a lot of it though."

Standing close to one another, they continued to peer into the room when a loud clatter from behind caused them both to scream and turn to face backward. A tall, metal shelf lay sprawled out across the hallway, spilling shattered glass vials onto the floor. From inside the room from which it fell, something stirred in the shadows, and the beams of their lights swung to reveal the black-eyed Gollum slinking out to sit hunched over behind the shelf. Tilting its head, it curled its blue lips into a sneer with its jagged fangs gleaming in the light. Paralyzed, they watched it slink closer with a yowl of an enormous cat.

Talking another step over towards them it got ready to pounce when it froze, turned, snarled, and scurried back into the room from which it came. Trembling, they watched the door slam shut on its own behind the creature as if being pulled by an invisible force. Huddling together, Charlotte brought her head up to see the pigman crawling down the hall towards them. Letting out a whimper beside her, Zack turned to run, but she grabbed hold of his wrist and pulled him back as the strange creature got closer.

When he reached the fallen shelf, the pigman stood erect, letting out soft grunts as it regarded them with his empty eye sockets. *There.* Charlotte heard his voice in her head as the creature pointed to a narrow hall on the left. Nodding her head, she held tight to Zack as she guided him past the figure clad in a black robe, and into the suffocating corridor.

The floor slanted and descended at an angle, leading down into the hospital's underbelly. She realized they probably used this before the days of elevators to wheel bodies down to the morgue and tightened her grip on Zack's sweaty hand. Craning her head to glance behind her shoulder, she noted the pigman was gone. They were alone again. Squeezing her flashlight, she pointed it forward, and headed down the path laid out before them.

CHAPTER FORTY-SIX

"The belief in a supernatural source of evil is not necessary; men alone are quite capable of every wickedness." —Joseph Conrad

S naking their way down to the hospital basement, they followed the path laid out for them by the brick, pipe-lined walls. Water sloshed under their feet as the beams from the flashlights skated across the onyx surface and bounced off the water-slicked walls. Aside from the pitter patter of water in the distance, no other sound echoed through the desolate hall. The walls were unmarked by vandals and the only indication of where they should go, were the paper-thin arrows etched into the brick with chalk. Rounding the corner in the direction of one such marker, they wound up in front of a set of unassuming double doors with *dodenakker*, scribbled above them.

Puzzled, Charlotte wondered if they meant the word as an indication of what this place was, or a warning meant to keep people out. Either way, she figured, this must have been the place they had been looking for. Pushing both doors open, she stepped over the threshold lined with salt into a pitch-black room covered in white tile. Blinded by darkness, she swept the beam of her flashlight past the metal lockers used to store bodies and stopped at a blood-gummed metal table. She knew they had used it for autopsies, but to see one still crusted over with blood was both unusual and unsettling at the same time.

"Hey, what's this?"

Charlotte turned to look at Zack crouching beside a blood-slicked glass jar with two silk tubes coming out from the top.

"A vintage device used by morticians to drain blood from the body. I saw the modern-day version at the morgue of the new hospital."

"Now, I'm no medical expert, but isn't this a tad unusual for a morgue in a hospital?"

"Maybe, hard to say what is and isn't normal in a small island town. For all we know, their medical examiner also doubles as the mortician. Besides," she glanced back at the doors they came through, "aren't you going to question the line of salt on the threshold?"

"That's used to keep evil out." Zack stood up and looked at her. "I'm surprised you don't know this. Superstition has it, that evil spirits can't cross a line of salt."

"Okay, so are they trying to keep these spirits in, or out?"

"Out... I hope, but let's look around in case it's the other way around."

Agreeing with Zack, Charlotte went to dig in one corner of the room while he searched the other. She had no idea what she was looking for; a death certificate, notebook, anything to give them even the slightest hint as to what was happening on the island. Coming across a stack of photographs, she flipped through them. In each one was a man in a doctor's coat with round spectacles and a curly handlebar mustache who was in the company of a tall, slender woman with her face scratched out. She was pondering what could have transpired between the two people to cause the destruction of the photos when Zack called out to her from the opposite corner.

"Hey Cherry, come look at this."

"What is it?"

"A ledger of some kind. Your friend wasn't kidding when she said no one lives here."

Getting up, she walked over to where he was standing and took the black, leather-bound book out of his hands, running her finger down the brown, water-stained pages.

"Huh, that's strange. This says this person came in for a stubbed toe and died of blood poisoning. How is that even possible?"

"I don't know. But look at all of these. These people came in for minor ailments and wound-up dead." Zack points out the names written on the pages. "Now, I am no doctor, but something tells me you don't come in for diarrhea and end up dead of cholera, at east not in today's day and age. And what's with the numbers at the end, in the column marked *extracted*."

"Hmmm... 5L, 4.5L, 5.6L. They all seem to correspond with the amount of blood in a human body in liters, but surely it can't be."

"Why not?" Zack turned to peer behind him. "Isn't that what that thing over there is used for?"

"Yes... but why would they be recording it like that, and what is the blood used for?"

"I'm going to go out on a limb and say that it's used for that tub upstairs."

"You suggesting we have our own Elizabeth Báthory on this island?"

"Well, it's either that, or we are dealing with the real Count Dracula, and he just happens to lap up the blood from the tub like a dog."

"I wouldn't be surprised if we were dealing with something Clive Barker dreamed up." Charlotte snorted. "And look at this, these strange deaths only happen every five years, and only for three weeks between August and September."

"Let me see that." Zack took the ledger out of her hands and flipped through the pages. "You're right, and, if I did the math correctly, the next cycle is... now."

"Indeed, this is all really peculiar, I wonder what it all means."

Looking over the pages, thinking about the numbers,

Charlotte was oblivious to the world around her until a faint noise coming from near the cooling lockers caused her to pause as she attempted to pinpoint where it was coming from. It was faint, as if someone was running something sharp on the wall, or across the floor. Looking up, she noticed one of the steel doors had been closed, revealing a black cross painted on its surface that she had not seen when they first entered. Walking over to it, she opened the door and pointed her light inside. A small mound of grout gathered on the bottom of the blemished tray, while the rest continued to cascade down like some gray snow from above.

Trailing her beam up, she spotted a tile which seemed to be loose in the wall, raining dust down from where it had been lodged. Picking at the cracked white square, she allowed it to drop with a clang that echoed through the locker and peered into the deep hole behind it. Something peered back at her from the dark crevice it had been hidden in, a parchment, rolled up tight from prying eyes. Pulling out the paper, she realized it was made of skin, but whose skin it was, she dared not consider.

"What you got there?"

"I'm not sure," Charlotte unfurled the dried flesh and stole a glance at the crude picture scribbled on it in black ink. "It appears to be a map of some kind."

"A map? Let me see."

Pulling out the tray of the locker, Charlotte laid out the skin and allowed Zack to take a closer look while she directed the beam of her flashlight at it.

"This looks like a map of this island."

"That's because it is. Look, here is the lighthouse, the hotel, and we are here, at the old hospital."

"What's with the little red 'X' at the center? Think it could be a treasure?"

"Maybe. Want to go and find out?"

"How? We don't even know where to start."

"I know where to start, can't you read a map, Zack? Just look, it's at the center of the woods that lie between Lighthouse Point, the hotel, and the hospital."

"The Autumn Falls Triangle?"

"I suppose we can call it that. Well, shall we go explore?"

Zack opened his mouth to object, but he never got the chance to reply to her. A loud clang coming from somewhere above them caused them to jump with a yelp, as faint footsteps ambled towards them, clacking rhythmically on the tiled floors above. The overlaying echoes rolling back to them sounded like harsh whispers spelling impending doom. Whoever was upstairs would catch them sneaking around at any moment, and Charlotte realized they were in danger even before she broke the uncomfortable silence.

"Who do you think that is?"

"No clue, and I don't want to find out. Let's get out of here, and after we regroup with your friends, we can figure out what to do next."

"We must find another way out; we can't risk getting caught by going back the way we came from."

"And where do you suggest we go? Can't you see we are trapped here?"

Darting her head about the morgue, Charlotte was getting ready to admit he was right when the scraping of metal on tile behind her caused her heart to stop. Spinning around, a steel bookshelf swung itself open, grinding to a halt to reveal a dark, brick-lined tunnel concealed behind it. The invisible force which showed them the map was now guiding them out of the hospital. Stepping inside the opening, she placed her hand on the metal pipe running down one side and felt Zack grab hold of her shoulder and pull her back.

"What the hell is this?"

"It's an old tunnel for transporting bodies, if I was to take a guess. It should come out to where the cemetery is supposed to be. Let's go find out."

"You aren't seriously suggesting we go down that way, do you?"

"You got any better suggestions?" She tilted her head to look back at him. "If we stay here, we'll get caught. If we go back, we'll get caught. I can hear them coming closer to the doors as we waste time arguing. This is our only chance of escape, unless of course you *want* to see what's going to come through those doors."

"Damn it! I hate it when you're right."

"Okay, turn your light off, stay close, and follow the pipe."

Stepping into the tunnel, she guided her hand along the slick metal tube while watching her footing on the crooked brick floor. A few feet in, and she heard the double doors creak open, followed by a shrill holler coming from behind. Zack's hand trembled on her shoulder as the ice crystals formed in her blood. Whoever was behind them seemed unable to cross the barrier of salt placed on the threshold. She was not sure how long it would hold the person or thing in place, but she didn't wish to find out and picked up her pace, tripping on raised bricks as she shuffled along.

Before long, a crisp sulfur breeze rushed past her, making her shiver, and she could see a faint hint of grayish-blue light ahead of them. Running through the narrow opening, they found themselves in a field of stones bearing nothing more than a number. The surrounding air stunk of rotten eggs and a fissure in the ground just beyond the cemetery billowed black smoke into the air. A groan escaped from the crack. It sounded pained and angry, and the earth quaked beneath them. A voice came after the shock, rising from the ground, telling them to run.

Heading its advice, she grabbed hold of Zack's hand and set off down the hill at a sprint without turning to look back. Following the shoreline to the spot where they parked, they drove home with their map, without running into the person, or creature who was at the hospital with them.

CHAPTER FORTY-SEVEN

"Why is it that when one man builds a wall, the next man immediately needs to know what's on the other side? "— George R.R. Martin, A Game of Thrones

S itting in the floral wing back chair by the crackling fireplace of the great room, Charlotte watched Chuck pace around the room as Zack recounted their adventure at the old hospital. The fire did little to warm the room with the broken window and Iris sat beside her, shaking half from the chill blowing in through the empty panes, and half from the fear of what they uncovered.

Sipping the tea from her mug, Charlotte turned her gaze out the window where clouds of gray gathered again, and inklings of thunder grumbled in the distance. The weather did not seem to be letting up; they would have to brave the storm to sail off the island. Putting her blue and gold porcelain cup on the table beside her, she turned her attention to her partner, wondering what vessel would aid them in their escape, or their death, depending on how strong the storm was.

"So, Chuck, did you ever find a boat for us?"

"Yes. Found a good old lobster boat. It ain't much, and it will be rough going to the mainland in this mess, but I think the old girl can make it. We'll go as soon as you're ready."

"I still want to check out the location printed on the map Cherry found."

"Dude, are you insane? We need to get off this island... like yesterday."

"Zack's right. Someone gave us this map for a reason. The least we can do is check it out and find out why."

"You wouldn't be saying that if you knew what I knew."

"And what's that?"

"That they have replaced us."

"Replaced? How?"

"I'll tell you how. I found this out when I went back to the station house to grab my bag. First, the place was deserted, and inside it looked like no one had been there in years. The dust had to have been five inches thick. Anyway, I went up to the lockers, and to my surprise, I found they were no longer ours. They had different name tags on them, an L. Fitzgerald and an H. Looman." Charles shot a glance at Iris. "I checked out your office next, and your desk tag was gone too. They have found replacements for all of us."

"But..." Iris stuttered, "how could they possibly know we were leaving?"

"I don't think we are leaving." Charlotte leaned back in her chair. "I don't think they ever meant for us to leave, at least not alive."

"Then that means... oh my God, "Iris turned pale, "they were planning to kill us all along. That's why they brought us here, isn't it? That's why we all got the same strange call at around the same time."

"Afraid so doll. Although I want to know why. There has to be a reason they chose the three of us. It's not like there isn't enough fresh meat on this island, and they actually had to go hunting for Charlotte since she doesn't use social media like we do."

"And the only way we will ever know the answer to that is if we figure out what's hidden behind the 'X' on the map."

"I hate to admit it, but you're right. Fine. You and Zack go dig up your buried treasure. I am going to put all our shit on the boat, then I will grab Iris and Kevin, and meet the two of you at Lighthouse Point by sunset."

"How long do you think we have? I don't want to keep anyone waiting."

"Not long, I'm afraid." Charlotte stole another glance at the fog pooling outside, obscuring the landscape in its milky veil. "All I know is that I want to be off this island before twilight sets in and the storm gets worse."

Agreeing to the plan, Charles grabbed the first round of bags and set off into the squall outside. As soon as he left, the rain reduced to a drizzle, as if trying to give them a false sense of hope like any good hurricane. Charlotte, however, was not the least bit fooled by it, she felt it deep inside her bones; she knew what the island knew, and it was playing games with them. An internal voice told her this was all a trick designed to make them feel safe before it struck, but she was not going to fall for it. She intended to keep her guard up until they were safely back on the mainland, and away from whatever the phantoms of Autumn Falls needed her for. Warning Iris to be careful, she followed Zack out into the rain to walk the short distance to the forest in hopes of keeping the curious eyes watching them from asking too many questions.

CHAPTER FORTY-EIGHT

"He supposed that even in Hell, people got an occasional sip of water, if only so they could appreciate the full horror of unrequited thirst when it set in again."—**Stephen King, Full Dark, No Stars**

By the time Zack and Charlotte made it into the forest, the storm had picked up again, bringing with it howling gale. Rain slashed through the trees while the branches creaked and groaned, bowing to the ground with each gust. Occasionally, lighting would light up the sky, scattering a kaleidoscope of light through the forest underbrush. The roar of thunder was always close on its heels and it shook the ground beneath their feet as they staggered along. A strange composition of odors permeated the forest, the metallic scent of steel mixed with the pungent aroma of wet dirt, but there was another fragrance in the mix—far more subtle and sweet, and altogether familiar—the scent of fresh blood. It saturated the forest floor with its sickly aroma as if the ground had lapped up gallons of it over the centuries.

Stopping in a clearing, Charlotte glanced over her map again to catch her bearing. The mark lay just ahead, but something entirely different drew her attention. The clearing, though devoid of darkness and engulfed in fog, was entirely familiar to her. Despite never having been there before, at least not physically, she knew where she was, and the cut on her neck tingled and pulsed as the scabs broke away to allow a warm stream of blood to trickle down her skin.

"Hey, what's wrong?"

"I've been here before?"

"When?"

"In my dream, the night I woke up with the cut on my throat. Remember, I told you a crazed old woman tried to kill me."

"Are you sure?"

"Positive. The creature ran that way," she pointed to her right, towards the old hospital, "and he came from the thicket of forest before me. I tripped and fell by that stump right there, and then the woman came out and attacked me. We should go check it out, the place where she was might contain some clues."

"No. It's too dangerous. Plus, the map has us going straight, away from where you think the woman came from."

"What if there is something there, something else that will help us shed some light on this puzzle?"

"Then it would be on the map. Come on Cherry, we came here to see what the map was trying to show us, not explore the woods. And we did promise Chuck that we would meet him at

Lighthouse Point before sunset, so that gives us roughly three hours to find what we came for and leave. Even you said you don't want to be here past twilight."

"I guess you're right." Charlotte groaned. "Fine. We shall go where the map wants us to go."

Walking forward another mile or so, they hit a dead end when a wall of briar stopped them in their tracks. The snarled branches were so tangled and interwoven that they had no visible way to walk through to the other side. Not even a hint of light could penetrate their defense.

Charlotte attempted to pull the knots apart, snagging her finger on one of the many thorns. A bead of fresh blood formed on the tip of her finger, and before she had the chance to pull it away, it fell, hitting the shrubs below. As quickly as it hit, it was instantly absorbed by the plants, and the branches moved on their own. They twisted, turned, and arched upwards and to the side, forming a tunnel as they went.

Once the briar stopped moving and forming the path, a gust of hot, stale wind rushed out from the other end, carrying on it the stench of boiled blood and burned flesh. Gagging, Charlotte covered her mouth and moved inward, looking forward to getting out of the icy rain which had soaked through her clothing and chilled her to the bone.

Trailing closely behind her, Zack looked up to study the mouth of the wood cave they found themselves in. The branches were firmly interlaced, and not a single drop of rain fell on their heads while they walked. The only sounds enshrouding them where the thundering echo of their feet crushing the dead leaves beneath.

Their trek was short, and they walked out into a small patch of forest with a fresh mound of dirt at the center. Behind it stood a crumbling, weather-worn, and moss-covered cross with a shovel stuck in the dirt beside it. Pulling the map from her pocket, Charlotte glanced over at where the 'X' was and realized it wasn't a letter, after all, it was a red cross, and someone left the shovel on the grave for them to dig.

"So," Zack looked at the grave marker, "what do we do now?"

"We dig."

"Are you serious? You really want us to dig up a grave?"

"Someone does, and daylight is wasting." Charlotte grabbed hold of the shovel and plunged it into the loose dirt, moving the soil to one side. "The faster we dig this up, the faster we can go home."

"Fine, move, I can dig a lot faster than you."

Handing the shovel to Zack, she stepped off the grave and watched as he shoveled away the dirt. An odd silence shrouded them. Not even the crows had dared to be out for the last few days, and the sound of rain was muffled by the canopy of the trees above. The hairs on her arms pricked and her skin tingled. She sensed someone in the tree line, watching them, but no matter how hard she squinted her eyes to see through the gloom, she could find no one there, at least not as far as she could see.

CHAPTER FORTY-NINE

"And for a moment it seemed to me as if I also were buried in a vast grave full of unspeakable secrets." — **Joseph Conrad**

T*he* grave was anything but shallow, and Zack ended up digging for well over an hour before the dull clang of metal against wood made him stop. Tossing the shovel up by Charlotte's feet, he stepped aside and allowed her space to hop down. Brushing the dirt off the ancient pine coffin, they found a single name crudely etched into the wood: Clarence Thornbern. Exchanging glances, they pulled on the rotted boards which peeled away with ease and the pungent scent of fresh dirt and death filled their nostrils. Looking at the remains beneath them, they gasped in unison at the sight of a human skull intermixed with the remains of a four-toed hoofed animal. Kneeling by the skeletal remains, Charlotte studied them over with a scrutinizing gaze. She knew little about animal anatomy, but she could tell both heads had been severed around the fourth vertebrae.

"What do you make of this, Cherry?" Zack knelt beside her, picking up the human skull. "Why is this mixed in with animal remains?"

"I'm guessing this is the pigman's skull and the remains of the unfortunate pig which gave him his face. I wish I could tell you more, but I don't know too much about forensic anthropology. I can only tell you the skull belonged to someone of Caucasian descent and that the animal definitely looks of porcine origin."

"Fair enough, why do you suppose he led us here, to his grave?"

"I don't know, I'm not even sure he was the one to guide us here. But, if it was him, I think there is something here he wants us to find."

Bushing away the dirt with the back of her hand, Charlotte glanced around the dark black soil, hoping something would jump out at her. At first, the only thing she saw were the cream bones, picked clean by the worms squirming around beneath them, glaring up at her from the gloom. She was beginning to give up hope, thinking the remains were the only thing he meant for her to find when a steamy gust of black smoke came from out of nowhere and swirled the soil by the animal skeleton. With the dust and the vapor-filled wind settling, she spotted something poking its way from between the ribs. A small, torn black-leather corner of a notebook almost blended in with the soil, but it was visible enough to see.

Sweeping aside the remaining dirt and gingerly moving the bones aside, she pried the small book from its hiding spot and studied its cover. It was old, at least several centuries, with the edges and corners worn down and peeling to the casing beneath, but she could tell it hadn't lived in the grave long as the leather was well-preserved, and the cream pages, though worn and water-stained still had eligible writing on the inside. Flipping through the delicate parchment, she saw some ink had blotted and smudged away, but there were still pages with well-preserved writing which told a remarkable story. Getting Zack's attention, she began to read the tale out loud as he hung on her every word.

June 6, 1628

Today my family and I boarded the Sophie Schreur, bound for the new world. Like many, my parents fled England to worship freely, and in the last couple of years, they have decided to make the journey across the ocean to this new promised land we were told so much about. We are the first wave to leave Holland in search of a better life, and look forward to establishing our own colony in a land which will be our own. I was told the journey would take close to two months, and we should arrive at our new home sometime in August. I shall survive the journey just fine, but I worry about my younger sister as she is frail and may not live long enough to see this new world we seek. Still, I hope we all make it to the promised land in one piece and that this land is everything we hope it to be and more.

July 14, 1628

Five weeks into our journey, and we have discovered a witch amongst our ranks, one who goes by the name of Geertruyd Abeel. The elders have discovered her one night deviating in the blood of the rats that are so prominent upon the ship, talking to the devil himself no less. Some of the passengers wanted to throw her off the ship, but everyone knows witches float, and there is no way we can burn her while on the ship. So, we decided we would throw her in the brig instead, and burn her at the stake once we set foot on solid ground. She didn't seem phased by her sentence, she simply smiled and said she would have her revenge. Since then, all she does is sit on the floor of her cell, brushing her long, ebony locks while she sings to the devil. Even now, three days later, she sings her unholy melody, filling the ship with her siren song, driving us all insane, and probably putting a curse on us as I write.

July 25, 1628

Yesterday I glimpsed at the witch with her bewitching eyes and a seductive smile. I caught her rubbing blood on her face, making the fine lines in the corners of her eyes vanish. She attempted to lure me in and have me open her cage, but I refused and ran away. Her melodic laughter followed me all night, and she haunted my dreams since. I wish I could say they are only dreams, but they feel like so much more, they are as real as if she is in there with me and I fear what she has in store for me.

August 8, 1628

We hit some foul weather last night, a raging storm descended upon us like the wrath of God, smashing rouge waves against the hull of our ship, rocking it violently from side to side. The captain did his best to maintain course, but we hit a cluster of jagged rocks in the fog and the ship took on water. Someone spotted land close to where the ship was going down, and we filled the smaller boats with as much of our things as we could and headed for shore. We left the witch to sink with the ship. I have little knowledge of witches, but I doubt they can drown given their pact with the devil, but at the very least she is locked up for all eternity...

We have managed to make camp on this strange bit of land we found ourselves on. No one knows if we reached the new world or not, but we intend to make a decent life here regardless.

August 10, 1628

I glimpsed a strange creature lingering in the woods last night, and I believe it to be a demon of some kind. It was the size of an adult man, perhaps a bit taller with a hairless head which appeared almost swollen. It was lanky, with sickeningly elongated arms with long fingers tipped by sharp claws. I sensed him long before I saw him, and I could have sworn the thing called my name from the woods before I woke. Once I opened my eyes, I spotted him, crouching in the tree line, looking at me with his glowing amber eyes, like those of a deranged house cat. He was naked, with translucent, ashen skin, to the point where I could almost see his ribs. He had no nose, just a sleek spot where it ought to be, and a gaping hole for a mouth filled with pointy fangs. He called my name once more in his shrill voice, and he told me to leave the island for we didn't belong there, it was his home. I did not respond to him, and after a moment, he tilted his head at me, and then slinked back into the woods, walking on his arms and legs like some animal.

September 5, 1628

I have seen the creature many more times since our first encounter. Every night he tells me to leave before he vanishes into the woods, but I dare not tell anyone else what I have been seeing. One day, I followed him inside the trees, but instead of the demon, I found the witch hiding in a clearing, living in a small hut she constructed out of branches and leaves. She looked old and ragged, but I recognized the hairy mole on her chin, it was the woman who tried to seduce me in my dreams. I tried to run, but she spotted me and grabbed hold of me, dragging me into her hut, binding me while she figured out what to do with me... she stole a pig from the settlement, my father's prized pig, and beheaded the both of us while muttering a spell, combining our bodies to make me a servant to do her bidding. But I was stronger, I was not going to serve the witch, no matter what she did to me, so I ran from her when she undid my ropes, hiding in a grove of trees. She seemed unable to follow me, so I snuck out during the day and buried my remains, and that of the swine in the very spot, creating a makeshift grave for us. Every day I hear my family looking for me, my sister calls my name, begging me to come home, but I cannot show my face to them, I can't let them see what that witch has done...

September 10, 1628

Today will be forever known as the Feast of Shadows on this cursed rock. An unholy holiday created by the witch and the devil when she slaughtered three of the villagers, including my mother to seal the monster of this land away under our feet, somewhere between earth and hell. From what I was able to learn, this creature I had been seeing was an ancient guardian of this land, sprung from the soul of a magic man who spent his time eating wayward souls, and he had been trying to warn me of things to come. After the slaughter, the witch unleashed a storm on the land, wiping away the structures, and killing half the livestock. The surviving settlers have gathered their remaining boats and braved the storm to depart this place. I am not sure if any of them survived, but I pray they found a safe haven away from this place.

September 10, 1653

It's been twenty-five years since the Feast of Shadows, twenty-five years of my cursed existence, and I am amazed I still remember how to write. Lately, there has been no point in keeping a diary as all I do is spy on the witch and wait for a chance to exact revenge. Today, however marks a special, yet somber occasion which caused me to pick up the quill again. The last time I wrote, I thought none of the settlers made it to the shores of the promised land, but it appears some survived. Three lads who were fishing nearby penetrated the fog and landed on this island. Exploring the place, they stayed too long and made camp until morning, remarking how strange it was they found the place as if the waves themselves carried them here. The witch waited until night fell, and struck to fulfill the deal she made with the devil to keep the guardian asleep. After all these years she is nothing more than an ugly, frail thing feeding on animal blood to survive. Yet, despite lacking in strength, she lulled the boys over to her alter with her song where she performed the same ritual she had when we first came to this land. The blood and souls of the boys—who were apparently our descendants—were enough to keep the devil happy and the creature locked up. From within his prison, the guardian talks to me in my dreams. He is getting restless, waiting to be set free so he can destroy the witch, and I am compelled to help him.

October 31, 1699

... There was a British vessel that landed on these shores a few years back, after it too suffered an accident much like the Sophie Schreur. These unsuspecting folks made settlement here despite my warnings. They have built a pleasant town, including the lighthouse which now keeps ships from hitting the rocks in the dense fog. They call this place Autumn Falls, and they are oblivious to the danger lurking in the woods, hidden in a strange clearing away from town. The witch, however, is delighted to have people here. She lurks and plots, thirsting for blood to restore her beauty.

November 5, 1872

I have found something strange over the last few years, some settlers seem to be getting possessed by the witch and turning into monsters. To the human eye they appear to look normal, as no one seems to notice their grotesque appearance. To me, they appear pale and sickly, with hollow eyes as black as coal and claws made for shredding flesh. They resemble creatures similar to the guardian slumbering beneath, except they live to service the hag until she no longer has any use for them. I have witnessed them turn on their fellow men, charming them into committing horrible acts of violence upon themselves, and those who are family. I have watched one man stick a sickle in his eye, while another one bashed his wife's head in with a rock, and even the lighthouse keeper leaped to his death upon the jagged rocks from the tower he was taking care of. Curious, I followed the witch around and watched her drain the bodies of the dead, so she could bathe in their blood, restoring her youth and vigor. Once she was beautiful, she joined the town after she caused another ship to crash upon the rocks, pretending to be a survivor and charming the men to believe her.

August 27, 1989

It's been so long, too long if you ask me, and yet the same cycle repeats. Every five years she bathes in blood to keep her youth, and every twenty-five years she sacrifices three souls from the descendants of the original settlers to keep the guardian at bay. These days she goes by the name of Victoria Owens, and she put herself in charge of the very people who are supposed to save the lives of their fellow men...

I must stop her, put an end to this madness, but despite working with the sleeping guardian to save souls and spoil the blood, I have found nothing to break her spell.

September 10, 1998

I think I did it, I think I cracked the spell she had on this place, and all it took was one soul which she intended to use in the Feast of Shadows. For years, I have been stealing souls from her, robbing her soul eaters of the untainted blood she needs to keep up her mask, but she always finds a way to kill without me knowing who it is. But now, now I have stolen the soul of one descendant and set another one free. A man, a healer of sorts, agreed to join the guardian and become part of this island in exchange for safe passage to the mainland for his wife and daughter, the daughter who is my direct descendant, or at least that of my sister. Agreeing to his terms, I gave his family a boat I had stashed a few years back and told the wife how to guide herself to shore. I told her everything I told the man and warned her to stay away from the island, keep her daughter away, and I watched as the man died by my hand, making the witch one soul short. One soul is all it took to wake the guardian, and now he fights, struggling to free himself. If the witch doesn't put him to sleep in twenty-five years with the *blood of three more descendants, he will break through his chains and devour her alive.*

December 23, 2022

The results of my efforts are showing more and more every day. Little by little the guardian is clawing his way out and breaking through his chains. I can see the cracks forming in the earth from where the entrance to hell is, the one by which he's bound. My new friend, my descendant, Cyrus sees it too. It won't be much longer until we set him free to take revenge upon the witch and release the people of Autumn Falls from their spell. I just pray the witch doesn't find the souls she needs, but I hear her plotting and I see her searching. This fight is only beginning, I can feel a war coming, one which we must win if we hope to survive. A deal was made, and now, the price must be paid. Question is, who will pay it, us, or the witch.

Reading the last intelligible words on the ink-streaked page, Charlotte dropped the diary from her shaking hands. Her boss, the woman who lured her to Autumn Falls was a witch who was after her blood, and perhaps even her soul. While she was not sure if the child in the pages referred to her, she had a strong notion she was the descendant of the original settlers, and that it was her father who was being referred to. This explained why the island called to her, she always belonged there, and this was why her mother didn't want her setting foot in Maine. All these years she was trying to keep her away from Autumn Falls, and the fate which was bestowed upon her. And now, she was right where the witch wanted her, in her clutches, and she had Kevin too.

CHAPTER FIFTY

"Don't lie to me. Don't deceive me. Give me the truth. Even if it breaks me. A painful truth is better than a pleasant lie."
—Yasmin Mogahed

Charlotte was still processing everything she read when a sickening thought insinuated itself into her brain, turning her blood into glacial ice. The realization cut through her like a knife, and her knees buckled beneath her weight. Quick on his feet, Zack caught her in his arms and lifted her up while she continued to shake. Her stomach filled up with rocks and bile sat in her throat. The stagnant air burned in her chest with her lungs unable to expel, and hot tears pricked the corners of her eyes while she gasped for breath as if she was drowning.

"Zack..." she mumbled, "do you realize what today is?"

"No, what?"

"It's the Feast of Shadows," came a voice from the woods. Charlotte didn't need to turn to know who it was, she recognized Cyrus' voice immediately. "So now you know the whole truth, Lottie, but unfortunately you learned it too late. And frankly, I wished you never did. I was hoping you'd leave this place before it got that far."

"Daddy? Is... is that really you?"

"I'm afraid so bug."

"But how... I thought you died in that ambulance crash."

"I did. Well, my body did. I, however, made a deal with the entity underneath us—a powerful native shaman—my soul in his service for your safe passage off the island, and away from the witch." Cyrus walked out to face her, the lines on his face appearing harsher in the dim light. "You were never supposed to end up here again, your mother was instructed to keep you away at all costs. Seems the witch's will was stronger than any of us have anticipated."

"Does this mean you are a ghost?"

"I guess in a way, I am."

"Then how come you look older, and" she grabbed hold of his frigid hands, "how come I can touch you?"

"Because I am not your average ghost. I am a servant of this island. We can appear in any way we wish. Clarence appeared to your mother as the young man he was when he died. To you he appeared as the creature he has become to scare you off. Me, I chose to appear as I would be now instead of how I was when I died. I hoped that if I kept my identity secret, you wouldn't want to stay and learn more about the hidden secrets of Autumn Falls. I even lured Zack here in an effort to guide you away."

"What? That was *you* who called me here?"

"Yes, afraid so. When Lottie said my grandson's father didn't know about him, I saw the longing in her eyes. She still wished to be with you. I called her mother straight away to find out more about you, and learned how you have called her several times, seeking to reconnect. That's when I knew you had to come here, so I got your number and summoned you here, knowing you two would run into one another, eventually."

"You called mom? Does this mean she knows what happened to you?"

"Yes. I have been calling her every night for the past twenty-five years to receive updates on you. I felt like I was still in your life that way, and your mom was always happy to fill me in, although my grandson was a surprise. Guess she didn't want me knowing you had him so young, or that his father wasn't in the picture."

"I see, does this mean you only called Zack because he was Kvein's father, or because you thought I needed him?"

"Both. I figured I'd give you two a second chance. I hoped that once he learned he had a son, he would drag the both of you off this cursed island before the witch had a chance to sacrifice you. But you are stubborn, much like your mother, and you refused to leave. That's when Clarence decided to show you the truth, hoping it would be enough to make you run, but unfortunately it came too late. The Feast of Shadows is already upon us. If all of you don't leave the island now, I am afraid every one of you will die, and everything will be lost."

"Kevin..." Charlotte's heart leaped into her throat, "oh God, Zack, we left him alone with Iris, we need to warn them before someone attacks them."

"You go grab them, and I'll go find Chuck, tell him to start the boat then meet you at the house, so we can all leave." Turning to Cyrus. "How long do we have?"

"Oh, about an hour I'd say," Cyrus glanced up at the sky, "perhaps less."

"All right, Cherry, we have to go."

"I know, but we will never make it through the woods in time, I'm not sure I can find my way out."

"You will if you follow Clarence," Cyrus nodded to the pigman standing in the tunnel's mouth, "He knows these woods like the back of his hand, he's lived in them for hundreds of years. Oh, and Zack, take care of my little girl, will you?"

Nodding, Zack grabbed hold of Charlotte's hand and set off after the creatures who shrank down to the ground, crawling and gliding on the forest floor. In minutes, he had them out by the old hospital, pointing down the hill, which would be the fastest way to the house. Splitting up, Zack headed for the docks to warn Charles, while Charlotte ran for the house, praying it would not be too late when she got there, but something in the pit of her stomach churned and told her she would not like what she found, and her skin tingled, causing the hairs on her arm to stand up.

CHAPTER FIFTY-ONE

"What is an evil man? The man is evil who coerces obedience to his private ends, destroys beauty, produces pain, extinguishes life."—Jack **Vance**

S he could see the Gambrel roof of the house peek over the top of the trees stripped of leaves. She was only a few minutes away when her feet stopped moving. It was as if the pavement had turned to tar, sucked her legs in, and prevented her from moving. Something pulled her back to the forest, compelling her to turn around and run from the house like a dog on a leash. She wanted to comply, but she couldn't leave Kevin behind, and she forced herself to keep moving despite the burning pain in her ankles radiating to her core with every step she took. Forcing herself to cover the short distance to the house, Charlotte stood on the front porch with her hand poised over the lock, trying to convince herself to open it. Taking a deep breath, she held the air in her lungs as she turned the knob and swung open the door, cautiously stepping inside.

A death-like silence filled the house, and nothing moved, not even a shadow. She stood still and listened. There was a faint creaking of a door coming from the kitchen, but she lost any other sound amongst the clanking of water dripping into the metal sink, and the moaning of tress outside. A shiver tiptoed down her spine and goosebumps pricked her skin as she continued to listen for signs of life. Her gut told her something was not right. Calling out for Iris and Kevin, she waited, but there was no reply. They appeared not to be home. Thinking it was possible Chuck took them to the boat, she decided to check the house over one more time before heading for Lighthouse Point herself. Walking towards the stairs, she caught a glimpse of something from the corner of her eye. Diverting into the adjoining kitchen, she gasped when she saw what had drawn her attention.

The black boot which poked out from behind the white island belonged to Iris, whose body was sprawled out on the tile floor. She lay unmoving, her cornflower-blue skirt fanned out around her body, her neck twisted to the side. This was how her body fell, and she hadn't so much as flinched since. Her pupils were dilated, she stared blankly into space, and a silent scream contorted her face. Charlotte did not need to check her pulse to know she was gone, but she did anyway out of habit before closing the young woman's eyes. Bowing her head, she sobbed softly out of guilt that her only concern was for Kevin and not for her friend who was murdered in the house while she was away.

"So," a booming voice and heavy footfalls came from behind

her, "you thought you could get away from me, did you?"

"Bret..." Charlotte fell to the floor, turned, and scooted away from the imposing man, backing herself up against a cabinet. His dark brown eyes looked almost black, and he flicked his long brown hair away from his shoulders as he continued to scowl at her, filling her with dread. "What have you done here? Where is Kevin?"

"Your little bastard is fine... for now. As for your skanky friend," he smirked through his patchy beard and glanced down at the body by his feet, giving it a swift kick, "well, let's just say she got in the way."

"I knew you were a monster. Ever since we moved to Seattle, I knew what you were capable of, and I am glad I left you when I did."

"You are a pathetic, worthless whore." Bret approached her, his board frame towering over her shaking body. "You didn't leave me. I allowed you to go so you could see you were nothing without me, and that your spawn needed more discipline in his life, so he didn't turn out as stupid and incapable as you."

"I'll ask you again, where is Kevin?" Charlotte stood up, finding the strength to shove him away. "What have you done with my son?"

"I said he's fine." Bret snarled. "Come with me and I will take you to him. We can be a family again."

"Fuck you. I wouldn't go back to you if you were the last man on earth, and I sure as hell won't let you lay another finger on *my* son."

An icy glimmer glaze over Bret's eyes as he gritted his teeth, flared his nostrils, and smirked. Clenching one hand into a tight fist, he reached out and punched her across her face as hard as he could, knocking the air out of her, and making her stumble back towards the sink. Pressing a hand on the burning skin of her cheek, she held back her tears, looking up at him defiantly. This wasn't the first time he hit her, and it wasn't the worst. At one time he broke her arm by beating her with a PVC pipe when she accidentally knocked his glasses off his face, all while her five-year-old son watched helplessly from the doorway as she lay on the floor trying to defend herself. He turned a bright shade of red, narrowed his eyes at her, and she knew what was coming next, even before he stepped closer, pinning her in place.

"Won't go back to me, huh? Yet you'd eagerly spread your legs again for that fagot, Zack Campbell." He spat in her face and brought a fist down on the counter next to her, making the dishes in the cabinet clank. "I always knew you were eager to get back with him. After all, you gave birth to his son and raised him instead of putting him up for adoption where he belonged. You thought some other man would step up and play daddy, but you were wrong, no man wants to take care of someone else's kid. Hell, Zachary didn't even want to take care of his own until now, and suddenly he is this big noble hero because of it. But you know what, Charlotte? He's just a fuck boy, always was, always will be. That man loves to look at himself in the mirror and hear himself talk, he won't provide you with what you need, only a real man can do that... only I can give you that."

"I'd rather you go to hell."

Snatching a knife from the counter, Charlotte swung it at Bret. Leaning back with a laugh, he dodged her and grabbed hold of her hand, shaking the blade free, and it fell to the floor with a clatter. Wrapping his free hand around her throat, he tightened his grip and lifted her up in the air, making it almost impossible for her to breathe. Struggling against his grip, she kicked at him and felt the pulse through his fingers that were digging into the pressure points on her skin. He paid no attention to her efforts to thwart him as he slammed her against the wall, causing her skull to crack on the plaster, giving her a splitting headache and causing her vision to blur into a dark tunnel before she forced herself back to consciousness.

"You think you can attack me? You are weak, like your boy." He sneered. "I could kill you right now if I wanted to, but I won't. I'll go take care of fuck face, and then I will come take what is mine, whether you like it or not. You got that, bitch?"

Not giving her a chance to respond, Bret balled up his hand and drove another fist into her temple with a loud thwack. Specks of light danced in front of her eyes before he delivered a second blow, sending her plunging into darkness. Her body grew limp, suspended between time and space even as he let go of her and let her crumble onto the floor. Floating in a sea of black, all Charlotte could do was think of Kevin, and Zack, but she was powerless to help them as her body released its grip on the material world and allowed her to sink deeper into a black fog, spiraling into the abyss of her subconsciousness.

CHAPTER FIFTY-TWO

"The mind is its own place and in itself, can make a Heaven of Hell, a Hell of Heaven."—**John Milton**

C*harlotte* felt weightless and free of pain, as if her soul disconnected from her body. She found herself walking in an underground cavern, with only a faint orange glow to guide her. Not knowing where to go, she followed the light to see where it would lead until she came upon a golden grotto bathed in warm light. Sapphires and rubies adorned the gold brick walls with carvings of silver depicting various erotic and violent themes. Sex and death intermingled into one magnificent picture as if pain and pleasure where indistinguishable from one another. Below her a pit of molten lava spattered and spewed up onto an onyx bride sprawling across a vast chasm. Winged statues of black gold lined the passage, their hooded heads bowed low as they leaned on their swords. At the center of a distant rotunda sat a scrawny creature bound in chains.

The beast, at least six feet tall, emaciated with arms that stretched down to its knees thrashed and struggled against its restraints. The rusted chains creaked and groaned as the metal twisted and bent, and the monster mewed and snarled as it continued to fight. Compelled to help free him, she took one step onto the bridge. Her footfall sounded like the thunder outside, and the creature turned to look at her with its glowing amber eyes and let out a harrowing screech. Feeling her heart leap in her chest, she took a step back, pressing herself into a solid mass behind her.

Turning, she saw a young man in a black robe, about seventeen or eighteen, standing above her. His loose, curly, shoulder-length hair fell across his gentle face and his dark green eyes regarded her softly. The young man shook his head, pressed two of his fingers against her forehead and pushed her back into the pit of lava. But instead of falling, she once again floated through space, lost in the cosmos until she woke up back at the house.

Laying on the cool floor, she felt sick to her stomach. Her head throbbed as if a hoard of tiny drummers had taken up residence in her skull. The left side of her face stung and burned, and her mouth had a familiar, sweet metallic taste in it. She heard someone calling her name, gently nudging her shoulders, and she pushed herself off the floor, forcing herself to sit up. Opening her eyes, she found her left eye swollen shut. She could barely see through the murky crack her eyelid formed, and it hurt to have it open even that much. Iris sat beside her, and Charlotte gasped a breath of relief as she looked into the eyes of her friend who continued to sit and smile at her.

"Oh, thank God he got you back here, I thought you were done for. Okay, on your feet," she pulled on Charlotte's arm, and she staggered to her feet, "we have to go now, before it's too late."

"Iris?" She mumbled while pressing a hand on her aching head. "I thought you were dead."

"I am." The girl stole a solemn look at the body sprawled out on the kitchen floor behind her. "Well, at least my body is. He pulled my soul before your ex snuck up on me and snapped my neck."

"Clarence?"

"No, the Skudakumooch. At least that's what the Native people used to call him. He is the being the witch trapped at the gateway to hell under this island. He's weak from the chains she placed on him, but he had enough power to pull my soul before I died."

"Where is Kevin?"

"That's what I'm trying to tell you, we have to go now, that nasty man has your son, and by Chuck's account, they got Zack too."

"What? Who has them? Where? And is Chuck okay?"

"Chuck's fine, I told him to fetch the boat, and drive it as close to Lighthouse Point as he can so you guys can escape. The witch has your son, and Zack at the sacrifice site. I'm afraid that with me gone, she needs Kevin now to restrain the Skudakumooch for another twenty-five years, and I think she plans to do horrible things to Zack after the ritual. She wants to punish him for interfering in her plan. You need to go there now if you wish to save them. Do you know where it is?"

"I... I think I can find it. But, what about you? I can't possibly leave you here like this."

"Charlotte, I'm dead. There is nothing more you can do for me. I belong to this island now, like Clarence, and your dad. But you can still save Zack, Kevin, Chuck, and yourself. You just have to move."

Nodding her aching head, Charlotte thought of her son and what Victoria intended to do to him. Her body screamed in pain, and her face felt like raw hamburger, but she had to get to them no matter how badly she hurt. Thanking Iris, she turned for the door and ran outside into the pouring rain, which had once more picked up with cold gusts of wind to batter her aching body.

Chilled and soaked by rain, she set off down the road, picking up speed even as her lungs burned and her legs felt like Jell-O. She knew what Bret was capable of, and she knew what the witch intended to do with her son. Fueled by a new purpose; a burning desire to stop Victoria and not let her father's sacrifice go to waste, she pressed on faster, fighting her instincts as she ran. *Someone* was indeed going to pay for the deal Cyrus made all those years ago, but she was determined to make sure it was not her, or anyone else she cared about.

CHAPTER FIFTY-THREE

"Son, the greatest trick the Devil pulled was convincing the world there was only one of him." – **David Wong, John Dies at the End**

Rushing through the twisted trees, Charlotte thought the fog had churned into a solid wall as she ran into a suffocating cloud blanketing the forest. Struggling to breathe, she paused and waved her hand in front of her face, coughing, and realized the mist was thin, gray smoke seeping out from the ground. Every pore of the earth bled the caustic vapor, filling the surrounding air with the scent of sulfur, singed hair, and boiled blood. The clouds snaked between the gnarled tree roots and up the crooked trunks, shrouding the forest in a hazy gloom. With no visible markers to guide her, she looked around, disoriented by her new surroundings.

"Where to now..."

Pondering what direction to take, she heard branches snapping ahead of her and turned to see what was rusting in the distance. To her surprise, a large, white Yorkshire pig walked out from the smog and looked up at her, grunting. She had not seen a single farm animal on the island until now, and she quickly recalled what her father told her.

"Clarence, is that you?"

The pig snorted, nodded, and turned, walking a few feet forward before it stopped to look back at her. It appeared he wished for her to follow him, and so she took a few uneasy steps towards it. Satisfied, the pig grunted and returned to walking, stopping occasionally to see if she was still behind him. The round moon above their heads turned a deep shade of crimson, bathing the smoke-covered forest in blood. All around her, the trees appeared to pulse and move in a trance-like dance. Their branches let out soft whispers with the gusts of the wind, and they moaned as they bowed down to the ground. Mist continued to swirl and flow under her feet like a bloody river, rising slowly up to the pink sky.

"That's strange. I didn't think we had a blood moon tonight."

No blood moon, she heard in her head, *Feast of Shadows moon always red, blood-red.* She knew it was Clarence talking to her telepathically, but she was still not use to him being inside her head. Suddenly, she froze where she was, her skin tingled and the hairs stood up on her arm. Something else was nearby, an evil presence she knew all too well. From the trees she heard whooping and yipping, as if a pack of coyotes were on the prowl. These, however, were no animals, they were once humans who transformed into horrible demons ready to do the witch's bidding. Listening to the soul eaters hooting around her, she heard something else much closer to her, something that shook her to the core.

"No," Kevin screamed at the top of his lungs from a clearing ahead, "let go of me."

"Let him go." Zack growled.

A dull thud, a soft groan, and silence followed.

"Dad..."

Swallowing the air she'd been holding, Charlotte rushed forward and stopped outside a perfectly circular clearing where nothing seemed to grow, not even a blade of grass. The moon bled its burgundy light onto a stone altar at the center, with Kevin tied up by his hands and feet sprawled out on to of it. A few feet ahead of him was Zack, slumped over and tied to a wooden stake with a pile of timber under his feet. Instinctively, she retreated into the tree line and watched as Victoria walked out from the shadows of the forest wearing a black hooded robe, lined with gold. In her hands, a large cream dagger glistened blood-red as she approached Kevin with it raised near her chest. Clarence didn't need to tell Charlotte what she intended to do with it, she already knew, and her body moved on its own.

CHAPTER FIFTY-FOUR

"But the Dark cannot claim what Light does not surrender."—C.L. Wilson, **Crown of Crystal Flame**

Victoria raised her hands over her head, getting ready to make her first sacrifice to appease the island and keep its guardian chained. Fixated on the kill, she didn't notice Charlotte dash from the trees to intercept, nor did she hear the crinkling of leaves as she ran straight for her. Wrapping her arms around the witch's waist, Charlotte brought her down to the ground hard, causing the dagger to go tumbling across the barren soil. The hood of the cloak fell back to reveal the woman's withered face with an ancient fire burning in her eyes. She hissed and clawed at Charlotte's face who was sitting on top of her, thwarting her attacks.

The witch mumbled something under her breath and pressed her palms to Charlotte's chest, sending a shock wave through her body, causing her to fly back. Hitting her head on the cold ground, she gasped for breath while attempting to get up. She felt like a car hit her head on, with every bone in her body aching, and every breath she took sent icy daggers through her spine. A sour taste filled her mouth as she continued panting and digging her nails into the dirt. Forcing herself to roll over, she watched Victoria scrambling for the blade, crawling across the infertile soil. Thrusting herself up, she crawled after her, grabbing at the hem of the cloak, yanking her back.

Turning around, Victoria's eyes flashed with rage, and she hissed again, kicking Charlotte in the face, causing her to let go of the robe. Stunned, she looked at the witch, and grabbed hold of her again, pulling he away from the ceremonial knife. The woman chanted in a language she did not understand, and suddenly something wrapped itself around her ankles. Letting go of the cloth, she glanced at her attacker and saw dried up roots snaking their way out from the dirt, their brittle fingers holding her in her grasp, and giving Victoria a chance to pick up the blade.

Thrashing and pulling, she attempted to liberate herself from the dried up roots, freeing one leg. It was not ideal, but it was enough to allow her to scramble to her feet and lunge at Victoria, grabbing hold of her silver hair before the trees pulled them both back to the ground. Clasping the witch's mouth as they were dragged towards the trees, she fought for an advantage which miraculously came when the frail root snagged on a rock and broke away from her. Quickly rolling on top of her former boss, Charlotte struck her in the face with her fist. A crack of pain radiated from her hand to her wrist, but the witch was mumbling again so despite the discomfort, she struck her again, rendering the woman unconscious with a jolt of heat shooting up her arm.

Shaking her hand, she ignored the dull throbbing and got up, running to her son who was flailing about on the flat slab of stone. Doing her best to calm the boy, she undid the knot on his left wrist when someone grabbed hold of her neck, lifted her into the air and hurled her away from the altar. Bracing her impact with her hands before her, the pain shot up from her right wrist, and she rolled over to see Bret standing over her, looking down on her with his dark brown eyes, which sparkled with a sadistic malice. He scowled at her as his body shook with rage, his hands clenched into fists and his teeth grinding so loud she could hear them from where she lay. It was a look she remembered well; it meant he was about to pound on her like a meaty punching bag, or violate her in other ways.

"Keep your hands off her." Zack struggled against his ropes. "Don't you dare lay a finger on her. You hear me?"

"Want me to knock the wind out of you again, fagot?"

"I don't give a damn what you do to me. Just stay the hell away from Cherry and Kevin, you damn prick."

"Rich, coming from the man who abandoned them. Now, suddenly, you want to play father of the year, and she is all over you like a fly on shit."

"I didn't even know I had a son. You can't blame me for abandoning a kid I was not aware of."

"Oh, that's right, you didn't know. Want to know why? It's because Charlotte didn't give two shits about you to tell you. At least not until you made some decent money. Why, I'm more of a father to the little bastard than you are."

"You are nothing more than an abusive, self-absorbed, manipulative asshole, Bret." Charlotte staggered up to her feet. "You will never be Kevin's father. You haven't even got the right to call yourself a man."

"Of course not. Because you were always planning to run back to pretty boy as soon as you had the chance, you worthless bitch. You are nothing without a man and you know it, that's why you were so eager to pounce on me."

Lunging at her, Bret went to tackle her to the ground when some instinct made her insert her knee between them as they fell, keeping him back away from her. His weight was bearing down on her leg while he attempted to grab for her throat. Wedging her other foot between them, she pushed him away, giving her a chance to kick him in the face. Roaring, he fell back, clutching his bloody nose, giving her enough time to grab hold of Victoria's knife. Pressing the dull edge close to her wrist, she swung her arm as Bret moved in on her again, running the razor-sharp blade against his throat. Gurgling, he fell to his knees clutching his neck as the sheet of blood flowed down his throat and onto his white shirt.

Panting, she looked from Bret—who was trying to crawl to

her as he gargled and spewed out blood—at the blood-streaked knife in her hand and gagged. She realized the polished ivory was made from human bones. The figure of the screaming man consumed by hellfire was carved out of the top half of a humerus. Dropping the blade to the ground in disgust, she returned her attention to Bret who collapsed by her feet.

He was motionless and the thirsty ground lapped up his blood, suckling it down beneath the surface. With the last drop of crimson gone, the island shook and groaned, forming cracks in the earth beneath her. Trees rocked, lighting rippled across the sky, and the stench of sulfur filled the air. Black smoke billowed from the veins in the earth and bright red lava bubbled out by the altar, sinking it slowly into the ground.

"Mom." Kevin screamed. "What's going on here?"

"I don't know."

Running up to her son, she worked on freeing the other knots still binding him to the submerging platform.

"You polluted her sacred ground with impure blood, it's all over now." Cyrus stepped into the clearing and untied Zack from his post. "Her powers over this place have shattered. Clarence and I are now free to step foot inside the circle, and the guardian is almost free. We have little time left." He nodded his head to the moon, which turned a tinge of dark pink in the time she'd been in the clearing. "When the moon returns to normal, the Feast of Shadows is over, the island can be free, and we must get you out of here before that happens."

"What happens if she doesn't leave?"

"Then she will be bound to this place forever."

"Why didn't you mention this before, old man?" Rubbing his wrists, Zack ran over to help Charlotte untie the knots. "Seems to me, like you enjoy leaving out useful information."

"I figured you would have been gone after the last talk we had. I never expected to run into another obstacle."

"Zack," Charlotte screamed as she spotted Victoria lurking behind him, "watch out."

Her warning came too late. The witch raised her dagger and drove it into Zack's back. Letting out a pained yelp, he sunk to the ground, reaching over his shoulder to grab hold of the spot she struck. She let out a hiss, and he turned to see her with a raised hand, aiming the dagger at his chest. Charlotte screamed as she ran towards him, but she would not make it. The dagger was coming down faster than she could run, ready to pierce his heart when both it and the witch dropped to the ground. Looking up, she noticed a large rock struck Victoria on the side of her head which was oozing black blood, and Charles stepped out into the clearing.

"You know, I never did like her."

"Nice throw dude."

"Thanks, man. I was the star pitcher for the paramedic's baseball team back in Arizona." Chuck stepped over Victoria's body and looked at Charlotte. "What the hell happened to your face? You look like you went a few rounds with Mike Tyson."

"I'll be fine, can you check on Zack while I grab Kevin?"

Freeing the boy's last leg, Charlotte scooped him up into her arms, and he buried his face in her shoulder, sobbing and trembling. Kneeling by Zack, Charles looked over his wound before helping him to his feet and slinging his arm over his shoulders. The ground continued to rumble, and they both swayed as they steadied their feet on the dirt crumbling into the craters forming around them.

"I got good news and bad news, Zack. The good news is, she hit nothing major and I can patch you up on the boat. The bad news is, you will probably require surgery once we get on dry land to repair any cut muscles and tendons."

"Where did you leave the boat, Chuck?"

"Anchored it not far from here, just down the hill by Lighthouse Point. We should probably move before this whole damn island splits in two right under us."

Tightening her grip on Kevin, Charlotte ran after Charles, who was dragging Zack along with him. The earth continued to rattle and crack, making them lose their footing more than once until they slid down the hill to the moist sand of the beach at Lighthouse Point. Lighting sliced through the sky with peals of thunder right behind it, and the sky released another bout of frigid rain that cut them like razors. Through the sheet of water,

Charlotte could see a red and white boat bobbing on the surface of the waves close to the shoreline, they were almost free.

CHAPTER FIFTY-FIVE

"Never leave a friend behind. Friends are all we have to get us through this life—and they are the only things from this world that we could hope to see in the next."—**Dean Koontz, Fear Nothing**

Running chest deep into the water, Charlotte lifted Kevin into the boat before climbing in herself. Not far behind her, Charles helped Zack steady himself in the current. Leaning over the edge, she pulled him up on the deck while their vessel bobbed and swayed in the water, making her a little queasy. Instructing Kevin to go inside the cabin to hide from the torrential rain battering the boat like a drum, she sat Zack down on a bench under the awning and went back to help her partner. Reaching her hands down towards him, she was getting ready to grab hold of him when something pulled him under the dark waters, making his hand slip between her finger before she had the chance to respond.

Watching him disappear below the swelling waves with a scream, she leaned over the railing following the trail of bubbles rising to the surface and moving away from them. She strained to see past the surf, but something else in the white-capped water caught her eye through the gloom. A soul eater with webbed feet rose to the surface, snarled at her, and dove in after Chuck, leaving her in shock. Another monster popped its head up above the crest of the surf and regarded her with its murky, soulless eyes. The skin of its blue lips curled into a thin smirk, revealing rows of snarled needle like fangs, and it let out a boisterous hiss before going back under the water as if daring her to follow them. She knew that was what they wanted, and without thinking twice about it, Charlotte leaped overboard after it, diving under the raging waves to try to find Chuck, she owed him that much.

Below the surface, in the ink dark waters, she struggled to see where her hands were, let alone where the creatures dragged her partner off to. Salt water burned her eyes, and the cold of the autumnal surf constricted her chest, making it painful to move. Swimming up to the surface she took a ragged breath as the waves battered her body before she dove back under, swimming down towards the continental shelf where she saw them drag Chuck last. Her lungs stung from the icy chill of the water, and she was giving up hope of rescue when she spotted faint movement in the shadows before her. Propelling herself forward, she could make out Chuck fighting off three soul eaters who were trying to drag him down the slope into the ocean's depth.

Grabbing hold of her partner under his arms, she pulled him

up as he continued to thrash and kick at the creatures pawing at him. From the murkiness of the storm-churned ocean, a clawed hand wrapped around her ankle, digging into her flesh, and yanking her down with it. Giving her free leg a swift kick down to her assailant, she connected with something hard and felt the grip loosen. One more hard kick, and the hand let go, allowing her and Charles to make it to the surface. Breaking through the waves, both of them gasped for breath and located the boat a suitable distance away from them. The soul eaters almost dragged them past the shelf, into the unforgiving depth of the Atlantic. With neither of them willing to get pulled under again, they made their way towards their craft, battling the swells, and a faint riptide trying to pull them back.

Reaching the boat, they clambered up the ladder while Zack helped them in with his uninjured hand. Away from the creatures, and out of the surf, the two of them sat on the deck, panting and shivering as their wet clothing acted like acid. The soaked sweater stuck to Charlotte like a straight jacked, snuffing the air out of her lungs, and her skin tingled and burned from the gusts of wind rocking the ship. Her cheeks stung, and her arms and legs were going numb, even as Zack wrapped her up in a warm wool blanket he found in the cabin. Glancing over at her partner clinging to the dry cloth he was given, she tightened hers around her neck and smiled.

"You all right, Chuck?"

"Yeah, thanks for coming in after me. I'm not sure how long I would have lasted under there on my own."

"Not going to let my partner die, at least not on my watch. Hey Kev," she turned to her son who was staring at her with a gaping mouth, "why don't you go start the boat, and we can get out of here."

Nodding, the boy ran back into the cabin. Charlotte waited for the boat to move, but all she heard was the sputtering and churning of the engine trying to start. Something was wrong. The boat wasn't starting, stranding them close to the island which was threatening to sink under the ocean like some lost continent of Atlantis.

Jumping up to her feet, she ran to the side and started to pull up the anchor with Charles close behind to help. At the very least, with the boat loose they might drift from the island to safety, but something below the surface was holding on to their mooring, pulling it back down. Looking up at the cloud-streaked sky, she noticed the moon had almost regained its silver glow, the Feast of Shadows was almost over.

"Get them, don't let them get away." Victoria's angry voice bellowed from the shore. "Make sure they don't get out alive. If we are going down, they are coming there with us."

Letting go of the rope, Charlotte looked over at the moon-washed sands of Autumn Falls with a woman in ragged robes standing on the beach as the wind tossed about her silver hair. Her eyes blazed with teal flames as she pointed a crooked finger towards them, directing a small army of soul eaters rushing down the wooded hill into the water, vanishing beneath the waves. Grabbing a paddle, she raised it above her head, waiting for the onslaught, and whacking the first creature which popped its head above the surface of the water. Screaming for Kevin to lock himself in the cabin, Charles grabbed hold of the second oar and began hitting the monsters as they swarmed the boat like ants, tipping the port side closer to the surf.

The soul eaters started overwhelming the boat, almost capsizing it, when a tremendous earthquake shook the island, rocking the boat, shaking the monsters off, and causing Charlotte and Charles to tumble to the deck. Jumping back to her feet, she sent a creature sitting next to her flying into the ocean with her oar before looking back towards the lighthouse. The cliff upon which the brick tower sat crumbled into the raging waves. Boulders rained down into the ocean as a flash of lightning split the sky, making the lighthouse glow. Black smoke seeping from the splitting ground engulfed the island, and it trembled, lurching the boat in the waves. Steadying herself on the railing, Charlotte looked towards the cabin of the boat and saw something slinking on the roof, getting ready to pounce.

"Zack, watch out!"

She reached out to him, hoping to pull him back as the soul eater poised above his head with its mouth wide open like a snake, ready to swallow him whole. Pushing her aside, Chuck yelled for Zack to duck, raised the paddle above his shoulders, and swung it towards the creature like a bat. The oar connected with the monster's chest with a sickening wet crunch and sent it flying into the ocean as it let out a wail. Giving Zack a hand, Charles pulled him up to his feet and sat him down closer to the action as he took a swing at another creature climbing up the side.

"Thanks again, man." Zack looked up at him, with his hand clutching the back of his shoulder. "Let me guess, you were the paramedic team's star hitter too?"

"Something like that."

Chuckling and winking, Charles joined Charlotte, who was cracking the monsters climbing up the hull as if playing a game of whack-a-mole. Close by, the island rumbled once more, and a giant wave leapt up from behind them, towering over the small fishing boat. It collapsed onto the tiny vessel with a deafening crash, washing over the deck, thrashing the hull, and sweeping the soul eaters clinging to it ashore. Drenched, Charlotte coughed up water, looking over at the landmass threatening to fall apart. The moon had returned to normal; the time was up, and she waited for something dramatic to happen.

At first nothing seemed to transpire, and the only thing heard was the sizzling of rain hitting the boat, but as the trio stood on the deck, they spotted rusted chains rip their way from the ground, whistling, and snaring the witch in their grasp. The metal links twisted and tangled as she screamed and fought against them, tearing away the paper-thin flesh covering her arms, drenching the ground in her inky blood. Once the iron serpents had her firmly in their grasp, the hill behind her opened its mouth filled with stone teeth, sucking her into the abyss beyond while she let go her final hiss.

Watching the wound in the earth close, they turned in time to see another rogue wave batter their vessel, snapping the rope attached to the anchor, allowing them to drift away from the shore. Floating past the continental slope, the engine magically turned and roared to life as the propeller churned the water with a harmonic hum. Running toward the bow, Charlotte glanced at the beach bathed in the silver light of the moon where the lanky creature she saw in her unconsciousness come into view. Hunkering down, it gave her a nod of its colossal, alien-like head before slinking away into the forest. With the Skudakumooch's blessing, she waved to the spirits of Iris, Clarence, and her father gathering on the cliff by the lighthouse and went into the cabin to stir the boat towards the mainland.

CHAPTER FIFTY-SIX

"Every story has an end, but in life every ending is just a new beginning." - **Uptown Girls**

Piloting the boat through the jagged rocks surrounding the fog-locked island, Charlotte waited for Chuck to finish patching Zack's wound. For the second time in one week, she thought how it was fortunate she carried a suture kit in her bag and stole a glance outside at her partner who stitched her son's father up for the long trek to the mainland. She wasn't sure how long it would take; it was two hours by ferry on a clear day, but she guessed with the remnants of the storm, and the cloak of night, they would not get to shore before dawn broke. The rough, choppy sea made the boat bounce on the wakes and sway with every wave, forcing her to keep the speed down until they cleared the treacherous rocks encasing the island. Having finished with Zack, Charles snuck into the cabin unnoticed, shut the door behind him, and patted her on the shoulder.

"You sure you know how to drive this thing?"

"Yes, I have my boating license, you know. How's Zack?"

"He'll live. The wound was clean with minimal damage to the surrounding tissue. After they patch him up at the hospital, and maybe repair any torn ligaments, he will be as good as new, and probably as cocky as ever. Your boy will be up making TV shows and hunting aliens in not time at all."

"Where is he now?"

"Outside with Kevin, showing him the constellations, and telling him maritime ghost stories now that the rain has let up." Charles rolled his eyes with a smirk. "At least it gives me a chance to check you out. You look like you have a baseball stuck to your face, and your right knuckle resembles purple hamburger."

"I'll be fine. I'm pretty sure I broke my hand punching Victoria, and Bret rearranged the bones in my face when he knocked me out. But the injuries will heal, unlike the guilt I feel over what he did to Iris."

"Wasn't your fault, Char. I was the one who should have never left them alone in that house to begin with. I should have taken them with me after everything we went through in there."

"You didn't know Bret was on the island, or that he posed a threat to anyone but me."

"Neither did you, so don't blame yourself."

"Then don't blame yourself either."

An awkward silence fell between them as they averted each other's gaze for a minute. Then Charles spoke again.

"So, what now? What do we do from here?"

"We go to the mainland. From there, I call my mom to tell her what happened, and I move to New York with Zack as planned. What about you?"

"Same. I told you we're partners till the end, and that my uncle will help us stay that way. Not to mention Iris said she had a little going away gift for us, a glowing recommendation from Autumn Falls emergency services." Craning his head, Charles stole a glance outside. "Although... I need to get you and Zack to a hospital first for a check up and have you put back to factory settings."

"What are we even going to tell the nurses and doctors there? We look like we fought a war."

"Tell them the truth. Tell them your ex-boyfriend turned stalker followed you to the island and attacked you in your home. I'm sure they will have to file a police report at the hospital. Then the cops will lookout for Bret, but they'll never find him, and he will have a warrant out for his arrest. As for us, we can get the hell out of this cursed state as planned." He shrugged and looked out at the water churning outside the window in silence. "Think we did the right thing by letting that creature loose again?"

"What choice did we have?"

"None, I guess, but..." he shuddered, "do you think it poses less of a threat to people than Victoria did?"

"I have to say yes. There is nothing in this world that can compare to the evils men is capable off, and she was the embodiment of that evil."

"What do you think will happen to the people left on the island? Now that they are free from her spell that is."

"They'll go on living. Life always goes on. And maybe, for the first time in their life, things will be different. They have a chance to start fresh, live life the way they see fit, and I'm sure the island will flourish because of it."

"Well, I can tell you one thing for sure. I am never stepping foot on that hunk of rock ever again."

"Me neither." Charlotte laughed recalling how she thought her mother was insane for telling her to keep away from Maine. "What do you say we get a clean start as well partner, far away from here?"

"Sister, I say drive on."

Sitting down on a worn-out, white vinyl cushion beside her, Charles tilted his head back against the glass and closed his sagging eyelids. She knew he was tired, and she was content to let him sleep as it gave her the much-needed time alone with her thoughts. Stealing one last glance behind her, she spotted the fog swallowing up the island thicken like curdled milk, hiding it from view, and she saw the seagulls heading to Autumn Falls for the first time since she got there.

Pushing the lever forward, the engine whined, and the boat sped up as she pointed it towards land, skimming along the waves which were smooth as glass now that they were away from the storm. As the night got darker, and all lights faded, Charlotte felt a chill in the air. The hairs stood up on her arms, and she heard a faint wail coming over the ocean. The island left her with a parting gift.

Author's Note:

Hi, I wanted to thank you for reading my book. It means a lot to me that you took a chance on my work and I sincerely hope you liked it. While I have written four full-length novels and three novellas, Autumn Falls is my first horror book. So why the leap? Well, one night I had a vivid nightmare and not one to waste an opportunity I decided to write it down and created what is now Autumn Falls. I figured it was not a leap going from dark fantasy to horror, and I hope I did a good enough job and that you enjoyed it. Please let me know how I did by leaving me an Amazon or Goodreads review. I always appreciate any feedback I get as it helps me learn and boosts sale. And if you liked this book, sign up for the newsletter at arkingston.com to get news on upcoming books, free chapters, and possible ARC copies.

A. R. Kingston

About the Author

Multi-genre author A.R. Kingston is a lover of all things dark and magical. She started out writing fanfiction in High School until going off to college to pursue her bachelor's degree in Psychology and spent a few years in the mental health field before her passion for writing called back to her. Now she spends her time weaving fantastical tales of magical worlds or planting terrifying beasts on earth. When she is not writing, you can find her enjoying tea with her potbellied pigs while she reads a book or hones a new skill. Eventually, she hopes to retire in her beautiful Colorado Springs, Colorado, and run her own pig rescue.

www.ingramcontent.com/pod-product-compliance
Lightning Source LLC
Chambersburg PA
CBHW051528250626
47156CB00001B/275